"Vanessa Carlisle's characters are sexy, f
tumble far from grace. *A Crack in Everythi*
a tender touch and serves up equal parts
other books may show up carefully dres
her underwear."

-SARK, Author, Artist, Creative Fountain
PlanetSARK.com

"*A Crack in Everything* introduces a new, exciting voice in fiction. Vanessa Carlisle and her quirky, intelligent, entertaining and fractured people come alive on these pages in a vivid, tight, confident and lapidary prose reminiscent of Yates or early Didion. The book's dialog is so perfect in its rhythms, word choices and inflections that you almost *hear* it, rather than read it. A truly impressive debut novel that announces Carlisle as a writer to watch."

- Rob Roberge,
author of *Working Backwards*
from the World Moment of My Life

"Every would-be Hollywood transplant should read *A Crack in Everything* first — Vanessa Carlisle simultaneously beckons and dissuades in a voice that is original, seductive, and uncompromisingly honest. The characters that inhabit this sharp and witty novel are troubled, impoverished, confused, lost, sexually frustrated, and intellectually unfulfilled. So…basically everyone I know."

-Mike Barker,
Co-Creator and Head Writer, *American Dad!*

"*A Crack in Everything* titillates with passion and arouses with intelligence. Carlisle taps into many young American women's struggle to guard their strong, independent identity while embracing their emerging vulnerability and secret desires. Her saucy writing yet tender and heart-felt characters expose America's hypocritical obsession with sex and sexuality and bridges an unusual but empowering sisterhood between girls-next-door and girls-on-stripper-poles. It's about time!"

- Jennifer Musselman,
author of *Own It! The Ups & Downs of*
Homebuying for Women Who Go It Alone

A Crack in Everything

A Novel

VANESSA CARLISLE

iUniverse, Inc.
New York   Bloomington

A Crack in Everything
A Novel

iUniverse books may be ordered through booksellers or by contacting:

iUniverse
1663 Liberty Drive
Bloomington, IN 47403
www.iuniverse.com
1-800-Authors (1-800-288-4677)

Because of the dynamic nature of the Internet, any Web addresses or
links contained in this book may have changed since publication and
may no longer be valid. The views expressed in this work are solely those
of the author and do not necessarily reflect the views of the publisher,
and the publisher hereby disclaims any responsibility for them.

ISBN: 978-1-4502-4392-6 (sc)
ISBN: 978-1-4502-4394-0 (dj)
ISBN: 978-1-4502-4393-3 (ebook)

Printed in the United States of America

iUniverse rev. date: 08/27/2010

Acknowledgments

"A good writer possesses not only his own spirit but also the spirit of his friends."

Friedrich Nietzsche

This novel originated during a maverick summer workshop of MFA students at Emerson College. I owe those friends, especially the group's later incarnation "Papes for Weins," a mountain of gratitude for the time they spent commenting, encouraging, and asking tough questions of the pages they read. I especially want to thank Tony Schaffer for offering such care to both me and my writing.

A Crack in Everything would not have become a readable manuscript without the guidance and revision strategies of my MFA advisor, Pamela Painter. Her believing kept me believing. Katherine Hunt, my fellow student and friend, had the generosity to copy edit on a tight schedule for the price of a coffee, and for that I will be always indebted.

I offer gratitude to the multitude of family and friends who have read early drafts, asked me how the writing was going, and generally been present throughout the process—you know who you are. Thanks to Jill Franz Gorelov for info on clinic work, Planned Parenthood for the educational training, Kelsey for the Los Angeles photo tour, and Erica for persuading her book group to read a draft.

My love and gratitude point straight to Anthony and Lindsey, who challenged the book to become more than I thought possible, and challenged the same to me. Also to Susan, whose courage and joyful risk-taking have taught me, among so many other important lessons, not to fear the behemoth of the traditional publishing industry.

Finally: thank you Roy Carlisle, Dad, publishing advisor and sparring partner, for your unflinching dedication to getting *A Crack in Everything* in print and your unshakable faith in everything else I do.

For Rowe Junior High campers and staff.

ONE

On that Friday morning, during an April heat wave LA natives didn't notice, I still believed that I had seen the limit of what could go wrong in my life. I found a clean pair of jeans and enough milk for cereal, folded a to-do list into my bag, and switched the extra-gel shoe inserts from my sneakers to my black platform boots. I left my roommate Janet a note about meeting me for lunch and overcame the impulse to scribble "we need to talk" at the end. The sun had already baked my Honda, so I steered down Sunset Boulevard with my fingertips. On the radio, an overexcited traffic reporter described in loving detail a three-car pileup that wouldn't get in my way. Arriving at the clinic right on time, I honked twice and waved at Todd through the front window.

We worked at the Silver Lake Life Center, known by its acronym as "The Slick." The SLLC was a privately funded, youth-focused, outpatient treatment facility that specialized in sexually transmitted infections. We saw patients in the clinic and also did sex education classes and assemblies for Los Angeles high schools. Although technically we were both medical assistants, Todd worked reception and billing and I spent more time with patients. He didn't like blood. Our office attracted young ones with secrets or no insurance: sexually active high-school kids, underage strippers, dropouts, and porn actors who were intimidated by the big Kaiser building and Planned Parenthood. Our school programs attempted to fix alarming deficiencies in young people's knowledge of sex and sexuality. Todd and I wore our matching SLLC T-shirts to school assemblies. I loved it when we matched.

Once, a nineteen-year-old hardcore actress who had seen her vulva

1

magnified on a TV screen came into the clinic worried that her labia were too big. When her exam came back clear, she asked if maybe she should cut down on fatty food.

"Labia don't really gain weight," I had to tell her. "Some swelling during sex is natural." I told her to buy a hand mirror and check herself out before, during, and after masturbating, to see her own normal changes. When she left, I wrote "normal exam" on her chart. I had no idea how to indicate "so uninformed it's as funny as it is sad."

We handed out free condoms both at the clinic and at the schools, which made us a few quiet friends and some very noisy enemies. Students and patients trusted Todd and me because we were still in our twenties. Parents and teachers tended to be more suspicious. School administrators liked our price tag. Conservative demonstrators liked to patrol our sidewalk with surreal and disturbing pictures of dead fetuses holding crosses.

That Friday, Todd and I were off to do a Basic Sex Ed assembly at a high school in the San Fernando Valley, where over half the students got bussed in from downtown LA.

Todd sang his hello and loaded our box of assembly props—condoms, lube, female condoms, dental dams, bananas, pamphlets, overheads, worksheets, and pens—into the trunk.

He opened the door, leaned in, and begged for a Starbucks stop.

I looked at my watch. "If there's fewer than three people in line," I said.

He flopped into my front seat and sighed. "Another packed house today. They're giving us all the tenth graders. Follow-up." Meaning, these kids had Sex Ed in ninth grade, but an administrator decided it wasn't enough. He pulled out the folder for Greenvale High School. "Are you sure you want to do the opening bit for this one?"

"I'm sure," I said.

"You don't have to prove anything to me," he said.

I told him I knew that. I was proving something to myself.

This was the first visit I'd made to Greenvale since a student assaulted me in the parking lot six months ago. I hadn't been talking about it.

Todd asked if there was a chance Nathan would be on campus.

"He's probably there," I said, "but he's not a tenth grader. There's also a chance I'm wrong about his name."

"What will you do if you see him?"

"I don't know."

"Can I kill him?"

"No. And I don't want to discuss it," I said.

Todd said okay, although it was clear he wanted to talk more. He read over the assembly request form while I drove.

I hired Todd originally to take care of the filing system because we were getting way behind and losing things. No one ever asked me about the other applicants, who were just as qualified but not as attractive. Todd was a little too ostentatiously muscled, but he held himself like a dancer, not a thug. His light brown hair stuck up in the front because he ran his right hand through it when he was thinking.

Todd saved me from the disorganization of our office and also watched terrible "Life Skills" educational videos from the 1980s with me when I was planning our booth for the one Adult Entertainment Convention we dared to attend. We dated for a few months. We broke up ostensibly because he finally admitted to himself and everyone else that he was "mostly" gay. I wasn't shocked, but I was sad. We had gotten along almost too well, considering that I'd started to reveal the subtle obsessions and compulsions that governed my daily life—like how much I cared that colors matched. That one in particular I kept under wraps. Todd and I stayed friends. Still, he'd left me for men in general, not for any particular one I could hate directly, and though I understood that taking it personally was irrational, I couldn't help it.

After a short Starbucks line and a three-highway drive, we exited Route 118 in the heart of the San Fernando Valley.

"You know this is officially the Ronald Reagan Freeway?" I asked Todd.

"Tamina," Todd said in a pseudo-formal voice, "We should have lunch out here somewhere special."

"What?"

"We'll find someplace unique, bursting with local charm, and commemorate your return to Greenvale." He stared out the window for three seconds while I tried to respond. "But all I see are Burger Kings."

I told him I already had plans to meet Janet at Bitsy's if she woke up in time.

"She will," he said out the window. "She knows how important it is for you to stare at that waiter."

It was true. Janet and I had lunch together regularly, and the place we went most often was Bitsy's. Today we had some serious roommate issues to discuss, but that didn't stop me from wanting to watch the cutest waiter in our part of the city work his magic on the sidewalk tables.

"How's your love life?" I said. "What's happening with Derek?"

"He's a flake," he said, "but he's very sexy. He thinks I'm going to save the world. Still wants to see other people." He sipped his latte and shrugged.

"Are you?" I said.

"Going to save the world? Probably not."

"Seeing other people."

"He is."

Normally I'd ask more questions, but we were nearly there.

"Damn," Todd said as we pulled up to the high school, "I hate the Valley."

In the 1930s, the San Fernando Valley's appeal was picturesque orange groves and the promise of a better life. Now it was parking lots and drive-throughs. You could arrive wherever you wanted to go and be greeted by a lot full of spaces, or an option not to get out of your car at all. Car-friendliness made the Valley a paradise, in the abstract, for those of us accustomed to routine parking nightmares in Hollywood, Silver Lake, and even Studio City. In reality the Valley demanded a steep tradeoff: those big beautiful parking lots were usually spread out in front of strip malls. Going over the hills into the Valley meant entering the same suburban sprawl, bloated with chain stores, that I'd left behind five years before in West Courtney, New Jersey. I counted on the California weather and palm trees to cheer me up, but I often wondered how long it would take for all of residential America to streamline into one-stop shopping. And once that happened, how long would it take for all of our personalities to follow?

My Jersey-born mother and father would have considered my neighborhood in Hollywood a ghetto. Teenagers in baggy pants smoked weed on the curb, trash lined the street, and bars covered every window, but I treasured the old Spanish architecture of my building, the banana leaves growing in the courtyard, and the way you could stand at the end of my block and see both a decrepit liquor store and the Hollywood sign.

We found a space in the parking lot marked FOR VISITORS ONLY.

"Wrapped up like a Christmas present," I said. I tried not to look down the row of cars, at the spot where Nathan Reggman had cornered me six months ago.

"Your AC is crap," Todd said brightly.

"You're welcome," I said. "I was happy to drive."

"Seriously," he said, putting his hand on my arm, "are you ready to do this?"

I told him yes. But as soon as we got out of the car, I started sweating. An itchy prickle crawled up my back. I was not ready. I should never have gone back there.

We headed to the office for visitor passes. A grim-faced woman in khaki pants led us to the cafeteria.

"What are you all here for?" she asked over her shoulder.

"Sex Ed," Todd said.

"Lord knows they probably need it," she sighed.

"I wish the Lord would communicate that more clearly to the school board," Todd said, and I stifled a giggle. She pressed her lips and ignored him.

Most high schools in the Los Angeles Unified School District didn't have real auditoriums or theaters. Students piled into football stadiums, gyms, or cafeterias when it became absolutely necessary for them to have large group experiences. I suspected administrators and teachers were afraid of the violence that might erupt if too many kids gathered in one place. Inside Greenvale's cafeteria an enormous, shouting mass of faces, arms, and backpacks swallowed us as our escort disappeared. Accustomed to the chaos of three hundred talking teenagers, I started unpacking at the front of the room. Fifteen teachers leaned against the back wall of the makeshift auditorium, ignoring their students to bitch with each other. Occasionally one of them would shout a student's name, "Guys, knock it off," "Come on," or "Quiet, please!" into the crowd.

Some schools booked us for health classes, during which we gave a more interactive forty-five-minute presentation, or even a series that lasted a week or longer. Most schools only wanted the big assembly, because it was the most cost-effective way to deliver Sex Ed, particularly AIDS education, which they needed to fulfill certain state laws. If they chose to do all their education in house, they'd have to send their teachers to specialized AIDS educator training, which was more expensive than hiring us. Every school that hired us took a risk, though, since we didn't do abstinence-only programs. Abstinence-only was still exclusively approved by the federal funding people. Apparently it wasn't cool in Washington to read statistical reports on the colossal failure of that right-wing brainchild.

I preferred doing small classes on principle, but at least our large assembly covered issues most teachers were too squeamish to talk about. My last visit to Greenvale had been for a class, not an assembly. It was disappointing to know they had cut costs, but I didn't want to remember any more Greenvale faces, now that I was scanning for Nathan's.

I wished we could do longitudinal studies and anonymous surveys, something to prove that our style of no-nonsense, gay/lesbian/bisexual/ trans-inclusive, statistics-based, comprehensive education actually influenced kids to make smarter choices. Our curriculum was culled from a few other well-tested Sex Ed methods, but we didn't yet have hard data of our own. We were certain that no other group in Southern California worked as hard as we did to get kids in to make appointments once the class was over. Even Planned Parenthood had become a bit too bureaucratic for my taste. We behaved like a community project, not a healthcare franchise. We distributed literature designed by a local graphic artist, did direct outreach with schools, and we were chronically understaffed and underpaid.

In four years, the only time I'd taken a break from work was after Nathan attacked me six months ago. He had figured out I was the person who helped his girlfriend schedule an abortion. He found me in the parking lot after I visited his health class. *That shit wasn't mutual,* he said right before he shoved me. *You had no right to kill my baby.* He punched, hit, kicked. He ran, I think, when I blacked out. A security guard held my neck steady on the ground next to my car until the ambulance came. I spent the night in the hospital. I talked to a cop who took a description.

"No tattoos?" he asked.

I said no.

"Blond, about six foot, black backpack," he read off his notes. "I gotta tell you, this doesn't look good. There's a whole city fulla them out there. Probably two hundred just at that school."

At the time, I had no idea who had come after me. I explained that he must have some connection to the clinic, but even that wasn't helpful. I didn't recognize him, because I'd never seen him before.

I returned to my job against the advice of my doctor and Janet. On my first day back I dropped a box of clean syringes on the floor and then sat at my desk and cried. I didn't talk to anyone but Janet and Todd about the attack. Other clinic employees thought I'd taken some days off and come back banged up because of a car accident. I didn't want them to see me as a victim. My job mattered too much to let one angry kid stop me. The police said there were no witnesses coming forward. They told me that if I came up with any more information, I should call before two years passed.

Within a week, I used my class list from the school, my clinic records, and the Web to figure out that the kid's name was probably Nathan Reggman. He was only sixteen, a junior. I didn't go back to the police. Even if I was certain it was him, my position in youth outreach made me deeply reluctant to throw a teenager to the law. Anything wrong with him would only get worse in jail.

Now, nearly six months after the attack, I was still trying to decide what to do. I'd gotten my life back into tenuous balance, and I'd become comfortable telling everyone the same lie about feeling fine. But standing in the cafeteria at Greenvale, feeling hot, nauseated, and light-headed, I wondered how much longer I could keep it up. The memory of the attack was like a blister suddenly rubbing raw on the inside of my chest.

Todd set up an overhead projector—a dinosaur provided by the school—a box of flyers, and our portable Pyle speaker with the microphone and receiver. I stared at a stack of pamphlets and tried to remember the opening monologue.

A bell rang, the teachers began shushing everyone, and I imagined an enormous fan blasting me. At least the heat might make them all lethargic.

Most public high schools had gone the way of strict dress codes to try and stave off gang fights, and this room contained a mass of solid-color shirts, jeans, and khakis squished together. In the first two rows there was a nice pattern of dark and light blue tops. I could function in it. One time in a smaller class, I'd made three students in clashing outfits get up and switch seats, ostensibly as part of a game, just so that I could concentrate. Somehow crowds usually ended up having a harmony of colors on the whole. The cafeteria ceiling seemed to sag in the middle, and the lumpy beige paint caked on the walls gave me the strange feeling that we were locked inside a large intestine. The room smelled like perfume, sweat, and ketchup.

Todd moved some dials on the Pyle, then gave me a thumbs-up.

When most everyone had calmed down, I took a deep breath through my mouth, blew it out, raised the mike, and smiled. "Hey Greenvale!" I yelled. They rumbled for a moment. "My name is Tam, this is Todd, and we're here to talk to you about sex!" A few whoops wafted forward. I introduced the SLLC and gave a ten-second overview of the issues we would cover: sexually transmitted infections, pregnancy prevention, sexual communication, and self-care.

"I need three volunteers for a game," I said. Over some rising laughter, I picked out two of the toughest guys I could make eye contact with, plus one pretty girl. I brought them up front. Their friends halfheartedly made fun of them.

I told them I was going to ask them each one question about sexual health. I held up a five-dollar gift card to a healthy burrito chain and told the volunteers they were competing for a prize.

The girl's face twisted into disgust when I asked her about STIs. Her name was Ashley and her answer to the "most common" question was gonorrhea. At least she knew the real name, and I complimented her for it. Often students answered either "the Clap" or AIDS. I interpreted these answers as evidence that their parents' 1970s phobia had trickled down without adequate education to counteract it, or their exposure to 1990s MTV and the California Education Code had perpetuated a ubiquitous fear of HIV.

Actually, I told the auditorium, the most common STIs are human papilloma virus, a.k.a. HPV or genital warts, and chlamydia, depending on your governmental source, with herpes I and II closing in fast. I threw in the fact that about one in four sexually active teens gets an STI each year. Then I explained what HPV, chlamydia, and herpes were, detailed their signs and symptoms (and the fact that they often had none), and described how we tested for them and other STIs at the SLLC. I wished we'd started doing the HIV rapid test, so patients wouldn't need a blood draw, but most of them didn't know the rapid test existed anyway. Todd moved toward a group of chatting girls, and they quieted.

"Getting tested for HIV is very simple," I said, "but it's not included in a regular exam, so remember to ask your doctor about it." There were a few items that I couldn't stress enough. "Many people who have HPV, chlamydia, herpes, and other STIs don't have symptoms at all," I reminded them, "which is why it's so important to get regular testing done."

I thanked the first student for her participation. She ran back to her friends. I'd forgotten something. "Chlamydia is a bacterial infection," I said, "which means you can cure it with antibiotics, but viral infections stay with you for life."

"Does that mean you'll have warts or sores all over your penis forever?"

Todd asked from the audience, holding his crotch. He was a born actor. The room tittered a little.

"Not at all," I said. I told them that with regular doctor's visits, and possibly a drug that suppresses symptoms, a person could have a healthy, active sex life, even with an STI. "Okay! If you are sexually active, what's the cheapest, most effective way to prevent pregnancy and STIs?" I turned to my volunteers, but the second guy was already walking to his seat, holding a condom over his head. It wasn't our brand; he'd pulled it out of his own pocket. "He's right," I said. "Aside from abstinence, the cheapest and most effective way to prevent pregnancy and STIs is still condoms, condoms, condoms."

"Can I keep one in my wallet?" Todd asked, patting his back pocket. He had moved to the front row.

When I said it was okay for a little while, but he needed to replace it about a once a week or the heat from his body would start deteriorating the latex, he rolled his eyes and sighed, pulled a condom out of his wallet, and tossed it over the front row of students into a trash can by the door. That got some laughs.

"How about you?" I said to the third student. He stared at me, arms crossed over his chest, feet spread wide. "What percentage of the women in this room have been forced into a sexual act against their will?"

"How many girls have been raped?" he said. "Here?"

I didn't correct him, although I was talking about sexual force that may not end in rape. "Take a guess," I said. "Let's say there are about a hundred and fifty females in the cafeteria."

"I know of three," he said, keeping his eyes on me. Light brown eyes with long lashes.

The stony expression on his face was like a hand grabbing at the front of my shirt. Was he guilty? Or angry because those girls were people he loved? It scared me that I couldn't tell. I had a quick, unbidden, and terrifying image of him winding up to hit me. It was stupid; he looked nothing like Nathan. The image dissolved, but my heart kept pounding. He was leaned back into his hips, bow-legged, immobile.

I turned to the audience, fighting to keep my hands steady. Everyone was paying attention now. "Statistically," I said, "about fifteen young women in this room have already been forced into a sexual act. The numbers go up as you get older. One in three women will be victims of sexual violence in their lifetimes." I watched them do the math, and almost regretted telling them.

"That's fucked up," the kid said. He shook his head and walked back to his seat. I wanted to shout my agreement, and launch into a speech about everyone's responsibility to stop sexual assault. I struggled to respond to the fact that he'd said "fuck" in front of the school. No words came. Plus I'd forgotten to give away the gift card. The students had started talking to each other and glancing around. I realized they might be trying to spot the victims, or perpetrators, in the room. I'd lost them.

"The best thing we can do," Todd said, gently taking the mike, "is to educate ourselves." I went to our supplies and pulled out the overheads of cartoon people in "real life" situations. While Todd took the reins I stared at the students and tried not to guess which of them had been victims. I noticed the way they sat, dressed, talked, and chewed their gum. I tried not to guess which boys had been the aggressors. I reminded myself that the girls at their age were just as likely to commit acts of nonsexual violence as the boys.

The mood lightened as we spent fifteen minutes getting the kids to role-play each situation on the overheads. One situation called for one partner to pressure the other for sex, and for the pressured one to say no. I found a couple holding hands and wearing black to volunteer. As they came forward, it calmed me to see their matching black eyeliner, black backpacks, black boots, and black hair. They switched hands to stay connected as they faced the auditorium.

"Show me how much you love me," the boy said to his girlfriend.

"No," she said.

Todd asked them if they thought that was a realistic conversation. They shook their heads.

"How might it actually happen?" he asked them. They looked at each other. The girl leaned in to the microphone.

"Come over tonight," she said. "I want to show you something."

"Nah," said the boy. "I'm just not that into you."

Everyone laughed, and then Todd reminded the kids that the reason this was a hard situation to role-play was that most people don't know how to say no. He challenged them to make a commitment to themselves to speak up if they didn't feel right about something. "Even if things have already been heating up," he added, and winked. The couple shuffled back to their seats.

Todd handed the mike back to me and I asked the kids if it was legal to have sex with a drunk person. They were shocked to find out that in California, if a woman had sex while drunk, she could accuse her sex partner of rape.

"With the potential for STDs, pregnancy, and serious misunderstandings," I said, "why would anyone want to have sex?"

"Money!" a blue shirt yelled. I had no idea how to acknowledge something so complicated with any political integrity. I ignored him.

We talked about how fun sex is, even though doing that routinely garnered us the most complaints from teachers and parents. We talked about love. We talked about pressure, popularity, and whether people liked you better if you were sexually active. A few very interested girls sitting in the front row had a lot to say on the matter of when it was a good idea to let a guy "hit it."

Most schools hired us in hopes that we would open up a dialogue with students on campus-specific issues like an increased prevalence of a certain STI, an outbreak of antigay violence, or pregnancy. The fact that the SLLC also had a reputation for discussing pleasure was not their main concern, and it was a risk we always took. We weren't in real danger of violating state education statutes, because the way we addressed pleasure was realistic and safe-sex focused, but some parents' group could cost us precious time and money if they brought a serious complaint.

Todd talked about how difficult it could be to discuss your health history with a potential partner. He stressed the importance of agreeing on your method of protection, at the very least, before you got too physical.

"What about a one-night stand?" one student asked. "When are you supposed to talk about condoms?" He was baiting me.

Todd answered, "I'll tell you what I do," over rising giggles. "Before the deed, I pull out a condom and say, 'This is how I roll.' If they don't like it, they can get out." He was always careful with his gender pronouns.

"No one-night stand is worth the risk," I said.

I gave them the SLLC guiding principle: whether you are abstinent or active, have just yourself, another person, or multiple partners, you deserve access to information and the means to sexual health.

Todd got back on the mike to talk about the SLLC and all the services we offered. He was so good at making it sound reasonable and easy to come on down after school one day for an HIV test. Or for a Pap smear, which he expertly and briefly described. He invited them to check out our options for counseling and birth control.

We split them up into small groups and made them put a condom on a banana.

We walked around, inspecting their progress. "What do you do if you start rolling the condom on and realize it's on backwards?" I asked one group. I counted three reddish shirts, one blue, one green, one white with orange stripes. All jeans and denim shorts except one black skirt. It was too hard to look at them, so I settled somewhere over their heads.

"Wouldn't you turn it over?" one of the girls offered. Her friend hit her in the arm.

"Stupid," Orange Stripes said, "you have to throw it away and get a new one."

"That's right," I said. "Do you know why?"

Orange Stripes explained that if there was anything on it you didn't want it touching you.

"That's the idea," I said, "but to be specific, if the man has an STI and there's any fluid on the condom, it could get passed easily to his partner." I added that if there was any pre-come in the condom, a female partner could get pregnant. Then, judging by the expressions on their faces, I explained what pre-come was.

"Nobody really gets pregnant like that," one of the boys said.

"It's not common," I said, "but it does happen." I walked on to escape the intrusive colors of their clothing.

No doctor had ever diagnosed me with Obsessive Compulsive Disorder. I learned early how to appear capable of a normal life. The one Rutgers mental health intern I'd seen about my "matching issue" when it was getting more severe in college told me I had perfected the art of keeping up appearances. He gave me no referral, even though he agreed my obsession with colors was a problem.

"Everyone has problems," he said, twirling his pen. Maybe he thought I was making it all up, or maybe he didn't know how to write up my case file for his supervising psychologist. "You seem like you're managing," he said. In fact, I was, but barely. I'd missed classes because of my inability to stay in the same room with certain color combinations. That was the only time I tried to get institutional help.

I was happy to see that the next group had a perfectly outfitted banana, and all black or neutral clothes.

"Yo," said the kid holding the banana, "what's that called when a chick is born with a dick too?" He used the uncovered end of the banana to scratch his head while he stared at me.

I told him that most of the time doctors do a corrective surgery on babies with ambiguous genitalia right after birth, but someone with both sex organs was historically called a hermaphrodite.

I wished there was a mainstream movie character I could reference. When students asked about cross-dressing or transgender issues, I had a few movies I could use as tools to talk with them. But ambiguous genitalia still didn't make it into mainstream entertainment often, certainly not in a normalized way, and that made it hard to discuss with high schoolers. I kept an eye out for movies that could help with my work, but I constantly fell behind in my knowledge of current blockbusters, since my real love was film noir. It was too bad noirs didn't have more variety in their representations of gender and sexuality.

Banana Boy said, "Man, if I was born like that I'd never leave my house," and then pantomimed how he would masturbate both a penis and a vagina at the same time. His group covered their mouths to laugh—the girls with their palms, and the boys with their knuckles.

"Too bad you got stuck with only one organ," I said.

I searched the cafeteria for Todd. I found him near the back, distributing the handouts for our end-of-assembly competition.

On each paper was a list of correct terminology: Penis, Vagina, Oral Sex (on a male), Oral Sex (on a female), Vaginal Intercourse, Anal Intercourse, Manual Stimulation (on a male or female), and my favorite, because of how creative the responses were, Breasts. Whoever could fill in the most slang terms for each won a prize. The trick was that they had to think of slang no one else had written down. It was like Scattergories, except instead of writing down places that start with the letter *R*, they were all writing down "cock, dick, schlong, wiener," or "pussy, cunt, cooch, poon." We gave them one minute per category.

The students were always enthusiastic about the game. It left them with an impression that the SLLC was not their enemy, like other adult institutions. My problem with the game was that it did nothing to counteract the strong cultural assumption that mouths, hands, breasts, and genitals were the only body parts involved in "real" sex.

Our SLLC presentations were carefully designed to be inclusive toward the gay, lesbian, bisexual and trans students, students with HIV or other STIs, and also students who were choosing not to be sexually active, but they were still failing to battle any prejudice against fetishism, BDSM, exhibitionism, voyeurism, polyamory, commercial sex, or any other alternative sex practices. Those issues were too fringe for us to discuss, but I wanted to at least acknowledge them.

I also wished we discussed the assumptions people made about their partners. Invariably, students thought they knew already if the person they were making out with wanted to have sex. "I could tell she liked it," they'd say, smiling to each other. How to explain that younger women in particular often got physical for reasons other than arousal?

But we had to teach basics first. Most students in the room had already been through some kind of sexual encounter, and many of them were terrified or totally unprepared. Even well-informed students often felt fear or insecurity in sexual situations. They needed help to realize they weren't freaks.

Todd's laughter broke into my haze—he stood over one of the groups, waving a diminutive banana. A line of sweat marked the back of his SLLC shirt, and I worried about mine. I wiped my face with my sleeve and checked the time. We still had so much to do.

The strangest thing about doing large assemblies was the persistent gap in information across students. Presumably they all took some kind of health or biology class before we got to them, but students who believed you could avoid pregnancy by douching regularly sat next to students who knew things as specialized as which companies made polyurethane condoms for people with latex allergies. What movies were they watching, and what were they telling each other? Did parents believe having one awkward conversation about how babies were made was enough? People had been asking this question for so long, and still sex discussions were laced with emotional and political land mines—HIV, gay relationships—maybe even more of them, in my adulthood, than there had been in my parents'. The most common pieces of our humanity are what we fear the most.

I told school administrators that abstinence-only education contributed to a culture of secrecy and shame that prevented young people from becoming sexually healthy adults because it taught, indirectly, that curiosity about sexuality was wrong. More than fifty years since the first Kinsey report, we were still fighting giants: the federal program, years of misinformation, age gaps and mistrust, funding problems in public schools, kids with unpredictable levels of knowledge, the deep and mysterious insecurities of adolescents, a historically conflicted national culture, not to mention outright prejudice from right-wing parents and demonstrators. The mere fact that we did regular assemblies struck me as a sort of miracle. It also occasionally made me want to flee to France.

Todd motioned to me, and I turned the mike on at the front. "It's time for our contest, ladies and gentlemen," I said. "If I could please have my volunteers from the first game?" We discovered that the condom guy had left the cafeteria. A resentful teacher slipped out a side door. The other boy volunteer sauntered up, a list of slang words in one hand, the other hand in his pocket. Our girl brought up a friend, both of them clutching one paper. They wore tight denim shorts and tiny white T-shirts. Momentarily distracted by their clashing denims, I fumbled through reading their lists.

The other students busily crossed off the more common pieces of slang on their sheets. Once I'd been through my volunteers' papers, other students raised their hands to giggle and say something crass if they thought they had an original name.

For Manual Stimulation, one student raised his hand and said, "Does anyone else have 'playing the banjo?'"

A girl across the room raised her hand and said, "I have 'picking the banjo.' Is that the same thing?"

They looked at me.

I couldn't help it. I laughed. "Any vagina will tell you they are *not* the same thing," I said. "You both get credit for that one." I imagined them running into each other in the halls, exchanging sheepish smiles, realizing they were the only two people in school who had heard that phrase for fingering. After a minute or so, I told everyone to mark their score.

The winner was a boy who could have been headed straight for a state school frat house. His gray UCLA T-shirt tightly concealed an athletic body. He'd either been blessed by the gods of puberty or held back a grade or two. I glanced at his answer sheet. Wild, imaginative, totally obscure phrases and cartoons swirled all over it. Instantly, my favorite was "silk purse" for vagina. Linda Rondstadt flashed through my mind, with her enormous hair and a pig in mud next to her on the album cover of *Silk Purse*. I was a list-maker, and his was a piece of art. I pretended to be counting while I suppressed an inappropriate buzzing in my body.

There weren't enough good slang words for vagina. Thousands existed, but most of them were derogatory or infantile. Many of them made vaginas sound disgusting, like "axe wound," "mouth with no eyes," or "fish taco." Rarely did our students come up with words that sounded sexy, gorgeous, or playful. In contrast, many of the words for penis had an inherent sense of humor. You could tell a man he had a beautiful dick and the word "dick" would sound sexy and nice. It was as if men and women had already agreed that the phallus was cool, and so it could take a joke now and then. Cocksucker, ha ha. But "carpet muncher" made everyone a little queasy, even people who liked to have their mouths buried in a pussy. I didn't like the word "pussy" that much either, although it seemed like a kind of compromise since "cunt," while sounding liberated to me—a lá Eve Ensler and Erica Jong—still sounded evil to the younger generation who hadn't heard of the *Vagina Monologues* or *Fear of Flying*, and might never. I had not come up with a word that felt authentically sexy to say in bed with someone. If I wanted something specific to happen to my vagina, I phrased it so I could use the personal pronoun: I want you inside *me*, go down on *me*, *I'm* a little sore. I'd known men who used the third person for their penises: *he's* happy, *he's* tired, *he* misses you. If we were both talking about our genitals, there were three *me's* and one *him* all in bed at the same time (*me*: Tam, *me*: Tam's vagina, *me*: Lover, *him*: Lover's penis). What a confused mismatch—all those personalities trying to interact.

When Todd and I were lovers, I had referred to my vagina casually, actually using the word "vagina," because he wasn't disturbed by it sounding too clinical. He'd been remarkably comfortable with my body.

I felt sorry for those tenth graders as I thought about the vocabulary they had to use for their experiences. I was sorry for all of us, and hoped for a time when there was clear, respectful, hot language to use for sex and bodies. Every time we played the game, I felt a bit older.

I told the kid with "silk purse" he'd won, and I handed him a ten-dollar Starbucks gift card.

"Sweet," he said, giving me a nod as he pushed the card into his back pocket. He was growing a goatee.

I asked him if he wanted his list back.

"Nah," he said, "put it on your wall."

"Thank you," I said, awkwardly. I would put it in a file. With a few other lists that were too satisfying to throw away.

The bell rang. A roar of movement drowned out the few people who clapped. We hadn't done our closing. I turned the mike back on and told everyone they could visit our information table on their way out. While they bottlenecked at the doors, Todd and I scooted out to the table near the last exit, throwing down piles of flyers about the clinic. Todd upended a small bucket of condoms and the kids swiped them all immediately.

A short brunette got squeezed against our table by the crowd. She picked up a business card. She smiled briefly at Todd before slipping out, and I felt a twinge of compassion, and triumph. I searched the students' faces, looking primarily for Nathan, but also for any other signs of anger. During those brief moments of chaos, we were vulnerable. Any kid with an issue could get to us. The distracted sense of purpose I'd felt during the assembly faded as irrational fear clawed through.

A boy in a baggy red shirt nodded at me. "I heard your place is full up with hos," he said.

I stuttered for a response.

"All the tricks from Deluxe go there?" He was asking about a porn studio in the Valley.

"We don't discriminate on the basis of a patient's employment," I said. The boy threw an elbow at this friend, and they shuffled out, laughing. Todd winked at me. It was a little risky, letting high school boys know that there might be porn stars in our waiting room, but if it got kids in the door, everybody won. I tried to smile back. The teachers followed the pack, ushering everyone back to class.

I stood gripping the table until they were all gone.

"That was pretty good," Todd said when the room was empty.

"The slang game took too much time," I said, and he agreed.

I suggested we play it at the beginning, with only four students up front competing, to loosen the room up, and then use the extra minutes to talk more about communication and deciding when to be intimate.

"You mean like having them brainstorm reasons why they want to sleep with whoever?"

"Something like that," I said.

"We also didn't talk much about sexual violence," he said, avoiding my eyes.

"That one kid at the beginning threw me off," I said, "when he stared at me and said he knew of three girls who'd been raped?"

"Yeah," Todd said, and started packing up, "what was that about?"

I said I didn't know, and it bothered me.

"Maybe he just needed someone to hear it," Todd said.

After an assembly, the enormity of the social disease we were fighting overwhelmed me. Parents seemed to aggressively turn a blind eye to statistics. Had I mentioned to this group that at least one in four people over the age of eighteen carry the herpes virus, and can pass it on without having symptoms? Yet every week I read letters from people who objected to what we did.

"How can they not care about this?" I said, looking over our flyer.

"Who's 'they'?" Todd asked.

I shrugged. Everyone. "I had a friend in college who was a vegan," I said.

Todd waited for me to make the connection.

"She used to tell me that all the meat I was eating was killing the world slowly."

"You still eat meat," he said.

I said I didn't care that much about animals, and Todd laughed. I told him I cared about the mistreatment of animals in general, and I cared about misuse of land and resources, but the fact that humans ate animals didn't bother me at all, morally.

Todd asked for the point.

"I care about them," I said, pointing out the cafeteria door. "I worry about them."

"So I should stop eating highschoolers for breakfast?"

I swatted at him.

"Pick your battle," Todd offered, nodding. "You think you'll work at the SLLC that long?"

I pursed my lips instead of snapping at him. I'd already been working at the SLLC longer than I'd planned. I was supposed to be in my second year of med school by now. Instead I had a pile of brochures and applications steadily collecting dust bunnies in my closet. Every autumn I pulled them out, ordered new ones, asked my boss Helena for an updated letter of recommendation, thought about how much more effective I could be if I was a doctor, and then shoved everything back in the closet once I'd missed the deadlines. It had once felt obvious and inevitable that I would end up in med school. I still coveted the prestige, the power to get things done, and the expertise, but as time passed I became increasingly intimidated by the work it would take to get in, support myself, and finish. However, I had not come up with a better plan.

Todd asked if I was going in to the clinic that afternoon and I told him yes, I had an appointment later.

I checked the time. I had to get back over the hill so I could meet up with Janet. We needed to talk about how we were going to pay off some of our three-months-late rent.

"Hey, since you're going to Bitsy's, could you get me that waiter's number and leave it on my desk?" Todd said.

I told him to fuck off.

He reminded me that stalking was a crime.

"I don't stalk," I said. "I observe nonthreateningly. During regular business hours."

"Right." Todd scanned the cafeteria for anything we could salvage for the next assembly. Then he asked me how I was feeling, while he taped up a box.

Reflexively, I told him I felt fine.

"No anxiety about being back here? You're totally fine?"

I assured him yes.

"So Nathan wasn't ..."

"No."

"Because there were a couple times I thought, you know, you'd frozen up?"

"I'm okay," I insisted.

"You're like a robot," he said.

I thanked him.

"It's not a compliment," he said. "But just so you know, when you finally do break down, you can call me."

TWO

Play an old noir film for five minutes and anyone can tell which character will eventually get shot. The information lives in his earnest face, clues in the music, or changes in lighting. Noir formula is reliable, even though the details in each movie change. Some scripts wrap themselves around a femme fatale, others sneak in with a secret weapon in a leather case. Some have explosions or car chases, a good cop, a bad cop. What holds true is that they all introduce at least one sad little stooge who gets killed to the chagrin, not the grief, really, of the rest of the cast. And you always know before it happens.

When I thought about movies, I never fit myself into the role of the dangerous woman with the money and the motive. Even if I'd had the sexual charisma, I wouldn't have known how to use it—my knowledge of sexuality was academic, theoretical. My sex appeal was pure niche: I was short, had curly brown hair cut messily at chin length, and looked more like a pixie than a vixen. I was too earnest to be the deceptively friendly rookie, doing dirty deals out back. I wasn't even the scruffy detective, unable to resist a stiff drink or a cold stare. If my life were a noir film, I would be the well-meaning but clueless friend who got shot.

That was what I was thinking when Janet plopped down at the table I'd snagged on Bitsy's piece of sidewalk. It was eighty-five degrees at noon, and I quickly became jealous that Janet got to sit in the shade of the building, with her back up against the bricks, even though I was the one who had taken the sunny side. I tried to think of a noir role Janet would play, but decided she'd fit much better in a musical.

"I'm totally starving," she said, turning over her coffee cup and checking the inside for stains.

At Bitsy's you could eat a great omelet while looking at local artists' photographs of local rock stars. Vintage posters from truck stops peeled haphazardly from the pea-green walls. I started coming to Bitsy's because it seemed like the kind of hipster diner where you could be hit with brilliant ideas while munching on wheat toast, where the cool kids wrote soon-to-be-legendary song lyrics on white paper napkins, and where the occasional well-dressed baby would flirt endearingly from a hemp stroller. It went on my list of "Places to Go in LA at Least Once." I still had a couple of other entries on the list: the Fredericks of Hollywood Lingerie Museum; the house where F. Scott Fitzgerald failed to write a screenplay; the Seventh Veil, where Courtney Love used to strip. Bitsy's was simultaneously a locals' spot and an area attraction. The fruit always tasted a little bit like onion because they only had one cutting board in the short-order kitchen.

One night I'd stopped at Bitsy's on a whim after closing up the clinic, ordered a burrito topped with avocado, and noticed the green of Bitsy's paint didn't match the green of the umbrellas which didn't match the green of the 1950s-diner neon clock over the counter. I almost left, but then I saw the gorgeous waiter. He rang my bill, brushed my hand as he handed me my change, and I walked out feeling like I should have done something. What it would have been, I had no idea. I came back to see him, and started sitting outside. He didn't acknowledge me more than any of the other regulars, except for bringing my coffee before taking my order and making extended eye contact every time I paid my check at the ancient register. I anticipated seeing him like he was Saturday morning cartoons and I was nine years old. Janet humored me because Bitsy's home fries made her happy. I'd been to Bitsy's at least once a week for almost four months, and made the mistake of telling Janet and Todd about my crush.

My favorite waiter's feet didn't appear to touch the ground as he moved from the doorway to our table. Wooden prayer beads hung from his apron—he was Buddhist. Or a Hollywood fashion boy who liked the eastern look.

I was a sucker for that adorable mop of brown hair and goatee. Janet didn't think he was sexy, but then she liked men with long greasy beards and alcohol problems. She would have married ZZ Top, all three of them, if they rolled up on old Harleys and asked. Her last guy, John, was constantly drunk, came on to me, and treated Janet terribly. He called himself a musician so Janet forgave him.

My waiter was a picture of calm as Sunset Boulevard zoomed noisily behind me. An umbrella directly above our heads was shading only Janet. I drank hot coffee anyway and tried to understand Janet's menu-reading expression. Halfway between concentration and tragedy. Something was on her mind. Probably our rent. At the table next to ours, a five-year-old wearing Dickies pulled the top off the salt shaker.

My waiter stood closer to my arm than Janet's when he took our order.

Janet fiddled with her silverware, and I wondered if there was something other than our debt bothering her. She chatted about the new shampoo girl at StageRage, the salon where she cut hair. Her phone rang. While she talked to Remy, her friend from work, I planned the rest of my day.

After we ate I'd give her a ride. Then I'd get a pedicure. Then I would go to the clinic for a few hours. One of our patients needed an annual exam and specifically requested that I be there. I managed so much information—much of it sensitive, confidential, complicated, and not my own—and covered so much ground every day running from clinic work to meetings, assemblies, and classes. I wondered if people outside of LA felt like their days were this long. Janet dipped a spoon in her coffee and grimaced at what she was hearing on the phone.

As an only child, I felt phony telling people I loved Janet like a sister, but we were a team. When she was happy, her nose scrunched up, and when things were bad, she picked her cuticles. She had an easy time expressing her emotions because she didn't have many complicated thoughts getting in the way—the opposite of me. We criticized each other, and bickered, and sometimes we laughed until it hurt. Janet had seen me through break-ups, illnesses, unemployment, and other dark things proud people like me tended to deal with alone. It couldn't have been easy to live with me, since I forbade any house decoration that didn't meet my approval, insisted that all the towels matched, and talked about work all the time, but Janet didn't complain. No one else would have taken care of me after my attack the way she did.

She hung up. I was about to ask her what we were going to do about paying three month's back rent when she said, "So this woman, in Boston? Died of cancer, it was on the news." She tucked a few pieces of frizzy red hair behind her ears and checked her nails, long talons painted cobalt blue with white, airbrushed flowers. My right arm was burning in the sun and I tried to tuck it under the table.

"So what?" I said. Our omelets arrived.

"She confessed to murdering her husband right before she died," Janet said. She liked collecting stories like this and presenting them in conversation. One of her endearing habits. She told me the woman on the news had killed her husband fourteen years ago in Ventura somewhere, put him in a freezer, and moved the freezer to a storage space in Boston, where it had stayed until yesterday. She paused to make sure I was listening. The woman confessed to the whole thing on her deathbed to a tape recorder and put the tape in an envelope on which she wrote: Don't Open Until I Am Dead.

I nodded to encourage her. There was something else more important in her eyes, but I knew better than to push someone to say more than they were ready to.

"Now her kids have to go get their dad," she said, "out of a freezer. Is that crazy or what? It's like TV but it's real."

I told her the news is still TV, and not always real. "Anyway, the freezer would have to be plugged in for fourteen years," I said, suspicious that no one in Boston noticed the dead body smell, "and she'd have to pay rent on it every month? Please."

"I saw the footage of the storage space and the crime scene guys putting a big black bag on a stretcher and everything."

I told her that was gross.

"I know," she said, and smiled. "It's like CSI." Janet had a habit of comparing everything to what she saw on TV. She was like a girl from the Dagara culture I'd studied in college, for whom the "realness" of perceived events didn't matter at all. What mattered was whether the event could keep her interest.

The waiter float-walked to our table with a coffee pot in one perfect hand and smiled serenely. He wanted to know if we were fine. We are fine, I told him, suddenly aware again of how much I was sweating. He seemed pleased. He filled our coffee cups. Away he went.

The heat rose in wavy lines down the block. I shifted toward some phantom umbrella shade.

"How were the kids this week?" Janet asked, referring to my students and clinic patients. I decided she got to make one more subject change before I pushed the rent issue.

"Dumb and horny," I answered, "per usual."

"Nothing exciting happened?" She always asked, even though she knew I couldn't tell her.

"One of our patients said he choked on a female condom," I said, and when she seemed disappointed, I added that now we were calling him Cunt-Throat around the office. She snorted a little. She didn't care if it was true, which it wasn't.

"Did you go back to Greenvale today?" she asked.

I nodded. She asked how it went, and I lied.

"It was cake," I said.

She put her fork down and sighed.

"Tam," she said, "I need to tell you something."

"Finally," I said.

She said she didn't want me to be mad, and she hoped I could be happy for her. "I'm moving out," she said.

"What?" I said, although of course I'd heard her.

"I'm moving in with John," she said. "He's totally clean now, and divorced, and everything's good, and we're ready."

She had to be kidding. Janet did not have real news about her own life. Maybe she got a new tattoo. I would believe she was pregnant, maybe. She broke my favorite wooden salad bowl, found a mouse in the kitchen, decided to quit wearing acrylics? But as she stared at her food I knew she was telling the truth.

"What about the rent we owe?" I said.

"I'm sure you can find a new roommate before the first," she said.

"I mean the past three months?"

Her phone rang and she answered it. Remy again. She told him it was a fine time to talk and avoided my eyes.

I couldn't believe Janet would leave me.

I had perfectly good reasons for not trusting John. He had tried to sleep with me after they got together. He had lied to Janet about still being married when they met. When he drank, which was every day, violence squirmed just under the surface of his skin. He probably had a sad childhood, and I wanted to be understanding, but he was a slave to his pain and rage. He wrote songs about killing people who disrespected his woman, then yelled at her for trivial misunderstandings, then called twenty times in a row to apologize. Janet loved that he was a musician. She loved how badly he "needed" her. One day he'd told Janet they needed to "take a break" so he could focus on his music. She found out he was fucking someone, told me she'd broken up with him for real, and we had made a deal not to argue about him again. Shortly after that Nathan Reggman attacked me, I installed a lock on my bedroom door, and hadn't thought about John since.

I wondered if they really had broken up. I wanted to be happy for her, but I wasn't. I considered the idea that she might be planning to leave without paying her half of the debt. We'd already received two thirty-day notices that our month-to-month agreement was being terminated unless we made rent. We were usually a little late with the checks, but neither of us had been able to pay at all the past three months, and so on the first of May, in less than a week, we would get a three-day pay or quit notice. If we could make a portion of a payment, and our landlord cashed the check, we'd be clear to scramble for money for at least another month. But I didn't have even the partial payment, and I'd been hoping Janet did. All my money went into a black hole of other debt. If we didn't pay, we could be forcibly evicted at the end of the three days, and we would have to go to court.

"Janet." I interrupted her.

She told Remy she had to go and hung up. "Don't be mad," she said.

"What am I supposed to do about the money?" I said.

"We'll figure it out," she said. "Don't worry about it."

The waiter was at my elbow. He had snuck up on me somehow, as if he sensed that I was about to start screaming. He was tan. The hair on his arms was dark, but not too thick. He wanted to know if we were finished.

Janet said yes as I said no. I cut into the last two inches of my omelet, and put a huge bite in my mouth. It was too crunchy. It didn't taste right. I must have grimaced. The waiter cocked his head to the side like a puppy, picked up my knife, and peeled back the top layer of egg.

Half a cockroach, about the size of my thumbnail, was still baked in. I retched, spitting my pile of half-chewed bug-egg onto the plate. Janet squealed. The waiter's eyes went huge. "Excuse me," he said, took the plate, and headed to the kitchen.

"Ugh, ugh ugh," I spit into a napkin, rinsed my mouth with water, and spit that onto the sidewalk.

"We're out of here," Janet said, and grabbed her bag.

I swished with coffee, and spit that out too. "What about the check?"

"Fuck that!"

She had a point. As a couple in matching bowling shirts started closing in on our table, I made a decision. I started writing my name and number on a napkin.

Janet asked what I was doing.

I told her I couldn't come back to Bitsy's after that. I'd have to switch to the créperie down the street. If the waiter never called I didn't have to see him again. It was risk-free, sort of.

"A Jersey girl who eats crépes!" Janet said, delighted, as if everything was fine between us.

I ran inside, checking my teeth for tiny legs, trying to imagine the waiter teaching me how to meditate, then sucking the gravity out of my toes. He was standing in the kitchen doorway, holding my plate, scolding someone at the stove.

"Here," I said, and held out the napkin. "I have to go."

"I'm so, so sorry about this," he said. He didn't take the napkin. "I can comp you another one."

"This is my number," I said. "I don't need another omelet."

"What?' he said.

"Just take this," I said. He took it.

Then I walked very quickly to my car.

I had no idea what to say to Janet. "I can't believe I ate that fucking bug," I said, and turned the ignition. "Give me some gum."

"It's a sign," she said.

Sure, I told her, a sign that Bitsy's had some health code violations. When she argued things like that don't just happen, I asked her how she could possibly interpret the symbolism of a cockroach wrapped in an omelet shroud.

"Things are changing," she said. "Even familiar things, like that same omelet you always order. You can't take anything for granted."

She was serious. Normally I would have laughed. This time, I was too hurt and angry. I had quit trying to convince her that "signs" didn't exist years ago.

I drove to StageRage, searching my memory of the past few months for indications of her wanting to move out while the neighborhood outside the car got more colorful. She said we'd work it out, but it was betrayal I felt, not hope.

"When was the last time you saw John?" I said. It had to be months.

"Yesterday," she said. "He came by the salon and we talked everything out."

That probably meant he brought her a teddy bear and told her he'd learned his lesson.

She said John had been clean and sober for a long time. He was working hard on his music. She really believed it. She rummaged aimlessly in her bag.

When I pulled up to her salon, she produced a sepia-toned, slightly crumpled flyer. "This is for a show that's on tonight, near the house. I thought it was the kind of stuff you'd like." She hopped out and the old Civic shook when she slammed the door.

I was double-parked on a side street that fed Hollywood Boulevard. Someone honked. I didn't care. On the flyer a girl in lace-ruffled bloomers, a black cat mask, stilettos, red lipstick, and nothing else stared steamily up at me. She held a whip across her chest at nipple-level. Bettie Paige meets Halle Berry, with some kind of Tiki god in the background. She had a gorgeous head of wild kinky hair, almond-colored skin in soft focus, and short black fingernails. Candles surrounded her. I turned the flyer over.

Fetish Art, Fifties Lounge Music, Exotica. A party-slash-art-show-slash-live-performance happening at Wacko, the bizarre book store, art gallery, and knickknack shop in our neighborhood. I tried to imagine a show fitting between the shelves of pin-up calendars, inflatable palm trees, vintage lunch boxes, and guns shaped like bull dogs that barked when you pulled the trigger. The guy behind me kept honking. I took my foot off the brake, rolled two feet, and stopped again. Janet was right; this was something I wanted to see. For a second I marveled at her ability to understand me even when she was getting ready to do something as thoughtless as move in with John, right before we got evicted. Then I gave in to the honking and took off to Fancy Nail.

THREE

When we met almost four years prior, Janet was bartending at Cheetah's. I was watching a stripper with a platinum pixie-cut scale the pole like a twelve-year-old boy. I sat alone at the bar, so Janet talked to me. She thought I was a lesbian, but was unaffected when I told her I wasn't. We did shots of tequila and talked about the etiquette of tipping the dancers.

"If you look, you tip," she said, "period. I don't care if you tip a girl you like more than a girl you don't, but you don't just watch for free, ever."

"You can't enforce that," I said.

"I can."

When I asked her how, she answered, "Shame." She said she embarrassed customers when they were stingy.

"And they come back here?"

She tucked the end of a bar towel into the back of her pants. "Yup." When I asked her why she didn't dance, she laughed at me. I wasn't brave enough to ask again.

Straight from New Jersey, I had moved into a surprisingly clean two-bedroom apartment in a cheap Hollywood neighborhood, naively thinking it would be easy to find a roommate. Then I had taken the clinic job, which paid considerably less than I expected considering I'd earned straight As in biology at Rutgers. I rejected everyone who answered my Craigslist ad—most for normal reasons: irritating, cats, etc.—but some simply on the basis of their inability to wear matching or neutral-toned clothing. I needed someone to help with rent who wouldn't hang garish paintings or unmatching tapestries, who didn't own furniture that clashed with mine. The second bedroom was a liability and I had been hubristic to pay for it in the first place, but everything else about the apartment was so calming to me—white walls, tile steps, painted-over kitchen cupboards and windowsills—that I couldn't leave. I'd planned to move to LA, work for a few years in the medical field, enjoy myself in the sun before the MCATs and an Ivy League med school and an illustrious career as a doctor, but those plans had begun to fall through at about the same time I met Janet. My savings were gone, and my credit card debt had begun to accumulate at an alarming pace.

I went back to Cheetah's the next night. Janet was leaving a bad relationship with John's predecessor and needed a place to stay. She promised to only bring her clothes (mostly black, I guessed, for work) and two boxes of toiletries. No furniture, no art. She made me laugh. I invited her to move in.

When she walked into the apartment the first day she said, "Not much of a decorator?" and ran her hand along the white canvas wall-covering.

"I like to keep it simple," I said, appreciating her matching purple manicure and pedicure.

I could have told her the truth: bad color combinations, especially ones that had symbolic associations like red and green, assaulted me. When the colors were right, I could think. When the colors were wrong, it hurt like Janet's long fingernails screeching down a chalkboard, in varying degrees of torture. I had to drive fast on the end of my street or I'd get light-headed looking at the brutal teal and yellow house on the corner. Wrong color combos had kept me at home under the covers, caused me to leave restaurants, pushed my head into my lap in movies, and forced me to spend hours and hours picking out my clothes. Around most holidays, I had to wear amber-tinted sunglasses in the grocery store to keep from panicking in all the decoration.

I could have told Janet about my hyper-sensitive feet, and confessed to getting sometimes three or four pedicures in a week. I might have even thrown in the detail about my to-do lists, how compulsively I had to finish them. Instead I told her the price of her room and my request that she not add anything to the common space.

"No problemo," she said. "But how about a TV? My ex doesn't deserve to keep it." So we got her TV and set it on a white stand.

Janet told me I was smart, and a good listener, but altogether too serious. She felt it was her duty to help me loosen up and find love. She took me on as her project and became my guide to the city.

I envied the way she experienced celebrity sightings, street performers, and vegan sushi as banal. I was simultaneously in awe of her social skills and filled with skepticism about the culture she navigated. She was from Studio City, the compromise for people who didn't really want to be in the Valley but also couldn't stomach Hollywood or West LA. Her parents worked in the entertainment machine; they owned a small lighting company and drove trucks with their name painted on the side. In many ways Janet embodied my stereotype of a Los Angeles native. She felt entitled to a lifestyle that included trendy restaurants, manicures, gossip, and disposable clothing from the imitation-designer stores on Melrose Ave—and she had never been truly rich. Rich people ate at even more expensive trendy restaurants. They got their manicures at spas, became the subjects of gossip instead of its spreaders, and disposed of clothing that cost hundreds of dollars. Same lifestyle, grander scale. What was most perplexing was how much Janet, and almost everyone else, seemed to trust this system implicitly.

Within our first few months of living together, and at my prompting, Janet started beauty school. She told me she hated bartending for so little money but knew she couldn't get a job at a nicer place because she didn't look like an actress. When she got her cosmetology license, she starting cutting hair, and told me that it was a much more fulfilling job than pouring drinks. It made perfect sense to Janet that at StageRage Salon she was styling hair for actors, musicians, and strippers who lived on cash and needed to look hot more than they needed to eat.

I parked in the lot behind Fancy Nail, shuffled inside, and wondered if it was too hot for a pedicure. Sun streamed through the windows and I held a magazine to the back of my neck in the vinyl waiting chair. A man in tight black jeans yelled in Vietnamese from the reception desk and the smell of acetone burned in my throat. I had driven for less than ten minutes and entered yet another world.

When I first moved to LA I was struck, like every newcomer, by the fact that it is not one city. I knew it would be enormous, but I was not prepared for it to lack a real city limit, to be comprised of hundreds of distinct neighborhoods, strewn over valleys and hills without much order. In New Jersey, driving for two hours meant crossing state lines. In Southern California, it meant leaving LA, entering Burbank or Santa Monica or West Hollywood for a few minutes, and then crossing back into LA. I had to learn the major differences between Hollywood, North Hollywood, and West Hollywood fast, or sound like an idiot. (Hollywood: touristy, but also full of bums; North Hollywood: officially in the Valley, but with an up-and-coming arts scene; West Hollywood: separate city, lovely, gay.) There was also a slippery caché of coolness that seemed to migrate from neighborhood to neighborhood. A bar might be packed for six months and then, like geese in the winter, all the hip kids would suddenly be feeding somewhere else. The longer I spent in LA the more complex it all became.

I wanted to find my niche in LA since I had not found one anywhere in Jersey. Before I moved, I had envisioned cruising down a ridiculously large highway, my curly hair flipping around in the wind, on my way to a function at a mansion overlooking the ocean. The problem was that my understanding of where I'd fit was about forty years and at least two socioeconomic classes off. I was so well versed in glam and noir, because of classic movies and mystery novels, that I thought I knew both the nice and ugly sides of the city. But LA didn't have only two sides, like it did in a 1950s detective story. It had hundreds. It seemed a strange pastiche of '50s glam, '60s chic, '70s hip, '80s cool, '90s slum, and millennial schizophrenia, all at once. This was part of the reason why my apartment was so important to me. I'd landed there, and made it my own. I could breathe there—no colors out of place, no patients, no students, no pressure, no cultural cacophony unraveling my identity.

LA shocked me by revealing how true most of its reputation was, at least in Hollywood and Silver Lake. The cityscape actually boasted stylish outfits, small dogs wearing jewelry, and big sunglasses. Palm trees and banana-leaf plants framed the streets in my neighborhood. Off the Hollywood and Sunset Boulevard strip, though, decayed pockets of poverty presented an astounding disparity. What made Los Angeles poverty so surreal was that it looked better, had more character, than New Jersey poverty. The thugs that ran the streets near my clinic wore new clothes all the time, and recorded themselves rapping into their cell phones. There were certainly ugly areas, but the poor sections of downtown included blocks of amazing old Art Deco buildings and Spanish tile roofs. The bums in Venice got to sit on the beach every day. Life in the ghettos, which was the same as everywhere else—try to find work, eat, pay bills, deal with street violence—had a peculiar backdrop of sunny skies. Even the dangerous downtown high schools, where angry kids leaned against moldy walls, were more inviting to me than the city schools back home. Maybe, the "bad" parts of town in LA seemed nicer because they reminded me of fictional movie slums. And they were never bleakly covered in a foot of dirty snow.

I came to Fancy Nail because of Anh, an especially talented foot-massager. The customers were all white, the employees all Asian, and I felt uncomfortable participating in whatever system perpetuated that segregation. I wondered if my perception that LA poverty was somehow more aesthetic than poverty in other big cities was simple reverse discrimination. Was I seeing everything with an imperialist eye—a conqueror come to claim her place in the glorious West? Was I one of those irritating women who fantasizes about the wrong side of the tracks and then pretends she belongs there, like Carmen Sternwood, the troublemaking heiress in *The Big Sleep*? I hated thinking I was yet another privileged white girl trying to get into trouble. On the other hand, as another memory of Nathan pushed through my thoughts, I was definitively of the middle class, and got into trouble without trying.

Even after four years of working with all types of people at the clinic, I still often thought about Los Angeles the city as it existed in books, movies, and TV shows. I didn't know if it was possible to have an "authentic" experience in a city where everything was for show. But I loved the show. There had to be a way to enjoy the beauty of the surface, and still navigate issues of race, class, gender, and so on, with a moral compass. Of course that question had been asked before, by a whole genre of movies like *Sunset Boulevard*, musicians like Tom Waits, poets like Bukowski, painters, photographers, and countless novelists and philosophers.

No one could resist theorizing Los Angeles. I'd read Baudrillard's *Simulations* for a postmodern philosophy class that met in a tiny, windowless room at Rutgers. My professor had stood up from her table and cut the air with her hands in her urgency.

"Baudrillard wrote that Disneyland was LA, and LA was Disneyland, and thinking you've stepped out of the illusion when you leave the park is the grandest illusion of all," she said. "Disneyland is presented as imaginary, so that we'll believe the rest is real, when in fact none of LA, no part of America even, is real anymore." Baudrillard made up the word *hyperreal* to describe American culture.

I believed it, but instead of feeling Baudrillard's disgust at this contrivance, I was drawn to the spectacle. In class discussion, anti-LA sentiment ran high, and my peers all seemed to believe they alone could see through the unreality of a place like Los Angeles. To defend the sheer aesthetic value of LA would have been sophomoric, so I stayed quiet. I kept my notes from that class because I had written a to-do list in the margin called "Places to Go in LA at Least Once," and I couldn't throw the list away until I'd crossed them all off.

Even though countless other people had done it, and thought more brilliant thoughts about it before, once in LA I couldn't help but love the feeling of driving around the city-sized carnival, noticing all the unlikely storefronts nailed to asymmetrical 1960s architecture.

Now I checked my watch. I needed to get in that pedicure chair, fast. I couldn't bring myself to pester. I pulled another magazine out of the pile and flipped to an ad for discounted Disneyland fees for Southern California residents. It would have felt predestined, if Disney wasn't so ubiquitously part of LA's visual culture as billboard, TV commercial, storefront.

One of Janet's first goals as my friend, not just my roommate, was to take me to Disneyland. According to her, it would be an amazing day because I wasn't tainted by the Florida park, like most East Coasters. Janet insisted that Orlando's Disney World was inferior, because it was not designed with magic in mind. It was flat and wide with dead space in between the attractions.

"When you go into the real Disneyland," she told me, "you'll realize that you can't see out. You can't see the highway, you can't see the power lines, you can't see anything but Disneyland."

"Sounds creepy," I said.

"You don't get it," she said.

Janet went so often as a child, she didn't need a map. She knew where to eat lunch (Bengal Barbeque, the most meat for your money) and she knew which rides would have the shortest lines at which time of day (Big Thunder Mountain during a parade). She pulled me around the park, pointed at everything, and gave me a tour that was a mix of two histories: Disney's and her own. I wished I'd known people like her back in college, so I could have suggested in class that anywhere you make formative memories is real.

"This is where I made out with Ben, my first love," she told me as we scaled the plastic-coated steps of the Tarzan Tree House. "Of course it was the Swiss Family Robinson Tree House then," she said, "not this Phil Collins bullshit."

"I just flew in from Tomorrowland," said our boat operator on the Jungle Cruise, "and boy is my hovercraft tired."

"This ride has been here since 1955," Janet said as our boat shuddered slowly forward into murky chlorinated water.

"So have their jokes," I said.

Every corner we turned was full of bright colors and smells and loud bands playing. I started to have fantasies about a noir movie set there, after hours, when all the hardhats came out from underground to tweak things with wrenches and hose the sidewalks. A mysterious woman would haunt the park, there would be a death, the police would have to search incognito. It could have starred Bette Davis. Or maybe someone younger. I started babbling aloud about this idea on our way out of the Tiki Room, wondering why it never happened when the park might have still needed the money a movie studio could offer.

Janet was horrified.

"I thought you liked scary stuff," I said.

"Not here," she said. And that was it—Disneyland was exempt, for her, from anything painful. No great tragedy had ever befallen her there. Her memories were all sweet, sparkly, full of orange popsicles and sunburnt shoulders, waiting for the parade, a special birthday dinner at the Blue Bayou, her favorite stuffed toy, a Minnie Mouse, that her father bought her when she was seven. Ruining any of that with a violent story crossed her line of taste. Probably it had crossed Walt's too. I felt like a heretic.

Despite her incessant asking, "Isn't this fun?" I had a great day with Janet. I told her it was almost too much fun. A place like that was too busy with color for my matching sensor to really process. I got claustrophobic in the chaos, and unbearably tired. I said something about how the guys in bow ties with the fancy brooms and dustpans might need a break too, and Janet rolled her eyes.

"They're helping set the stage," she said, like there was no way they could resent the job. "They're cast members." She pointed at an inconspicuous door with a cute sign that read: Cast Members Only!

I decided not to lecture her on the complex injustice of the minimum-wage system.

On the way home that night, I worried that my childhood memories and games would always be inferior to someone who had grown up with Disneyland as their playground. Seaside Heights, the beach boardwalk I went to on the Jersey shore, was a crusty, smelly, junky heap of scrap metal next to the burnished, polished brilliance of Disney. That I liked Disneyland as the imagined setting of a noir film had only reinforced my belief that I was doomed to desire an alternative lifestyle forever. Feeling lonely in the car while Janet slept against the window, I thought about philosophers, murder mysteries, and postmodern concepts of visual reality. I wanted to argue to someone that I'd had just as fun and amazing a day as Janet, that seeing Disney the way I did didn't ruin it at all, but she wouldn't care, and there was no one else to talk to.

Finally Anh's pencil-thin fingers wielded a large file on my toes. Because of a near superhuman skin sensitivity on my feet, pedicures were the most pleasurable experience I could pay for, legally. I had to have them nearly every other day, or I became uselessly preoccupied with a disgusting feeling that my toenails were growing too fast. I'd been to almost every nail place within a ten-mile radius of my apartment, including StageRage, Janet's salon. The nail "specialist" there caused me to grip the chair and breathe through my teeth while she scrubbed my heels with what appeared to be a cheese grater.

But not Anh. Anh gave a foot massage that would make anyone an addict. She used jasmine lotion and pushed into my arches with her knuckles, never too hard. When she spoke in Vietnamese to the other women she worked with, she sounded bawdy, like she was asking rude question after rude question. When she talked to me in English she smiled and her volume dropped fifty decibels. I pretended to read whatever magazines were floating around her table while I eavesdropped on her voice. I always chose the same color polish as my skin, a pinky-beige that gave me Barbie feet when I flexed just right.

My phone rang as Anh lowered my feet into a bucket of tepid suds. The screen blinked a local number I didn't know. I considered myself brave to answer.

It was the Bitsy's waiter, calling from the restaurant. I could hear the kitchen. He said his name was Bow.

"Like a bow tie?" I said, stupidly.

"More like the simple beauty that is created by the human mind interacting with raw materials," he said. I choked a little. "My mother was a weaver," he continued. "She loved the impermanence of a bow, how quickly one could turn a bow into a knot."

"Oh," I said. First of all, he called too fast. Secondly, he was crazy.

"I'm kidding," he said, and the way his voice relaxed made my shoulders lower two inches. "It's short for Bowen. It was my mom's maiden name, she liked it, she gave it to me."

When he apologized for the cockroach, I realized he might be calling because we hadn't paid for Janet's food. Of course we hadn't tipped him either. Plus I had handed him my number in the most awkward way possible.

"I hope that little guy had a good life," I said.

"Me too," he said. We both waited for a second. "So are you the kind of girl who gives a guy her number and then makes him do all the work?" Then, "Sorry, I need to get this." He clicked over to another call.

I had been to so many professional trainings for sex educators, read so many books, and researched so many bedroom behaviors I had become a sex-and-relationships snob, at least in theory. I felt most guilty for behaving predictably, like a musician who hates to love pop songs, so Bow's challenge made me feisty. The gender roles of the heterosexual mating dance bored me so much that I was filled with self-loathing whenever I caught myself lowering my eyes or giggling around a man. I should have been too smart for all that. Of course I occasionally still acted like a coquettish girl-programmed robot, but I tried hard not to. This definitely contributed to my lack of dating prospects.

At least Bow hadn't seemed to be warning me I was about to be arrested.

He came back on the line, and with a ball of terror in my gut, I asked if he was busy tonight.

Nope, he said, and asked me what I wanted to do, like we'd been hanging out for years.

I thought about the flyer. I told him there was a show I wanted to go see at Wacko. I tried to describe it without scaring him away, although clearly it was odd to invite someone to an erotic art show for a first date, especially after coming to his work and watching him so often. But he was the one who had called right away. We might have been tied on the Creepiness Scale.

"The fifties fetish show?" he said. "Have you been before?"

"This isn't the first one?" I asked, feeling silly for describing something he'd already seen.

"Oh my God!" he yelled. "This is going to be fun. Want to meet there? It gets going around eleven. Oh, wait, should we eat dinner first?"

I told him to pick the restaurant. Meeting at the show might signal that I was only interested in sex. Of course I was interested, but I also didn't want to preempt any possibility of a real date. They were such a novelty. I suppressed visions of his naked body carrying a coffee pot to me in bed. That only produced visions of him in a moment of ecstasy, fucking me from behind in the Bitsy's kitchen. My heart was beating too hard.

"They don't mess with the food too much at Lala's," he said. "I can pick you up. Like eight?" I thought about him driving, and imagined his feet hovering over the pedals. Did he walk on the ground outside of the restaurant? I had a hard time making the voice on the phone match my image of him presiding over Bitsy's like a sexy monk. Was it a bad sign that he'd been to this show before? I decided not.

I told him how to get to my apartment while Anh toweled off my feet.

"Bye, Tam-jam," he said and hung up. No one but Grant Rose, my childhood best friend, had ever used that nickname with me. She'd be jealous if she knew someone else had come up with it. I had a strong pang of missing her. We hadn't spoken in over two years. She'd be jealous if she knew I'd gotten so close to Janet, too.

I had to get to the clinic by three-thirty, and be home by six, since it would take me at least an hour to get dressed. For a second, I wanted to call Janet and tell her about the date. I focused on my feet. I wondered if I had been thinking about sex with Bow because I was getting a pedicure when he called.

Anh yelled something to another manicurist who was sitting across the pink padded table from me, leaning on a white towel. They both cracked up. I wondered if they talked about customers, or their husbands and boyfriends, or if they were secretly planning a way out of that tacky room with its chemical haze. I wondered if they were lovers. From the walls, 1980s-era posters of cartoon women with solid black, punky hair stared down at me. They looked like they should sing backup for Robert Palmer, with hot pink on their lips, fingernails, and roses held in their skinny hands. I could deal with it all because the pink on the tables was exactly the same color.

I had to call Janet. She was my only close girlfriend now, and even though I was angry, I didn't want to add more drama by keeping things from her that I would normally tell.

"StageRage Salon," she answered, sounding bored.

"I have a date with the waiter tonight," I said as I moved a miniature nail fan around so that it pointed at my face.

"No fucking way!" she said. "Come over here and let me do your hair!"

I told her I didn't have time. I had to go back to work. I asked her if she could find another ride home.

"Of course," Janet said, "you go get some ass!" I heard Remy, who hopefully was not with a customer, start singing 1970s porno-soundtrack guitar—bowmn-chicka-bowm-bowm—in the background. Janet yelled to him that I was on my way to get some straight-boy booty, which was a way of making fun of me for dating Todd.

"Get it, girl!" Remy hollered.

"Charming," I said. "Thanks." Anh tapped my feet and I put them under the UV dryer. Then she held out her hand for my credit card. I suddenly wanted to yell at Janet. I felt a rising panic about the apartment, my apartment, the only safe place I had.

"Have fun," Janet said, in her you-know-what-I-mean voice.

I told her I had to go and hung up.

I hadn't had sex in almost a year, since Todd and I broke up. It wasn't grief that kept me alone, but a queasy suspicion that every man I'd be attracted to would somehow turn out to be fundamentally, on principle, against the idea of being with me. I wasn't worried about the soft mysteries of the human heart—"I don't know what happened," "I just don't feel the same way anymore," "It's not you, it's me"—those rejections were cake. Todd and I were close, but I'd still hidden most of my problems from him, and I was sure he would have left me eventually even if he hadn't been gay. In addition to the colors issue, and the toenails, and the to-do lists, I had an inability to control my spending, which had led to terrifyingly deep credit card debt. I opened one of every five threatening letters that came in, paid down a bill so I could use one card, then piled the rest of the mail in a corner in my room. Now that I was battling the aftermath of being attacked, it seemed even less likely that another human being should take on the weight I carried around. My attractiveness as a potential mate had hit a minimum.

I always overtipped Anh, and she always patted my shoulder and said she'd see me soon. Anh may have laughed behind my back, but she had a graceful way of not openly shaming me for getting a pedicure every two days. I convinced myself that one date with Bow was still worth it, if only for the story I could tell Todd and Janet later.

FOUR

Heading out on Sunset to the clinic, I watched the red taillights on the red car ahead of me and wished they were the same red. Helena, our clinic director, didn't need me to assist on an annual exam, but Layla, the patient, had requested that I be there. Layla was one of our true sex workers, a fairly major porn star. She'd shown up at the SLLC a few years ago with a yeast infection, and kept coming back. Adult industry standards required "players" to get tested every thirty days for HIV, which Layla did at a free clinic in Sherman Oaks. She came to us like she would a regular doctor: for the flu, check-ups, annual exams. She had a strong head for business and a surprising sense of self-respect.

Other young porn stars generally depressed me, even though I supported their right to work in the sex industry and the general idea of erotic entertainment. I probably supported them more wholeheartedly and idealistically than any other woman they knew. I wanted good, sexy movies to get made. The problem, if my patients were any indication, was that it was a rare director who made his actresses feel confident, respected, and protected on set. It was a rare cast or crew member who made the decision to make porn out of some creative impulse—most liked the parties and the money. And the industry was not helping us promote public health. Even with a recent outbreak of chlamydia at one of the larger production companies, most sets didn't require condoms. Layla, in contrast, worked for a small production company that appeared to treat her well.

She paid taxes, owned a house in the Valley somewhere, and came to the SLLC because she liked the staff. She told me once that she didn't feel uncomfortable discussing her work with us, and that was most important, even though she could have afforded a fancier doctor. She made a very nice living traveling between LA and Las Vegas shooting movies and escorting Hollywood men to snazzy parties. Layla invested money for when she "retired" in a year or two.

Layla smoked weed, which I also generally supported, especially since she had somehow avoided becoming a drunk or a cokehead. Most incredibly, she never allowed a man in her circle to become her complete financial support. Whenever I caught myself wondering why a girl like her would stay in porn, I remembered that she probably made three times what I made in a year, for a tenth of the hours. It was my job not to judge her. Anyway the industry would never become more safe and equitable unless women like Layla stayed in it.

The two girls who worked the SLLC front desk had already left. I unlocked the doors and flipped on the lights in the waiting room and the hallway. When I'd joined the staff, the building had needed a new coat of paint. I showed so much interest in decorating the place that I was put in charge. All the rooms got painted a light blue that blended very nicely with the brown vinyl furniture we'd been unable to throw away.

I opened the metal cabinets where we kept the charts, found Layla's, and set it in the box outside an exam room. I pulled a Pap smear kit from over the sink, replaced the wax paper on the table and checked the clock. I was early. I reviewed Layla's chart.

The date of her last exam jumped off the page—I'd seen her on a Saturday afternoon, and been attacked and admitted to the hospital by the same time two days later, on Monday. Of course. Schools tended to book us once a semester, with a six-to-eight month gap in between visits. Layla had an abnormal Pap six months ago. That I would visit Nathan's school and see Layla on the same day was a meaningless coincidence. Nevertheless, my body responded like Nathan had just come up behind me and twisted me into a headlock.

I tried breathing slowly, but kept sipping air and holding it. I felt like I was at the top of a roller coaster, in the slow moment of tipping over to the other side. I tried to flip the pages of the chart to distract myself, but it was too late. The memory of the attack, which had been pushing into consciousness in disjointed bits of physical panic all morning, blazed in my body like it was happening all over again.

That day we had booked two schools for the same time slot so Todd and

I had done them alone. The SLLC shirts seemed more official when I was with Todd. People often mistook me for a student, so to gear up for going it alone, I wore black platform boots and dark eyeliner. I scrunched my short curls with a lot of gel.

The tenth grade at Greenvale High had spent one week talking about "Reproduction and Your Choices." The health teacher had requested a succinct, apolitical discussion of "how to avoid pregnancy and disease." I told him it was impossible to be totally apolitical, but, I assured him, I was trained to adhere to state education standards and would be happy to discuss pregnancy prevention, STIs, and the resources available to teens in their area. When I arrived at the classroom, one of the students was visibly pregnant. She wore a burgundy velvet dress over black leggings and had pulled her long brown hair into a ponytail. Her notebook and pen were poised on the desk, ready to take notes. No one was talking to her.

Usually pregnant teens were shuttled into alternative programs, got home schooled, took their GEDs, or dropped out. I wondered how she'd stayed in regular classrooms this long, and why. Maybe she knew she'd get an even worse education if she let the administration push her out. I did my best to keep my eyes focused on the kids' faces. They sat close together at old chair-desks in a bungalow classroom that would crumble in a heavy rain. A few of them slept on their arms or leaned against the back wall, desks tipped up at perilous angles. Black, blue, burgundy sweatshirts. Brown sweater. White T-shirt. The brown had to go.

I introduced myself, wrote our clinic name and number on the board, and passed out a stack of my cards.

"I'm here today to talk about sex," I said. I told them I wouldn't be able to cover everything they needed to know, so they should come visit us to ask questions, see a doctor, or find out more about any services we discussed. "We're going to do some group work later," I said, and then I asked the girl in the brown sweater to move to a group a few rows over. She did. I could focus.

When I asked the class to brainstorm the major ways to prevent pregnancy, the only ones they knew of were "pulling out," which I debunked and didn't write on the board, abstinence, condoms, and the Pill. None of them had heard of an IUD, a contraceptive sponge, a Nuva Ring, or a female condom. They'd never heard of Depo shots. I wondered how long it had been since their health teacher had updated his curriculum.

While discussing pregnancy and STIs I carefully used the conditional phrase "if you choose to have sex," to make sure it was implied that they could choose not to. That way, abstinence itself didn't come off as a joke. To be in compliance with the permission slip all their parents had signed, I had to "emphasize" abstinence, even during what was legally determined to be a comprehensive education presentation.

I drew a pie chart on the board that represented everyone in the classroom.

"Right now," I said, "national statistics predict that about half of you are sexually active." I filled in half the pie with vertical lines. "Over the next ten years, those numbers go up drastically." I filled in nearly the rest of the pie.

"Of these people," I said, pointing at the filled-in section, "it is predicted that nearly 75 percent will be exposed to HPV, or genital warts, at some point in their lifetime." I cross-hatched 75 percent of the filled-in section. I explained that not everyone would develop warts, in fact most of them wouldn't, but they could still pass the virus on. We went over chlamydia, herpes, and the other common STI symptoms, treatments, and implications.

I discussed ways to be intimate with a partner that didn't involve pregnancy or STI risk. I distributed a stack of pamphlets that recapped some stats on rates of STIs in student populations and ways to protect yourself and your partner. The pregnant student wrote a few things down. At the time, she was the only student I truly noticed, apart from a terrible combo of reds and browns in the corner that occurred when a boy pulled off his sweatshirt.

In my memory now, though, Nathan Reggman's blond hair shone from the back row of the classroom like it was on fire.

Although there hadn't been time to talk about good communication in sexual relationships, I thought I had done a pretty good class. More faces turned toward me than didn't, no one called out anything particularly offensive, and I heard some actual laughter when I said, "What's a four-letter word for fun? Lube!" during the brief section when I stopped emphasizing abstinence and talked about ways to safely enhance pleasure.

As the students left, the health teacher, a rounded fiftyish man who had been innocuously polite until that moment, approached me with an uninvited critique.

"You should have shown them pictures of genital warts or syphilis," he said.

"Are you serious?" I said.

He shrugged.

I reminded him that most people with HPV didn't have visible warts. "Some of this stuff is scary enough already without pushing extreme cases at them. We don't overemphasize unlikely outcomes."

"You could have told them that once they have a kid they will never get to hang out with their friends again," he said.

I told him I didn't think that would be particularly respectful to the experience of the pregnant girl in the class, who was obviously choosing to carry her child to term. I zipped up my bag.

"She's a sad one," he said. "These girls just keep burping out babies."

"It takes something pretty terrible to shock me," I said. "Congratulations."

"What'd I say?" he asked, hands open, blameless.

"Burping out babies?" I said. "Really?"

"Relax," he said, "don't get all uptight."

I said goodbye and left. No doubt his assessment of my presentation, which would be mailed to my clinic and reviewed by my director, would be scathing anyway. He must have been the one teacher who taught Sex Ed in the school for the past thirty years, and was threatened by new blood.

I was loading my bags into the trunk when Nathan walked up to me. At first, he seemed like any other kid who had some embarrassing question he wanted to ask without everyone overhearing. His backpack sagged around his thighs, straps straining.

"You from the SLLC?" he asked. He was tall. His straight blond hair, matted like a surfer's, fell into his eyes.

I answered yes and closed the trunk.

"Your name's Tamina?"

I nodded. I'd said my name only once, at the beginning of the class.

His face changed. He was getting angry, shaking his head, tensing. I asked if I could help him, but already my gut had gone cold.

"You didn't even fuckin' call me," he said.

"Wait a minute," I said, trying to understand. As I glanced over his shoulder to see if there was anyone else around, he raised his right arm over his chest. I met his eyes for a split second—bright, painfully bright blue—and then he hit me across the cheek with the back of his hand. My head down, arms over my face, I smelled my own soured sweat while he punched my side. He grabbed my wrists and tried to pry my arms open. I lost my footing, yelling "please, stop, please!" smacked into the asphalt, there was another sharp pain to my side before all the pain became the same—dull, throbbing, everywhere, I tried to curl up like the smallest insect, keep my face and stomach inside a shell, he wore brand new red and black Nikes, the scent of my own hair gel confused me, it didn't belong, he was yelling, he was crying, blaming me for something, his dead baby, he spat, it hit my arm, he crushed my temple, the asphalt cut into my face, he kicked, I coughed up a terrible bitterness, and then, with a whoosh that was blood in my ears or something more supernatural, I was lifted away, and all was quiet.

Freezing and sweating, short breaths keeping me from throwing up, I stayed in the clinic chair, unable to loosen my muscles enough to move.

Nathan had gotten a girl pregnant. I'd helped his girlfriend, ex-girlfriend, or whoever, get an abortion. If she was the girl I'd seen most recently before the attack, she was one of the easy cases—mind made up, very calm, and articulate about her reasons. She assured me that the father didn't want to be involved. It was her right.

When I filed a police report from the hospital, the cop told me we probably wouldn't be able to find him. No witnesses.

I started with Greenvale High's website. They posted photos of all their sports teams. Eventually, I found a boy, a junior, named Nathan Reggman. He played baseball. He smiled in the team photo, his hair sticking out from under his cap like straw. Looking at him, my heart raced, my stomach lurched. I wondered how his girlfriend, or whomever, had told him she was pregnant—before or after the abortion? I wondered if he had anyone to talk to about it. I hated him. I worried for him, too—a young man with that kind of violent streak would likely lose control again. But maybe not. Maybe he'd so horrified himself that he was already in some kind of behavior management therapy. If I went to the police and gave them the name, and it led to his being arrested, I was complicit in the trauma he would suffer, and nothing about him would improve. He would likely emerge from the California penal system worse than before: more violent, uneducated, outcast. I would have to retell and relive the attack again and again. But if I didn't tell the police, I was complicit also, in letting someone dangerous go. I told myself I didn't need to decide until all the physical wounds healed.

Six months had passed, and still I had done nothing, except go back to Greenvale for a bad assembly.

I hadn't read any more of Layla's chart when the bell at the door announced her arrival. I wiped my eyes, took a few seconds to control my breath, and met her in the waiting room.

Her new hair was bright red underneath, platinum blonde on top, and curly. Tight black capris, studded arm bands, a ripped tank top, and dark, shiny red lip gloss.

We said hello, and I walked her into the exam room, checking the time again. Helena was late. My heart would not stop racing.

"So, how've you been?" Layla said.

"Busy," I said, fighting the urge to cry. "You?"

"I'm awesome," she said. "I'm great. I got married!" She held up her ring finger, on which sat a very large, very yellow diamond.

I congratulated her. "I didn't know you were engaged," I said.

"We weren't!" she laughed. "I met this guy when I was out with some friends and we all decided to go up to Vegas together, like, spur of the moment?" She shook her head. They had fallen in love, stayed in Vegas for the week, and gotten married.

"Wow," I said, simultaneously horrified by this apparent lack of judgment and jealous of how thrilled she seemed. Her story reminded me of Janet. I walked to the sink and washed the clamminess off my hands. I willed myself to focus.

They had been married for two months, Layla said, and it was amazing.

Maybe if Janet didn't have to apologize for John, and could convince me he was amazing, I'd be able to support her. I briefly imagined Nathan ten years in the future, staggering out of a Vegas chapel with some faceless girl.

I told Layla I was happy for her. "So you feel like getting a follow-up Pap smear to celebrate?"

"Right," Layla's face softened. "I'm really glad you're here, because I wanted to ask you about something."

I sat in the chair across from the exam table and asked her what was up.

"There's something wrong with me," she said, "and I am, like, freaking out."

"What kind of thing?"

"Okay, I like sex, right?" She told me she was one of the only girls she knew who wasn't constantly wasted on set. She knew she was a porn director's dream. "I'm a good sport," she said. "I'll do, you know, the stuff that's hard to book?" I assumed she meant double penetration, anal/oral, things like that.

"You are a good sport," I said.

"But I don't like sex with Martin, my husband," she sighed. "It's boring. And so then I go dry and of course I don't want to stop in the middle and be like, honey, can you get me the lube because you're not turning me on enough to enjoy this right now."

"Ah," I said. I always told people that needing lube didn't necessarily indicate a lack of attraction, but she sounded very clear about it.

"He's a sweet, sweet guy, and he's totally supportive of me and has no problem with what I do, but he's not into bondage or toys or anything like that. Like nothing. Like he's not even into a threesome."

"That surprises me," I said.

"I know! I know!" She started picking at a loose thread on her pants.

I wondered if I needed to be taking notes.

"What is he doing falling in love with a porn star when he doesn't even want to get freaky?" she asked. When they'd first met, she had been happy with how calm he was about her job. Now, she wished he was more interested. "He doesn't even want it every day," she said. "God, what should I do? He's like Mr. Perfect, you know? Do you have any idea how hard it is to have a good relationship when you do what I do? No one can deal with it."

I wanted to tell her I knew exactly what she meant. Instead I said, "Maybe that's how he's dealing with it." I suggested that he might think she got enough bondage, toys, and threesomes at work, and when the two of them were intimate, he wanted it to be different.

"Then why doesn't it turn me on?"

"I don't know," I said. I asked her if she'd ever lubed beforehand, with a jelly instead of a water-based product.

"Then he wouldn't go down on me."

I didn't want her to leave without some new ideas. "What do you enjoy, that you never get to do on the set? If you feel okay telling me," I said. She waved her hand to dismiss my modesty while she thought for a few seconds.

"I like talk," she said. "Like not 'fuck it, yeah, eat that pussy' kind of talk, but like 'you're my angel, you're so beautiful, I'm so in love with you' talk. I had this one boyfriend a few years ago who had a southern accent? He would always say that stuff to me."

I suggested she try that with Martin, and she worried it wouldn't work.

I suggested she try a marriage counselor, and she said she'd rather leave him than try to find a therapist who wouldn't judge her for being in porn. I offered referrals but she just rolled her eyes.

"I wish I could help you more," I said. I told her what she was going through was actually pretty common.

"I'm sexually dysfunctional!" she wailed. "I'm a slut! I'm only turned on when people are watching me!"

"Maybe," I said, "you and Martin could try public sex? Bathrooms? In the car?" I almost said "parking lots" but swallowed it. "The risk of getting caught might rev you up some. Of course I'm not officially recommending this, since it is illegal." I winked.

"You know what?" she smacked her leg with a realization. "He keeps his eyes closed."

"Aha!" I said, like I knew why that was relevant.

"I need him to keep them open. I want him to watch me while we're doing it."

"Well, there you go," I said.

"You are so fucking brilliant," she said and hugged me.

I told her I didn't think I'd helped much.

"Bullshit," she said. "You probably saved my marriage."

As I insisted it was no big deal, Helena knocked and opened the door.

"Girl talk?" she said.

"Tam is a fucking genius," Layla said.

"I'll get you a gown," I said.

Although Helena worked efficiently, I tried to help by organizing, labeling, and preparing things for the lab. I should have taken Layla's blood pressure, weight, and height before Helena showed up. I was shaking a little, still. As Layla dressed, and Helena puttered in her office, I made a notation in Layla's file: April 25, some probs adj. to marriage—and signed my name. I checked the appointment book to make sure I could leave. I dreaded asking Helena to let me go early. She had written me letters of recommendation for med school for two years. She thought I was busy getting ready to be a doctor, having a rough time because the Rutgers program wasn't premed. She didn't know I had never been brave enough to apply. I read her letters and then put them in the stack of other mail I couldn't deal with in my room.

I knocked on her door. She let me in.

"Would it be alright if I came in to do paperwork for a few hours tomorrow and got going early this afternoon?" I said in one breath.

"No more appointments?" she said.

I shook my head.

"I can take care of the phones until the desk staff come back in," she said. "You go on."

"Thank you so much," I said.

She told me to have fun.

In my office, I added "Look Up Post-Traumatic Stress" to my to-do list. There was a name for the kind of memory I'd had in the office and I needed to know what it was.

I couldn't help but think about the fact that I had five days to find a new, color-compatible roommate or come up with a substantial portion of a full month's rent, which led to some familiar anxiety about how I was going to pay any of the back rent we owed. I needed to stop getting pedicures, but when I thought of it my toes itched deep inside, and I could feel the nails pushing out, growing. I'd considered asking my parents for a loan, but they barely had any savings as it was. They didn't have a few thousand dollars to spare, plus, the idea of owing them money made me nauseous. To pay for college, I had taken out student loans, all of which were now in forbearance. I had never asked my parents for financial help.

I wanted to call Bow and cancel, hide under the covers in my room, and watch some old detective movie. But it was my first date in a year. I had to go. I planned to stop thinking about money, at least until the morning. I also planned to stop thinking about Janet, and her betrayal. And Nathan. Period. It would ruin my chances of appearing charming to have those thoughts blipping across my face every few minutes. I needed to get home and figure out what to wear.

FIVE

Our place was on the second floor and as I walked up the Spanish tile steps, I rifled through the mail. Bills, junk, bills, and a sex toy catalog. Somehow one of the companies had gotten my home address, instead of the SLLC's. What to wear to meet Bow? I was digging in my purse for keys when John opened my door from inside.

"Lovely Tamina!" he said.

"Janet failed to mention that she'd given you a key," I said.

"Just helping out," he said, and backed away so I could get in. John had the sort of pickled look of a lifetime alcoholic. He was almost the same as the last time I saw him—scruffy beard, tan, prematurely wrinkled skin, beer in his hand—but he'd gained some weight.

"Starchy jail food?" I asked, and poked his gut.

"Still a bitch?" he said, poking back. He leaned in the arch between the living room and the kitchen. A few ratty cardboard boxes sagged behind him, randomly packed with an assortment of both my and Janet's things. He ran a hand over his stomach.

"Did you do that?" I asked, nodding at the boxes.

"Didn't I say I was helping?" He jiggled his beer can, then swigged.

I told him I thought he'd gotten sober.

He smiled at me. He said he was.

When I headed toward my room, he moved in front of me.

"It's so, so good to see you," he said softly.

"You smell like beer," I said. I tried to walk around him, but he dodged in front of me, laughing, like we were playing a game. I backed away, sat on the couch, and sorted through the mail. After standing still for a few seconds, he sat next to me.

"My mom died last month," he said.

I got up and ran for my room. "I'm sorry about that," I hollered over my shoulder. No wonder he needed Janet to move in. He couldn't possibly take care of himself and his brother alone. As I locked the door I felt guilty for my lack of compassion. A Prince CD sat on my stereo. Perfect. I turned on my fan and wished I'd thought to flip on the air conditioning before retreating.

"Don't have to be beautiful," I sang, "to turn me on." I opened the closet. I thumbed through the black section and pulled out a dress. I slid the mirrored doors closed, held the dress up, then put it back. Too boring. I moved to the red section. I pulled a red top and black skirt. I closed the doors and held them up. No. I put the top and skirt back. I moved to the green section.

Outside my room, John sounded like he was pacing.

I couldn't wear any colors together that had thematic associations (no red and blue: too patriotic, no black and white: zebras). I couldn't wear colors that reminded me of a brand label or anything patently unattractive (no red and white: Coca-Cola, tampons). I couldn't wear two clothing items of the same color unless they were exactly the same. I couldn't wear colors that obviously clashed. It was complicated. I put on a blue dress. Somehow, I bore too much of a resemblance to a flight attendant. I put it back.

I heard the front door slam. I turned down the music for a second, heard nothing, turned it back up.

We'd been living together for over two years when Janet brought John home. Their first night together followed the storyline of a bad eighties movie. He wandered into her salon, wanted someone to trim his ponytail, they got to chatting, he came back after she got off work and played her a song on his guitar. They went to a bar and ended up at our house with Remy, Janet's friend from StageRage, some underage boy Remy was seducing, and two bottles of Bacardi Razz. I walked in from a night out with the SLLC staff to find them all screaming in laughter at Remy doing a terrible impression of Conan O'Brien.

"I mean, okay!" he yelled, and bobbed his black pompadour. He shook his head around and bugged his eyes out. "I'm Conan! I'm Conan!"

"Tammy!" Janet yelled.

"Hi, guys," I said, hoping to walk past them into my room without having to hang out. John's eyes ran over my body.

"Hey, girl!" Remy said. I generally liked Remy. He was a transplant from the East like me. However, earlier in the day I'd handed out two positive herpes results to baby-faced kids like his boy toy. I was burdened by the consequences and regrets of meaningless hookups, and I knew I'd ruin the party. More than anything I wanted to get into my room, lie down, and sleep off the Jack and Cokes I'd been drinking.

When I did lie down, the room started spinning. I tried to sneak into the bathroom.

"Tam!" Janet called. "Come in here and tell that story about the school nurse with the flavored condoms!"

I told them how tired I was. Still wearing my work clothes, I felt gummy with sweat and bar dirt.

Remy's little friend said, "You look like you've been partying."

"Tam's a party *an*-imal," Remy said. He knew I wasn't.

I told him to fuck off, as lightheartedly as I could, and closed the door to the bathroom so I could throw up in peace.

Later that night, I woke up to Janet and John having sex. They probably thought I'd succumbed to a dead-drunk sleep. Back home in West Courtney, houses were built to keep out the cold: double-paned windows, wall insulation, and doors that sealed at the bottom. What keeps out cold doubles as noise protection. My Hollywood apartment had single panes with no screens and gaps under the doors, which allowed cockroaches, drafts, and noises to slip in and out as they pleased. All tenants could hear everything that happened, anywhere in the building. Janet and I both put towels between our beds and the wall so we didn't usually hear sex thumping from each others' rooms, but we heard grunts and moans and breathing—and the volume of Janet and John's sex was higher than her usual. I didn't feel happy for her.

What bothered me over the next months was that John was so practiced as a drunk he could walk and talk fine even when I could smell him sweating beer. He and I developed a tense, joking acquaintance. John sapped Janet's energy and money, but they made each other laugh, and he wrote songs for her, so my hating him was admittedly unfair until he tried to sleep with me. I hovered in total disbelief for about three seconds when he got in my bed one night, before I settled into rage.

I asked him what he was doing.

"What do you think I'm doing?" he said. He was scooting toward me so I sat up.

"Get the fuck out of my bed," I said.

"You're kidding," he said. I couldn't tell if he was too drunk to know I wasn't Janet, or if he intended to rape me, and had been planning it all along.

"Get the *fuck* out of my *bed*, asshole!"

"Relax, baby," he said.

"I swear, John, I will knee you in the junk."

"Jesus, calm down," he said, rolling out of the bed. He grabbed his pants off the floor and called me a frigid bitch as he left.

The next day, I confronted Janet in the kitchen after John left for a "job interview," which, I was sure, was a lie. Despite my anger, I reveled in having my instincts about him validated, since most of the time I was overreacting or having some kind of idiosyncratic response to the world.

I told Janet her boyfriend tried to have sex with me.

"He was drunk," she said.

"He's always drunk," I said. "I don't see what that has to do with it."

She asked what happened.

"What do you think happened? I kicked him out! Like you should!"

And that was when she argued that he was trying to get his life together, and was so, *so* talented, and if I ever really was in love with someone I'd try to understand him, and some other asinine things. She was right that I'd never given him much of a chance, but at that point I no longer felt guilty for it.

The conversation changed us. We pitied each other. Even though the seed of it was caring, there was something diseased about how we always tried to make the other person act differently. I wanted Janet to get smart, get ambitious, get self-protective. She wanted me to get happy, get relaxed, get laid.

I resolved to put up a fight about her moving in with John, for her sake as much as mine. I'd talk to her tomorrow, after she got home.

I was having more than usual difficulty picking out an outfit. The pressure of preparing for a date, especially with someone as effortlessly adorable as Bow, made my color sensitivity particularly acute. I imagined him arriving in perfectly rumpled linen pants, groomed to his eyebrows.

The only people who knew about my obsession with colors, to its full extent, were my mom, one Rutgers health center intern, my childhood best friend Grant Rose, and Janet. No lovers, no casual friends, no coworkers. Even Todd, who had some idea, had never spoken with me about it. It was usually pretty easy to camouflage my color discomfort with other excuses. I was controlling, opinionated. My bouts of eccentric behavior—refusing to eat in a certain restaurant (with red checkered table cloths and floral print walls), for instance—were usually forgiven.

As an only child, I'd never had to share a room. My mom kept my walls white, my furniture all one kind of wood, and let me dress myself. My dad never asked me questions other than "How was school?" or "Did you forget to lock the door last night?" He wasn't cold, he was just clueless. I kept the secret from my college roommate by putting up a curtain and wearing the same solid black dresses every day—a style that Grant Rose, who witnessed my obsession develop since we were children, had explicitly encouraged.

Janet found out when I was on Darvocet after Nathan attacked me. Even while heavily medicated, I noticed that the hospital gowns matched the hospital walls. Apparently I talked about that more than the attack, more than my family, my love life, my religious beliefs, my philosophy about death and the connectedness of all living things—the importance of color coordination, in my brain, trumped all other popular topics for the benignly stoned. In an admirable show of friendship and abnormal level of discretion, Janet honored my request that she keep the colors thing a secret.

In our apartment, my room was decorated in all-matching sage greens and royal blues. Calming colors. Our living room had white walls and a brown couch. When I left the house, I felt compelled to mentally comment on how all the colors around me were fitting together. Some people count stairs. It's impossible to know what small-scale obsessions are working under the functional surface of the people around you.

After trying on many other options, I settled on a black skirt and green top. Janet hadn't called, so she must have gotten a ride from work to somewhere else. First-date nervousness crept around my stomach. I walked through the apartment, straightening things, checking my face in the mirror every few minutes. The mascara level was appropriate. Possibly the lipstick was too much. I squeezed the last of Janet's hair gel into my palm and scrunched up my curls. It was too hot for blow-drying. I didn't want to think about my hair again. Running cool water over my hands, I slid my feet in and out of my little black sandals.

I packed some money, credit cards, my license, and a lip gloss in a tiny black bag, another difficult task considering I was used to carrying a large purse with the world inside. My phone was staying home—I wasn't on a leash like everyone else. Anyway the only person who would call me would be Janet, trying to find out if I was having sex yet. I folded the fetish show flyer in quarters and stuffed it into the bag. I drank a glass of water. I turned on the TV.

Live from Studio City, a pretty brunette reporter, yellow crime scene tape in front of a pink stucco duplex. A murder, blood seeping through the ceiling, a man held hostage in a bathtub. Janet would tell me about it tomorrow. It was eight-fifteen. I tried to feel casual. Maybe I should be getting a condom from my always-less-than-a-month-old stash, just in case. Maybe I'd rather not have a condom pop out of my purse on the first date, even if we were going to end up watching girls in vinyl whip each other at the fetish show.

He knocked, I answered. I said something about how it was nice seeing him without an apron, accepted a compliment, my eyes slipped for a second to his feet, checking to make sure he was on the ground, and then I felt self conscious. The floating hallucination appeared to be over—he was human. I had been right about the linen pants—a pleasing blue-gray color. Ivory shirt with the top buttons undone. He looked ready for a trip to Greece. We walked down the stairs.

He drove the same car as me, but a few years newer, blacker, louder, with a stick shift. I enjoyed not driving. I scooted the seat back to line up with his, so I wouldn't feel too short.

"Been to Lala's?" he said as he turned the key.

"On Melrose?" I said.

"That's the one." He put his hand on the back of my seat as he twisted to look behind us.

"I love that green tapenade they give you with the bread," I said.

"It's chimichurri," he said.

"What?"

We headed down the street toward Sunset.

"Chimichurri. It's an Argentine condiment. Tapenade always has olives."

"Always?" I said, trying to remember a tapenade without olives.

"I do know my condiments," he said, shaking a finger toward the ceiling, a mock professor. "Ask me what's in it."

"What's in it?"

"Thank you. Olive oil, vinegar, parsley, oregano, onion, garlic, salt, and cayenne pepper."

"It might be faster to take Santa Monica part of the way," I said, tapping my window.

"Hungry?"

I hadn't eaten since the cockroach omelet.

"Finding shortcuts is the big LA project, isn't it?" I said. I studied the dashboard. No dust.

"Are you trying to tell me you're from somewhere else?"

"Not trying to, no."

"But you aren't from LA," he said.

"Right." I wondered how to make the conversation normal. Was I the one making it strange?

"So," he said, drawing out the O-sound, "where are you from?"

"New Jersey," I said. I did not elaborate.

"Where's that?"

"Funny."

"Are you a Scientologist?" he said. "Are you originally from another planet?"

I fake-laughed. I said the East Coast sometimes felt like another planet and then asked where he was from.

"Guess," he said.

I said no way, it was too easy to offend someone I didn't know, and then I asked him if he was a Buddhist, since, I said, asking people about their religion wasn't quite as risky as asking them about their region.

"*You're* funny, and I'm from San Francisco," he answered.

"I've never been," I said. "All I've got are stereotypes."

"I'm not gay, if that's what you're asking," he said. I tried to protest my innocence, but he cut me off. "No worries, I get that a lot. I tried having sex with men for a while just to make sure, since so many other people seemed convinced I should."

I blinked a few times.

"And, to answer your question, I'm only an occupational Buddhist."

"Someone pays you to be a Buddhist?"

"Sort of," he pulled on his goatee and turned briefly to me. My stomach tensed up nicely. "I stay unattached to outcome, take nothing personally. I remember the transience of all restaurant things. It's the only way to wait tables. Once I'm out of Bitsy's, I'm as dissociated and egotistical as everyone else."

I thought about that for a second. "What do you really want to do?"

"What makes you think I want to do anything else?"

"The waiter gig seems like a cover now. You'd quit in a heartbeat if your other thing came through. But I don't know what the other thing is. Acting?"

"I like you," he said.

"I'm having a hard time taking you seriously," I said.

"Is that okay?" Somehow, he was being sincere.

"Sure," I said, and it was the truth. "I've had a long day and this is pretty entertaining."

He asked what happened to make my day feel long, and I answered, work.

He grabbed a parking spot right outside Lala's, and when I congratulated him, he told me he had made a dirty deal with the street-parking gods. They're vampires, he said, so he bled a little every month for the good parking. I told him bleeding every month was no big thing; he must have been doing something way more salacious.

We sat at a table in the middle of the restaurant. Orange walls, rusty red tables, tons of noise. The wrong orange with the wrong red, which meant I'd have to work very, very hard to concentrate on the conversation. We both had to wedge ourselves in, the place was so crowded.

"If I fall over," I said, "at least someone will be there to catch me."

"Comforting?" he said, and raised one eyebrow, "or claustrophobic?"

"Isn't that the enduring urban question?"

"Yes," he said. "I think it is." He drank a whole glass of water in one breath. "What exactly do you do in this city? When you aren't eating bugs?"

I described seeing patients in the SLLC, booking and running an assembly, the rare "down day" without many appointments when we all filled out paperwork and filed things. Realizing I'd veered away from seducing him, I told him about the clinic's mysterious funding source. Our founder and administrative head was a porn star-turned-activist, and I suspected all our salaries were originally paid with royalties from her biggest hit, a movie called *Graduating Cum Loud*. I had never met her, because she was rarely on-site, and she usually dealt with Helena, the doctor who served as clinic director.

Since I was on a roll, I mentioned that I had originally planned on med school.

"What happened to that?" Bow asked.

I gave part of the truth. "It takes so long," I said. "I'd come out about as well-prepared to tell high-schoolers they have herpes as I am now." If I left for a few years to get a medical degree who knows how many kids would fall through the cracks. There would always be doctors around to sign the forms I had to fill out. I tried to sound happy that I'd chosen clinic work over becoming a doctor. I said that maybe when I was older, and the kids started thinking of me as an automatic enemy, I'd consider it.

Bow nodded and poked the ice in his glass thoughtfully. While I talked, he paid attention and asked questions. Most impressively, he never said, "I don't know how you people do it." "You people" always referred to the speaker's assumptions about medical personnel who chose to work with difficult populations like the homeless, at-risk teens, sex workers, and so on. People thought we were naïve and idealistic. Saying they didn't know how we did it was a way to make themselves appear respectful, while they pitied us who were headed to disillusionment and burnout.

"So you're not scared of med school?" Bow said.

"Why would I be?" I hated the question.

He shrugged, "I'm not sure."

"Med school should be scary," I said. We could talk about my getting attacked and stuck with huge medical bills, having no credit with which to bargain for school loans, the slow process of my becoming enraged by how much work it took to help everyone, and all the rest, later. If there was a later, which I doubted.

"Your work is really amazing," he said, and I forgave him.

We ate steak with garlic mashed potatoes. We drank merlot. We dipped tiny round slices of baguette in the chimichurri and smiled at each other. Despite his unnerving questions, I was feeling better than I had all day.

"You were right about my job," he said, when the conversation broke for a moment. "What you said in the car?"

"It's a cover?"

"Yes." He waited a dramatic few seconds. "I'm actually here on a diplomatic mission."

"You're Princess Leia?"

"I'm an out-of-work carnival clown?"

I told him I tried not to joke about clowns.

He said he was a film student.

"I almost believe that one," I said. Our waiter came over and filled our water glasses. Bow made eye contact with him while he said thank you.

"Tam-jam," he said, and I had a flash of missing Grant Rose again, "you are going to want to leave this table if I tell you what I do outside of Bitsy's."

I told him I'd spent thirty minutes earlier that week listening to a nineteen-year-old girl talk about how much easier it is to fuck for money if she stays drunk.

"Fine," he said, "clearly you're tough. But my other job's not titillating, it's technical." He waited. I motioned with my hands for him to go on. He said, "I write user manuals."

Bow told the truth with his face. When he was kidding, he gave it away, so I didn't feel left out or tricked. When he was serious, his eyes were clear, like now.

"What does that mean?" I said.

He told me he solved logic problems, connected A to B to C. He consulted, wrote, edited, and proofread for companies who were having complaints about their manuals. When people couldn't understand how to work their gadgets, a company would call Bow and he would fix up their literature. He felt like a silent superhero, making the technological world a safer place for everyone. He had done cars, DVD players, power tools, micro transducers, EKG machines. Theoretically, he knew how to work everything he'd read about. He'd always been good with mechanical things. He didn't want to be an employee of a big company or get stuck reading about only one product, so he was a self-employed, freelance technical writer. And a server at Bitsy's to help pay the bills, who meditated while he waited tables.

When I asked him what his career dream was, he answered, "Renaissance man." Then he told me he wanted to write a book about do-it-yourself home maintenance that empowered people to keep their garbage disposals, air conditioners, electronics, and so on, in working condition. The goal was to help Americans "connect" with their belongings. He had a BA in Asian Religions from UCLA.

"It's an environmental and spiritual imperative," he said, "that we quit throwing away so many appliances. I want to help people learn the mechanisms, appreciate craftsmanship, hopefully change the market demands toward more sustainable manufacturing, more durable goods."

He excitedly described a perfect relationship with the material world: equal parts appreciation of and freedom from the tyranny of objects that improve our lives.

Then he briefly got embarrassed. "I'm a total geek," he said. "The goatee is supposed to distract you from it."

He got sexier by the second, and so I got more nervous.

SIX

On the way out of Lala's, Bow suddenly gasped and smacked his forehead.

"Ohmygod," he said, "I forgot to go to the Eidel sale."

I had no idea what that was. He checked his watch.

"I'm about to have some really bad manners," he said. "Do you mind if we stop at Eidel for like ten minutes before we go to the show?"

I asked him what that meant.

Eidel was an organic body products store in West Hollywood. Bow thought they made the best shampoo you could buy, period. They held a biannual sale with everything in the store marked half off, before their new product lines came out, and every time, Bow had bought enough shampoo to last until the next sale.

"You're kidding," I said.

He wasn't.

"I'll buy you a soap," he said. "I swear you'll never use anything else again."

"Let's go then," I said.

On the drive, Bow described the environmentally friendly company. Soy inks, recycled paper, rainforest sustainability. They never tested on animals. He bought lotions from Eidel that were so pure they needed refrigeration.

"And the scents are amazing," he said. "Nothing smells like perfume, it's all natural smells like cucumber, pine, fennel." He held out his arm. "Smell this."

I leaned a few inches to his forearm. The heat from his skin and the sweet, nutty smell inspired a desire to bite him. I told him it was very nice.

"Cocoa butter," he said, "and some other stuff—olive oil or beeswax."

I thought about the ersatz hippies at Rutgers, who used no deodorant, rubbed honey or mayonnaise into their fine hair trying for dreadlocks, wore baggy, patched up clothing, and smoked everything and anything "natural"—unfiltered cigarettes, pot, cloves, hash, hookah tabac. They took mushrooms because they were natural, too. When their favorite bands came to town, they decided it was okay to do pure synthetic MDMA, which they bought with money they pretended they didn't have. Bow didn't strike me as the type, and I told him so.

"I'm not really that kind of hippie," he said.

"I'll bet that deep down, you're more of a real hippie than the Phish fans I knew in college."

He shrugged and said, maybe. Then he told me he thought that deep down I was really a Californian, not a Jersey girl.

"I think I love you," I said, meaning it to be funny, but realizing too late that it was insane, too much, embarrassing. I blushed red hot.

Bow winked and kept driving.

There was no parking outside Eidel. The three walls were painted solid chartreuse, the brightest, most ugly yellow-green color ever invented. No way I was going in. Customers crowded the store. I offered to wait in the car if Bow wanted to double-park. After arguing with me for a few seconds, he gave in. He didn't even ask if I could drive a stick. I assumed this was a sign of respect.

"When I get back," he said before running into the store, "it's time for you to tell me something you wouldn't normally reveal on a first date. A guilty pleasure, or secret shame, since you're seeing mine." Then he was off.

There wasn't a big difference between the things I wouldn't reveal on a first date and the things I wouldn't reveal, period. One was how much I hated being from New Jersey.

The area where I grew up had one claim to fame: it was an hour from New York. While not the seedy Jersey everyone is always afraid of—you'd have to head into Trenton or Newark for that—it wasn't Princeton, either. West Courtney was a nothing-place, a small stretch of perfectly desolate middle-class sprawl, and when I was preparing to leave, no one asked me why. What they did ask was why I would go all the way to LA. For West Courtneans, New York was the primary destination for anything important. There was no reason to move there, since the commute was easy by train or bus and the cost of living was so much lower in Jersey. Secretly though, the city lifestyle, with all those sexy people, wood-paneled restaurants, and parties where Woody Allen and his friends drank expensive wines and got into luxurious trouble, was a community wet dream.

New Jersey was limbo. Purgatory. Not ivy-covered, educated, self-congratulatory New England, not leather-clad, artistic, audacious New York. Jersey had no identifying characteristics except being the middle child in the east coast family. Maybe it was that underdog status that made it subject to fierce regional loyalty. There was always conflict in describing it. West Courtney could be so beautiful, especially in the early summer when everything was green and plump. You could stretch out on balmy June nights and listen to the crickets, or, in the fall, watch the trees turn fire-colored and blanket the roads with leaves.

On the other hand, Jersey seemed to exist for the express purpose of being the butt of everyone's joke. Bruce Springsteen fought to legitimize the scruffy, poor white, blue-collar image the state smeared everyone with. He may have succeeded for himself, but everyone else back home was still fighting. And how could they win, as long as New Jersey accepted New York's garbage into its own landfills?

Amidst the identity crisis I suffered as a West Courtney girl who couldn't conform to West Courtney standards, Los Angeles had been about as real as Jupiter. I'd been so busy trying to appear normal I hadn't had time to consider the notion that what "normal" meant in my town might have been too restrictive for me. I'd relied on Grant Rose, my best friend, to help me. She had an ability to navigate our Jersey microcosm that I lacked. She was the glue that kept me in place.

Before we went through puberty we were partners in everyday fantasy games and pranks. We made dresses for our dogs, snuck into our neighbors' backyards to pick flowers, spent the night in sleeping bags in each others' living rooms. If other girls played "Princess in a Castle," Grant Rose and I played "Superhero princess who can pull frogs from her ears in a castle made of Flubber." Our mothers would occasionally call each other on the phone to find out if the other one had already fed us both dinner, since we tended to graze at both houses like wild cats.

Our differences surfaced in middle school, when Grant Rose became lovely, and I stayed impish. There is that fine line, once a girl starts edging into adolescence, between cool-different and outcast-different. Other kids respected Grant because she was as pretty as the popular girls but told better jokes and could burp on command. I still had a mop of curls, didn't wear the same soccer sandals as everyone else (the sensation on the bottoms of my feet was too distracting), became increasingly compulsive and secretive about colors and lists, and felt the imminence of my exile from acceptable social functioning in the way you can sense your own house coming up on the block. Grant made sure I had hoop earrings big enough, grades just low enough, and a giggle just cute enough to pass for anonymous in middle school. But keeping me that way was work for us both.

High school was a tiny bit easier—not because I changed (except maybe for the worse), but because I was given more space in which to bounce my oddity around, and Grant felt less responsible. In high school it occurred to me that I didn't have to stay in West Courtney forever.

Grant Rose and I made a habit of complaining to each other every day on the phone, our discontentment making us feel grown up. We weren't completely certain of what we didn't like about our lives, so we blamed West Courtney for being boring, lacking cute boys, and having no fun events for teenagers besides sneaking out at night to read romance novels in someone's basement. Later, in college, I decided our unhappiness with the town sprang from a truly great instinct, and I was grateful that I'd hung on to it as a young adult, instead of succumbing to the nesting fever that spread among my peers.

Once Grant got a license we occasionally drove out to the shore to do our complaining. We drank Mickey's Big Mouths, which we'd stolen from my parents, under the pier. We tossed pennies into the water while we argued about what kind of pizza to order later. I never drove, even though I had a license too, because according to Grant, I was way too cautious to get anywhere.

My favorite days in high school were during the summer, of course. At least once a week we'd trek out to Seaside Heights, a stretch of shore two hours away, where the boardwalk was big and busy. I would get Grant all to myself, since it was rare we'd run into neighborhood kids that far away. Seaside Heights was where both Grant and I learned how to have hurried sexual encounters in public bathrooms with our bathing suits on. I didn't have intercourse, although I couldn't have explained exactly why. I still hadn't questioned the idea that real sex was somehow special, and dangerous, even though my family wasn't particularly conservative or religious.

Grant and I called finding boys to make out with "hunting." We spent the day on display, laying in the sun in various poses we thought enticing. Aside from being taller than me, which everyone was, Grant had the long silky hair, pouty lips, and slightly rounded hips of an adolescent femme fatale. I had the curly hair, compact body, and dark eyes of a best friend. About once an hour we would dip in the water, pick up our basket-weave bags, and take a walk up by the food stands and rides, casting around for a pair of boys we could tolerate. If we found them, we followed them. We took our time closing in, laughing at everything the other said in wild, demonstrative exuberance, suggestively licking vanilla soft-serve cones and tucking our sunglasses artfully into our hair. I was excellent at this part of the hunt.

Once it came time to talk to the boys, Grant had to take over. She would slide next to one in a corn dog line, ask him his name and where he was from, and invite him and his friend to sit with us.

"What do you guys like to do?" she'd ask, arranging her shirt to show her bathing suit.

The conversations were never memorable, but somehow they always progressed to our going somewhere more private, and I never had to say much before the friend of the guy Grant liked was trying to kiss me.

One time, when we were sixteen, we scored a pair of tanned blond locals, guys who had immediately spotted us too. It was the end of the day, and teenagers ruled the boardwalk. We stood in line for the Ferris wheel leaning against the boys, wrapping their arms around our waists. We hopped into separate bucket-shaped cars and rode to the top, our skin sticky with salt on the wooden bench. I tried to chat with my boy about his football team. He had platinum blond eyebrows, eyelashes, arm hair. The trail of hair from his belly button into his shorts was only a faint shade darker. The ride stopped.

After a few dry kisses, he started scooting my bathing suit bottom down my legs with one hand. Somehow the fact that he had completely ignored my breasts, neck, and tongue excited me. He knew what he wanted. He parked his face between my legs and moved his tongue up and down doggedly while our bucket swayed gently on its squeaking frame, and kids elsewhere on the ride yelled complaints about being stuck. I tilted my head back and tried to make soft, sexy noises. He was only the second boy who had tried it, and was decidedly gentler than the first. My body relaxed.

I stared into the deep twilight blue of the sky, trying to focus on an airplane or a star. Down over the pier, the neon lights turned the surface of the ocean into a flickering collage. My gaze wandered to Grant in the bucket-car below us, grinding on the lap of the other boy. The way she was circling her hips sent shock waves through me. I stared at her, watched her arch her back, open her mouth for his tongue, and after my body throbbed for a minute, I grabbed the back of my guy's head and had my first orgasm. Terrified that I'd peed on him, I yanked my bathing suit back on, but instead of pulling away from me in disgust he wiped his mouth and started untying the drawstring on his shorts. I refused to have sex with him, and he shrugged. Whatever, he said. Like he didn't care either way.

When I started reading books about human sexuality for my clinic work, I realized that in addition to being my first voyeuristic thrill, that experience showed some untaught resistance to our adolescent gender dynamics. I knew I didn't want to have sex with a stranger, based on some West Courtney morality that made me afraid of being a slut, but in our local taxonomy, receiving oral sex was much sluttier than giving it. I felt no guilt about receiving pleasure without satisfying the partner I was with. This was also against the rules. My parents never talked to me about sex, not once. I had no idea if they cared that I stayed a technical virgin in high school. I had no compass with which to navigate gender, desire, and intimacy. My sexual history became a scattered array of experiments, conducted silently. I didn't get any solid information about pregnancy or STIs until college orientation. And once I did, I was furious no one had tried harder to help the kids in West Courtney.

When we got back home that night from Seaside Heights, Grant and I went for a walk. The lightning bugs made frantic circles above our neighbors' lawns.

"Those guys were so hot," Grant said.

"Not bad," I said.

"Do you like giving blow jobs?" Grant said, giggling.

"Not really," I said.

She said she didn't either. "They always push on the back of my head, like my throat is going to get longer. Gross."

"I get freaked out when they look at me," I said.

"Have you had a guy go down on you, and stare at you the whole time? All you can see is his nose and eyes down there?"

"I keep my eyes closed," I lied.

I masturbated to visions of Grant, but it only turned me on to think of her with someone else. I never kissed Grant, never wanted to. I wanted to watch her be kissed.

During our senior year Grant got a boyfriend and I finally cemented a two fold reputation as both a nerd, because of getting good grades in science, and a tease, because I would have oral sex but not go all the way. Grant's continued friendship buffered me somewhat from the gossip, but I hid out in the biology classroom and read murder mysteries during lunch for the rest of the year.

Bow's face appeared at my window.

"The line's ridiculous. Do you want me to park somewhere so you can come in?"

I glanced inside the fluorescent yellow-green store and told him I was fine, I'd turn on the radio and keep waiting in the car.

"Thanks for being so laid back," Bow said.

I almost laughed at how incredibly inaccurate that was, but it felt nice to have someone think that about me, however briefly.

Once he knew me, he'd never say it again. I thought about Janet, and imagined her with John, drinking cheap beer in his house, watching bad TV. Laid back.

After Nathan attacked me outside the high school and Janet found out about my obsessive matching at the hospital, her suspicion that I was "pathologically uptight" was finally given good hard evidence. At her insistence, and because I found it irresistible once she suggested it, high as I was on painkillers, we made a list together called the "Index of My Mental Problems," as they had appeared in chronological order. Janet sat with me in the hospital room and took my dictation. I simultaneously hated and loved what the list represented: both my inadequacies as a human being and Janet's sweetly misguided expression of caring and concern. And of course, making the list was pleasurable. Once we got home, the list went in a desk drawer, but not before I'd memorized it.

Issue number one: sensitivity to colors in clothing and décor, especially non-matching color combinations or those that have some symbolic significance. I confessed to Janet that one of the reasons I'd asked her to live with me was her lack of furniture or beloved artwork.

Number two: highly sensitive feet. I stopped reading Reflexology texts when my anatomy class debunked the practice, but I still experienced hypersensitivity and the unbearable sensation of my toenails growing. This issue was later compounded by my addiction to pedicures. I spent over a hundred dollars a week at Fancy Nail, not including the gel soles, special "mercerized cotton" socks, and thick-soled shoes I had to buy.

Number three: to-do lists, and compulsive finishing of tasks on lists. This included an inability to throw lists away with unfinished tasks still written on them. A drawer in my desk was stuffed with lists, some nearly ten years old, because I'd capriciously written something like "travel to India" or "kiss Prof. Rochard" on them.

Number four, or three subsection one: aversion to leaving tasks unfinished. This was not a hard-and-fast obsession, because it was not always a determinant of my behavior. But when it surfaced, like in my junior year of college when I started organizing my shared kitchen alphabetically— from left to right, bowls before cups before plates—I couldn't stop in the middle. That activity took me four hours. I had also stayed late at the clinic, sometimes after midnight, if I started a certain filing job too late in the day, even if it didn't need to be finished for a week.

Number five: slight hallucinations/visual exaggerations. They never interfered with my ability to *also* accurately perceive physical reality. I saw little, inconsequential things like squirrels that weren't there. Bow's feet hovering above the floor.

Number six: credit card addiction. Janet and I argued for a while about whether this was truly a "mental problem." I made a case for overspending as a generational disease many people in their twenties shared. As such, it could not be considered my own individual pathology. Janet countered that I routinely paid bills late, spent more than my paycheck every month, and that my credit card habits were the same as a strip club addict's: secretive and excessive. She wrote it down.

She also wanted to add "voyeurism" to the list, but I refused.

"There's nothing wrong with that," I said, a little disturbed that she knew about it. From my hospital bed, I waved in the air near her to indicate I would swat the pen from her if she tried to write it down.

"What I don't get," she said, "is why you like strip clubs more than porn?"

"Most porn is boring," I said. The fantasies didn't appeal to me, and I didn't like the idea of searching through tons of bad sex to find the good stuff. Even the independent studios often made bad movies. I told her I'd rather watch dancers and then fill in the naked partners in my head. "Plus," I said, "I know how sexist the mainstream porn business is."

"Strip clubs aren't a sexist business?"

"They are," I said. "But there's more room for the women to take power, I think. Plus, I like the artistry of really good pole work."

Janet rolled her eyes. "Have you ever seen a psychiatrist about any of this?" she asked. "Like to see if you're bipolar or something?" Bipolar was the current catch-all for any psychological issue that couldn't be called simply depression—it was slipping easily from the mouths of my patients and students, too. Janet's protective concern ran higher than normal, because my face was huge and purple. (My best Darvocet-inspired joke: What's the cheapest way to get "I'm a Victim" tattooed on your forehead? Get someone to hit you there!)

I told Janet I wasn't bipolar. "I don't have clinically diagnosable mood swings. I don't have OCD. I don't have Tourette's. I'm not schizophrenic. I've been to many doctors," which was a lie, I'd only been to the one intern at Rutgers, "and I'm just weird. I'm functional and subclinical. Know what that means?"

"Everyone just has to put up with you?"

"Yes. Exactly."

"You just reminded me of something I saw on the news," she said, and our one conversation about my needing to "get help" was over. She told me a story about a four-year-old kid who was so flexible he could squeeze in and out of places his parents couldn't reach. "They did a story on him because he crawled up into one of those claw machines they have at arcades? The ones that never pull out the teddy bear you want? You should have seen the face on that kid, he was so proud of himself, in his glass case surrounded by stufties. You knew his mom wouldn't punish him because what he'd done was so crazy."

Although list-making distracted me, it wasn't my idiosyncrasies worrying me at that moment. I wanted protection from Nathan, although I hadn't yet learned his name. Working at the clinic had sharpened my bullshit sensor to almost superhuman strength. The fact that I had not predicted he might be violent when he first approached me scared me almost as much as the fact that he had attacked me. How would I stop another attack, if I couldn't see it coming?

I reminded myself that I'd decided not to think about Nathan while on the date with Bow, but sitting in the car alone, there was no stopping the memories.

I focused on Janet, and how well she'd taken care of me after I came home from the hospital. She'd practiced with so many drugged-out, alcoholic men that my tidy bouts of nausea due to double-dosing Vicodin on an empty stomach were a cakewalk for her. Janet made mac and cheese, the only thing I wanted to eat, for a week. She did both our laundry and ran to the pharmacy for my anti-nausea pills, sleeping pills, pain pills, and antibiotics. I tried not to become too dependent on her help, but because I wasn't broadcasting the news, there wasn't a lot of other help arriving.

My mother and father probably would have jumped on a plane if I had called. But I didn't, partly to prove to them that I wasn't in need of rescuing, ever, partly in fear that they'd find a way to blame me for what happened, and also partly to avoid the guilt of worrying them. I stayed in bed reading Raymond Chandler mysteries and watching the classic movie channel.

When I was healed enough to walk comfortably, Janet decided it was time to go shopping. She had three types of uniform: work clothes, going-out clothes, and staying-home clothes. Work clothes were black and sexy, going-out clothes were glittery and sexy, and staying-home clothes were stretchy and sexy. She owned more pairs of strappy sandals than any woman I had ever met. She wore heels all the time—except at home, where she wore platform flip-flops. I allowed Janet to fashion-coach me, since I had decided to branch out from my all-black wardrobe shortly after arriving in California.

In Jersey, black was invisible—East Coasters wore black all the time, and Grant Rose had helped me see it was the obvious solution to the matching problem. But in LA, especially Hollywood and Silver Lake, black made me look like a waiter. This wasn't fundamentally a bad thing, since looking like a waiter was synonymous with looking like an actor. However, conforming to LA's service-industry chic wasn't the way to convince people I was a friendly medical professional. Everyone at the SLLC who wasn't a doctor wore jeans or shorts, and my style appeared severe and serious next to them, which I certainly didn't want. Janet heralded my fashion revolution into dressing like a business-casual West Coaster. The only sacrifice was how long I took to get dressed. The green top I was wearing on the date was one of Janet's picks.

On shopping day, Janet told me we were going to do something "really exciting." We were going to walk. Our apartment was in the small limbo-land where Hollywood bled into Silverlake: simultaneously Thai Town, Little Armenia, and discount-store central, where all items were labeled in Spanish. We made our way down Hollywood Boulevard and I developed an intense fascination with the curvy mannequins sporting track suits in every window. I adored the fad—everybody walking around in perfectly matching velvet or jersey pants and hoodies was very satisfying.

"So cozy!" I said while standing outside the Ladies' Discount-O-Mart.

"You need one," Janet said. "Let's find one in baby blue."

I asked why I would need one.

Her answer: it would look hot. "You have exactly the right body for those," she said. "All the over-the-hill women trying to hide their fat asses in them are ruining the look."

Armed with the confidence that I could be part of some Cuteness Army that saved the track suit from corruption, I got brave.

"I want a red one," I said. "Red would make me look fast."

Janet shook her head and sighed.

We ended up buying matching pink terry suits. Pink was the compromise made tolerable by the hilarity of us both wearing them, even though, with my Barbie toes, it should have been too much. We put them on at home, still smelling like plastic, plopped on our couch, ate cereal at three in the afternoon, and watched a *COPS* marathon. She sang the theme song to the TV, while I tried to convince her that we should watch something that wasn't so blatantly racist.

"You're awesome in that suit," Janet said.

"I feel like a real LA bitch now," I said, snapping my elastic waistband.

"All you need is a teacup dog," she said, without moving her eyes from the show. Then, "Oh shit! They're going to beat the crap out of that guy!"

Hanging out with Janet was a kind of vacation.

We hadn't done anything like that for months. A pang of sadness about her leaving me for John was followed by fear about money which led to frustration at my inability to keep terrible things out of my mind for one night.

The sound of Bow opening the trunk made me jump. I wondered if he was hiding a ridiculous number of bags full of organic products from me.

He slid into the driver's seat and held out his fists, palms downward.

"Pick one," he said.

I pointed at his right. He opened it, and handed me a small bar of white soap.

"Smell," he said.

It smelled like the beach. "A nice beach, like Malibu, not a polluted one," I said.

"People shit-talk Malibu," he said, and I wondered if I'd shown some ignorance of local custom, "but I love the dolphins."

"What?"

"You haven't seen them? Sometime we'll go there when the sun's going down. There's pods of dolphins that swim by. It's magical."

I didn't believe him. I also balked at him using the word "magical."

"It's one of the most beautiful sights of the city," he said. "It's like being in a kid's book to stand there, with big, busy Los Angeles at your back and all these fins coming out of the water."

"Thanks for the soap," I said.

"It's the least I can do, for making you wait for my vanity." He closed his eyes and pressed on them. "I think my vision is damaged from being in there too long."

"Chartreuse is the color most visible to the human eye," I said in awkward agreement.

"Isn't chartreuse orange?"

I told him no, but I knew why he thought so. "You and I grew up with a crayon called 'chartreuse' that was orange," I said. "Crayola had it wrong for thirty years. Chartreuse is actually right in between yellow and green."

"You're kidding."

I shook my head. "They fixed it in 1990."

"What's the orange crayon called now?"

"Atomic Tangerine," I said.

"Fucking nihilists," he said, reaching into his pocket. "Let's teach our kids that 'atomic' is a perfectly safe, friendly word."

"Atomic energy is safe," I said. "Don't get stuck in the fifties."

"You think Crayola is really trying to help kids become proponents of atomic energy? 'Cause I don't. I think they're implicitly reinforcing the idea that it's okay for America, and really only America, to own atomic weapons."

"Or atomic citrus fruits," I said.

"Touché."

"I think you're probably right," I said. "Sometimes my idealism gets in my way."

Bow nodded sagely, pulled out a small bottle of lotion, rubbed it into his hands, offered it to me, and then put it away. I hoped he'd forgotten about making that request for a confession before running into Eidel. I hoped he wasn't going to ask me why I knew so much about chartreuse. I hoped he wasn't going to keep trying to convince me about the dolphins. I feared he might be the type of guy to have a dolphin or a butterfly tattoo somewhere— sort of ironic, sort of not. I glanced at the clock on the dash.

"Let's go check out some naked people," I said.

"I like your style," he said, and started the car.

SEVEN

Hollywood was slinking into its Friday night clothes. The club-goers, indie-band groupies, coffee-house screenwriters, and kids from the Valley walked the same few streets, never more than two blocks from their cars, in categorizable outfits. Men in shiny shirts hooted out the windows of silver SUVs, while girls in tight jeans and high heels pretended not to hear them. Occasionally a couple in sneakers, studded belts, and asymmetrical haircuts would strut by, hands in their pockets, eyes on the ground. This was a neighborhood where you would be judged by the humor value of your vintage T-shirt or the level of luxury associated with your handbag, depending on the audience you sought. As we got closer to Wacko, the crowded streets thinned out. Fewer streetlights flooded the sidewalks. The only knot of people was directly outside Wacko, trying to get in.

Bow grabbed another very nice parking spot, right across the street.

"So you heard about this from a flyer?" he asked as we got out of the car. "You don't know anyone involved with the show?"

Not that I was aware of, I said. But it was always possible I'd run into a patient or student. "If that happens," I said, "I give them a reassuring smile and pretend I don't know them. Unless they initiate a conversation."

"Show me the smile," he said. I showed him. He said he suddenly felt very much at ease. I punched him lightly on the arm.

Approaching the crowd outside, I realized Bow and I would be part of a minority not in costume. Mostly I saw black vinyl on both the women and men.

"I do know someone in the show," Bow said. He was heading for the front of the crowd. "Her name is Naomi. She does a Tiki-theme burlesque thing."

I pulled the flyer Janet had given me out of my tiny bag. "This girl?"

He nodded.

"She's a goddess," I said. He agreed. The streak of courage, which had begun with giving him my number, suddenly ended. Of course Naomi was a goddess. Of course she was also his ex-girlfriend.

"Not exactly an ex," Bow said.

His face stayed totally friendly, as it had been all night. "She's currently your girlfriend, like right this minute?" I said, bewildered and shrill.

He told me they were not in a committed partnership, sounding a little like a politician. "We were monogamous for a while," he said, "but it just wasn't right for us. So we opened the relationship up. Then she fell in love with someone, so now we're very close polyamorous friends." I remembered the first line he'd given me about his name. He met my eyes. It was no joke.

"I don't get it," I said.

"We're really more like best friends who take care of each other when there's no one to be with on Christmas, or it sucks to sleep alone, or you need a ride to the dentist?"

I was already rolling my eyes and starting to walk back to the car.

"Hey, wait," Bow said, "maybe I'm not being clear."

"You don't call me up and get me to ask you out if you already have a girlfriend," I said. "You just don't." I was almost running. He kept up.

"So you are kind of traditional," he said, and for a second I wanted to hit him. "I'm sorry I was so ungraceful about this," he said, "but she's not my girlfriend, and anyway, I got the feeling that you weren't the normal mission-style monogamist."

I pointed behind me at the line of black vinyl bodies. "Obviously not," I said.

"Are you sure?"

I stopped at the car. He'd called me a chicken. Turning to face him, arms crossed, I said, "Don't act like I'm the coward here."

"Clearly, I did a bad job of representing my intentions," he said. He said he liked me, and he and Naomi weren't in love. They were best friends and occasional sex partners.

"And so what happens if you want to date someone?"

"You mean if I wanted to be monogamous with someone? Then she would respect that boundary. End of story." He opened his hands. "I'll tell you whatever you want to know."

While I marveled at the oddity of our standing on the street outside a fetish show having a lovers' quarrel on our first date, a car crawled toward us with two mowhawks inside. They were stalking the parking spot. Bow said it was up to me. I waved them on.

"I think you're adorable," Bow said. "I'm curious about you."

"I'm not adorable," I said. "'Adorable' is for children and baby animals."

"I'm glad I'm saying everything right tonight."

I asked him if he'd hidden Eidel bags in the trunk.

He nodded, and laughed. "Addictive personality," he said. "I don't do coke anymore. I binge on avocado extract now."

I leaned against the car. People were slowly pushing into Wacko. A bass rhythm floated underneath the sound of the crowd.

I'd wanted to see the show even before Bow called. I told myself it didn't matter if he was with me or not.

"Let's go in," I said.

Bow's brief expression of disbelief was replaced by delight, then something like sadness. "You're giving up on me," he said.

"I'm not," I protested. But I had, and his instinct unnerved me.

He stared at me, not talking, like he was trying to telepathically hear everything I couldn't say. Out of defiance, then bewilderment, I stared back.

"Okay," he said.

I wanted to ask him what he'd seen in my face, but I didn't.

We walked across the street. He picked up my hand as I started for the end of the line and steered me toward the entrance. We were on the guest list. As we walked up the steps, I could feel people staring. I smiled sheepishly at everyone we passed, trying to let them know I really was one of them. If they ran into me inside, I said with my expression, I would be a nice person, not a pushy LA elitist who didn't stand in lines.

The club scene in Hollywood was organized like a dictatorship, with Connections in top office. As Tamina, a moderately pretty, short young woman with curly hair who didn't wear skimpy skirts, I might have to wait outside bars and clubs for an hour or more. As Tam from the SLLC, a gatekeeper for the sex industry and sex encyclopedia for the young and clueless, I had a guilty hook-up almost anywhere trendy. I discovered this perk when I was giving a young actress her HIV results in my second month of work.

"I'm a cocktail waitress at the Standard downtown," she'd said, overjoyed that she was still virus-free and employable in the porn world. "Next time you go there on a Thursday tell them you're on my list!"

Janet always urged me to lean on my contacts.

"You deserve it," she would say to me. "All those people burdening you with their fucked-up stories. Let's get shitfaced on Grey Goose martinis and find Clooney or someone to pay for us."

I took her advice a few times. It made Janet so happy. I had done my share of walking to the front of a line, saying my name, and being ushered in. I was a bit dazzled by the scenes. But I knew I belonged in the crowd behind the velvet rope. At least at Wacko, I was riding the coattails of Bow's popularity, not feigning my own.

To his credit, Bow was busy making eye contact with people in line, nodding and smiling hellos, as we got patted down outside the door by a three-hundred-pound man wearing bunny ears. The noise began to envelop us.

Bow told me we were going to see great art tonight, if we hurried. There were so many people doing this kind of photography, painting, you name it, the show always had hundreds of people sending in slides. We'd missed the mellow part where everyone walked around being snotty about the exhibit, and we'd have to rush through it before the show started, but he reminded me to sniff my beach-scented soap if I started resenting it.

"Naomi and her girls will do a burlesque," he said, looking at his watch, "there might be a topless fire-dancer, some of the models from the photos do a fetish fashion show, there's a lounge band, we'll see what else."

The doorway cleared and we made it in. Normally, Wacko was three high-ceilinged rooms crammed with stuff. Tonight, half the stuff had been moved, and it was instead crammed with people. The main room usually housed rows of books, a wall of homemade beauty products and kitschy household items, a wall of offensive and funny T-shirts ("I'm huge in Japan," "Gay Marriage? Only if both chicks are HOT") over the cash register, and glass cases of costume jewelry. Farther in was the entrance to the gallery, and through the gallery was a back room, where all kinds of odds and ends, like drink umbrellas and Jesus action figures, spilled onto tables and burst out of cardboard displays.

The colors were completely cacophonous. With no way to control it, no place to start fixing, I could try to get lost in it like everyone else. If I looked too long, the hot pinks, yellows, and greens from a day-glo disco suit to my right screamed in the face of muted mustard and brown Hawaiian shirts tacked up on the wall. Black vinyl outfits blended together. Posters and costumes and colored lights bouncing off the ceiling turned the room into a mismatching soup. I had to keep my eyes moving.

Someone had moved the book stacks out and set up a bar, so a motley club scene replaced most of the store. To the side of the bar, a makeshift stage with a half-kit, bass, guitar, and 1950s radio-style mike waited in front of a banner proclaiming "The Black Orchid Band" in vintage bamboo font. People stood very close, yelling in each others' ears over the music. A DJ, set up where the cash register should have been, mixed a dance beat with Esquivel's "Mucha Muchacha," resulting in a sound like a sexed-up Jetson's Theme. The room was warm, and smelled like Mai Tais and latex.

"This is crazy," I said.

Bow seemed excited to be a tour guide and squeezed my hand. I wondered if he fancied I'd forgiven him. We turned sideways and scooted through the bodies to the bar. Halfway there, a tall woman in a long black wig turned around and saw Bow.

"Honey!" she squealed, and I realized she was a finely-featured man in very expensive Bettie Page drag. Even though I'd responsibly filled in "MTF," or male-to-female, on her chart instead of "male," the first transgendered patient I'd seen at the clinic had lectured me on the importance of respecting someone's demonstrated gender, regardless of whether they popped in and out of it, like drag queens did, were committing to a sex change, like she was, or simply wanted to pass as the other. Now, pronouns referring to whatever gender someone was "doing" at the time came more naturally to me than pronouns referring to a perception of their biological sex.

I'd loved Bettie Page when I was younger, and there was something simultaneously familiar and disturbing about speaking to a real-life version. Bettie's thick black wig-bangs were cut straight across her forehead. She opened her arms to Bow and revealed a stuffed black push-up bullet bra, long black opera gloves, black shorts on tiny hips, a black garter belt holding up black thigh-highs, long thin legs, and red heels. Her red lipstick sparkled.

"Tam," Bow said, "this is Bettie!"

I put my hand out and said it was nice to meet her. She seemed to fall forward into me.

"You are so cute!" she said, and tapped my nose with one gloved finger.

Reflexively swatting her away, I spilled her champagne on our feet. She reached to tug on one of my curls, and I caught her hand.

"Sorry baby," she said as I let her go, "I like to touch the pretty ones." Then to Bow, "Are you coming to my party?"

"Monday?"

"Bring this kitten," she said, pointing at my face again. Then she made a claw with one hand and did that annoying cat-growl-and-clawing-gesture-thing at me. "Rowr, ffffft-fffft," she said.

"Catch up with you later," Bow called to her as we kept on. He was amused. "I assume you don't like being called cute."

"Same problem as adorable," I said.

"Franco makes a lousy Bettie anyway," he said. "He should pick a taller icon to impersonate. But he throws a great party, and you just got invited!"

I didn't respond for a second. "You're right about him being too tall," I said.

Bow asked if I was a Bettie Page fan.

When I nodded, he asked me if I knew her middle name.

"Mae," I answered. "Real height?"

"Five foot, five and one-half inches," he said. "Drink?"

"It's got vermouth and cherry and something else, but she had nothing to do with naming it," I said.

"No," he said, pointing at the bar, "what do you want?"

"Red wine? A merlot, if they have it?"

"Done," he said. Then, "There's a drink called the Bettie Page?" He waved at the bartender, who smiled and nodded in friendly recognition.

"I guess I'm more of a nerd than you," I said. Then I wagged my finger like he had in the car and added, "I do know my pin-up history."

Bow pulled an imaginary pen and paper from his pocket and started scribbling in the air. "A point for Tam. I think you're ahead now."

I said that Grant Rose, my childhood best friend, was the one to push me toward the decision to move to LA. But, I told Bow, it was Bettie Page, the queen of all pin-up models, who had led me first to consider the idea of leaving New Jersey and doing something with my life.

He accused me of joking.

"I'll tell you the story if you promise not to laugh," I said.

He couldn't promise.

I told him anyway. I found a copy of her 1955 *Playboy* centerfold issue in a box of unmarked odds and ends in my family's basement when I was fifteen. She was exotic and trampy, but she also seemed so sweet and approachable—I fell under her spell, and stole the magazine. I kept it for ten years in plastic in my closet. Neither of my parents said anything, if they ever noticed. Franco made a lovely thin woman, but the real Bettie had no hard edges. The real Bettie, I said, was also very well-read and unlucky in love.

"Didn't she end up a Christian?" Bow said.

"She did," I said. "Isn't it a fantastic mystery?"

The bartender finally leaned over to us. His tight blue shirt was unbuttoned to the middle of his chest. "Bow," he smiled, "welcome home."

I didn't know Bow had been out of town. The chasm between our first meeting and my getting close to him, or to anyone, felt suddenly vast.

Bow got up on his tiptoes, leaned over the bar, and hugged the bartender like they were brothers meeting at a train station. "Juno, this is Tam," Bow said, reaching back to me. I held out my hand, and Juno kissed it.

"What a little fox," he said. "You look familiar."

I thanked him, wondered why people kept commenting on my looks since I was the least made up of any girl I'd seen that night, and tried to recognize his vaguely familiar face.

"I know you," he said, "you work at the SLLC."

Bow looked at me expectantly, and I put on the practiced smile. This was the risk of going out in the neighborhood near work. I couldn't place Juno, though—had I counseled him? Tested him?

"Thanks for the way you handled that situation with my little brother Nate," Juno said, "poor kid." I kept smiling through the unbelievably uncomfortable moment of realizing who I was talking to. Nathan Reggman had an older brother, who was friends with my date. My stomach hurt. I felt victimized by an unmerciful god. I hated the way Janet called coincidence "fate," and I hated that this one had layered so perfectly upon my anxiety attack at the clinic, and knew I wouldn't tell her about it. The noise in the room exploded behind me. Juno's face swam in a circle. I felt very, very tired. And underneath it all, there was some kind of grace in knowing for sure that Nathan Reggman was the demon who'd knocked me out. I had found him, on my own, and I was right.

"We do what we can," I said, dumbly.

"Hey, are you discussing your patients?" Bow said.

"I'm not discussing him."

"It's okay," Juno said. "I'm sure he'll be thrilled to know you've forgotten about him."

"I haven't forgotten," I said. It was not the time or place to cry. It was not the time or place to berate Nathan's older brother for his reckless insensitivity. I rationalized: he doesn't know what really happened. No one in his right mind would speak to me, the victim, that way—like Nathan was the one who got hurt. I picked up a few bar napkins and bent down to blot champagne off my foot. Bow leaned down.

"Are you alright?" he said low, in my ear, like we were off-camera.

"Let's get those drinks," I said, standing up. I asked Juno how he'd recognized me as he poured wine into two plastic cups.

He said he'd driven Nate to the clinic a few times after "everything." Like, no big deal. "Kid was always too shy to talk to you, but, you know, I saw who you were."

I nodded and picked up the wine. I couldn't think of an acceptable way to ask Juno what the fuck he was talking about.

"Thanks man," Bow said as he put down a few dollars.

"You coming to Franco's party?" Juno asked Bow. "I'm bartending."

Bow said maybe, then excused us and nudged me toward the gallery room.

So I would have to get a restraining order on Monday. I envisioned a good-natured Juno driving his homicidal brother over to the SLLC, unaware of the gun in Nate's backpack, then the horrible trial after my death when Juno tried to convince a jury he'd had no idea. I imagined Nate sitting in a car across the street from my work, cracking his knuckles in his lap, and then telling Juno to keep driving. Too shy to talk to me? What did it mean? What if Nathan was stalking me? Maybe Nathan had given Juno a bullshit story that he wanted to find me to apologize. Probably Juno had heard a very watered-down version of the attack, with no physical violence. Nathan was waiting for me to be vulnerable, so he could come after me again. What else could it be? Why would he need his brother to drive? It didn't matter. I would get a restraining order this time, and everything would be fine.

Once we were out of earshot, Bow asked me what all the weirdness was about.

"A crazy coincidence," I said. He waited. He expected me to explain. "This is not really the time," I said, gesturing around us. I would have been counseled to remove myself from an emotionally threatening situation such as this, had I elected to speak to a counselor after Nathan took out his teenage-father rage on my body. However, at the time, I had believed my experience with traumatized young women was enough training to deal with my personal trauma alone. I had not planned for the trauma to swirl into this kind of insane synchronicity. Back to Greenvale, and now this? It wouldn't have happened in West Courtney.

We made our way into the gallery. I drank my cheap wine too quickly, envied the glittery, toned abs of a girl in a purple feather bikini, and imagined scenario after scenario involving Nathan, Juno, and my violent death.

"Hey," Bow said, "come look at these." His hand warmed the small of my back for a second as he slipped behind me and guided us to the first in a series of brightly painted lounge scenes. Their glossy cartoon style was vaguely familiar. The pieces resembled animation cells, with impressionistic stone fireplaces, rounded modern furniture, and stark, solid-color shapes of sleek people. The occasional tropical drink in hand, the occasional 1960s go-go girl on a slightly off-perspective coffee table. All signed by SHAG. "I love his stuff," Bow said. "I don't know if the Santa one is here," he started scanning the walls, "but it's like the greatest adult Christmas party scene, ever."

I asked about the burlesque.

He said it should start any minute now.

Every third person in the gallery was wearing an elaborate get-up: retro, leather, goth, girls in rubber dresses, men in drag. It was as if every sexual subculture had a representative present, in full uniform. Under different circumstances, which did not involve Nathan's brother, perhaps, I would have loved everything. This was what I had always wanted: a community of friendly deviants. I tried to keep that in mind while I watched Juno flirt with everyone, sent Bow away for more wine, got more tipsy, and evaluated the sexual tension between myself and Bow, and everyone else and Bow. I couldn't tell if it was higher with me. Everyone was smiling and touching each other so often.

The music seeped through cracks in the noise. I tried to compare the scene to a movie. We were the back lot party at a studio where a sci-fi, a porno, and Andy Warhol's bio-pic were being shot.

Bow maneuvered us up to the band right before the DJ faded out. He stood next to me, but just slightly behind my right side, pressed in by all the other bodies. The band started up while Naomi and two other girls came out from the audience. Of course Naomi was as amazing as her photo, and the other girls were tight-bodied and sassy. The Black Orchid Band had a real slack-key guitar. They wore matching black and white Hawaiian shirts. I wasn't fond of black and white together, but four guys in matching shirts I could enjoy. Naomi and her girls vibrated in bright blue fringed hot pants, blue bikini tops, and platform stiletto heels. They also wore black eye-masks and studded collars. They vamped around, bumping and grinding in unison, kicking their legs up high and flipping their hair to the music. They had cute, 1950s shoulder-shaking choreography, but the band's sound was a little dark, like a Dick Dale beach party for old-time gangsters. Somehow the masks made the whole thing more sardonic than silly.

"Her heart deceived me," the singer crooned, Elvis after a night of especially heavy smoking, "she was a goddamn cheat." The girls turned their backs to us, pulled the strings on their tops, tossed them over their shoulders, then turned around. Their blue tasseled pasties glittered in the low light. Naomi produced a leash, which she clipped to the other two dancers at their collars. She held the middle, steering them around while they crept up toward the crowd and back again. One of them nearly clawed my shirt, leaving a moment of candy-flavored scent behind her. Finally, Naomi let go of the leash, and the two girls started orbiting each other with it taut between them. Naomi spun to the front, ran her hands down the shoulders of the Black Orchid lead singer, gave the audience a second to stare into her teasing eyes, then bent over and grabbed her ankles. The girls spanked her, hard. Naomi tossed her hair as she came up, put a hand on each girl's head, and pushed them to the floor right on the last beat.

I was transfixed. At one point, Bow reached over and gently closed my mouth. When his hand touched my face my body responded with a heated ache. I liked Naomi's face, the way she smiled, and I couldn't bring myself to feel angry about her existence. Insecure, yes. The woman could move. She shimmied her whole body and the fringe shook like a tiny car wash. When the number ended, she and her dancers disappeared through the Employees Only door.

"What do you think?" Bow said, happy as ever.

I almost said, "It was worth it," but stopped myself in time. "Hot," I said. I told him I'd never seen anything like it. The Black Orchid Band went into a slower lounge tune, but the increasing crowd noise swallowed it up. We were packed in, and I thought about going back outside as people next to us started dancing. Naomi appeared with a lavender satin robe thrown over her costume and a white scarf taming her afro. She headed straight for us.

"Thanks for coming," she said in a velvet voice, her fake eyelashes swishing. She and Bow kissed the air next to each others' faces. "I'm Naomi," she said as she held out her hand, "and I'm thrilled to meet the Bitsy's mystery girl!"

"Tamina," I said, and took her hand. Instead of shaking it, she pulled me in for the same air kisses. She was a warm cloud of glitter and sweat and vanilla. I told her it was a great show. She had an utter grace about her. Perfectly comfortable balancing on stiletto Lucite heels in a crowd that had seen her nearly nude.

"It's fun, right?" she smiled. "I thought it might be too crowded for pasties, but what the hell?"

"I had no idea Wacko had a license for all this," I said.

"I've never gotten arrested," she laughed. "At least not here." Wink.

"Are you going on again?" Bow asked.

She said not for a while. "The fashion show got canceled, so," she shrugged.

Bow asked what I wanted to do. I wondered if he was bored, or if he wanted to steal me away, or if he was waiting until he could drop me off and get to Naomi. In spite of the girl inside that desperately wanted them both to think I was adventurous, if not absolutely comfortable in their world, I said I needed to get home. Bow and Naomi said effortless, affectionate goodbyes to each other.

"Next time," Naomi said to me, and kissed the air next to my right cheek.

As we got into his car, Bow asked me if I'd been disappointed.

I tried evasive answers, alternately implying that there had been disappointing events but none of them were his fault, and that I had been enjoying myself tremendously with no specks of disappointment in the evening at all.

"I understand that we don't know each other that well yet," Bow said, and I noted his confidence that we would be knowing each other sometime in the future, "but if you want to tell me what that coincidence was with Juno I'm here to listen."

"And if I don't?"

"No problem," he said.

I recognized the tactic. Make the patient feel that you won't push them, and then wait for them to open up. I resented being the patient. A little drunk, tired of worrying about Nathan, humming with the vibrations of Naomi's body shaking and snaking over the dance floor, I sighed in response. I sounded like I'd been holding my breath for two minutes. My heart thumped harder, my gut burned with adrenaline, and I could feel the words before I said them.

"Your bartender friend has a little brother, named Nathan, who assaulted me six months ago," I said.

Bow blinked quickly. "What?"

"I'm about to get evicted. That's not entirely connected."

"Okay—"

"This is the first date I've been on in a year. That whole normal first-date anxiety about whether we'll kiss has been completely replaced by this bizarre extra anxiety about whether, if you do end up kissing me, you will then immediately drive to Naomi's house and get laid."

Bow pressed his lips together, then opened his mouth and took a slow breath. "Can I ask a few questions?" he said.

"No."

He nodded. We hit a red light, and I felt his gaze on me while I stared down the block. Something was wrong in my throat, but whether it was tears or nausea I couldn't tell.

"Do you mind one other little stop?" Bow said. "I promise it won't be crowded, and you don't have to wait in the car."

I shrugged. "Whatever."

"You sound like you're under a lot of pressure," he said, "and there's a place not far from here that I like to go when I feel that way. Of course I'll take you home if that's what you want."

The lack of horror or blatant rejection in his voice baffled me. I couldn't understand why he wasn't speeding toward my house, doing his best to make innocuous jokes until he could toss me out in front of my place. I told him so.

"You don't scare me," he said. "We're a lot alike, I think."

"Juno's brother kicked your ass too?" I pressed my palms into my eyes.

"No. And I'd really like to know what happened to you. I meant that I tend to hide the truth under the surface until I lose control and it explodes out like that. I've only recently started a campaign against that habit."

I asked him what he was hiding from me at that moment.

After a few seconds he said, "I'm embarrassed."

I found that very hard to believe.

But then he described how the evening had gone, from his perspective.

He'd left me in the car for a half-hour, offended me by talking about his relationship to Naomi, then introduced me to someone who made me uncomfortable. He was worried he'd made a terrible impression, didn't like being a worrier, and couldn't get his mojo back.

The impression wasn't perfect, I told him, but it wasn't so bad.

We'd driven far past my street, on Sunset, and Bow took a left on Fairfax. He took my hand, held it gently, and let go of the wheel for a second to reach over and switch gears with his left. A gesture that had turned me on reliably since high school.

He drove to the Grove, a ritzy shopping center built next to the old Fairfax Farmer's Market. He went all the way to the top level of the parking garage and pulled the car into a corner spot near the elevator.

The late-night LA sky, an inky navy blue under the roof, faded into purple against the city lights. I could hear movie theater people scuttling to their cars, after action flicks and romantic comedies. People who went on normal dates.

"This is it," he said.

"Are we going to Nordstrom?" I said. "Retail therapy?" He shook his head and we got out of the car. I followed him to the concrete wall we'd parked against.

"Cross your arms and lean forward like this," he told me. We faced the Hollywood hills, elbows resting next to each other, me on my toes. We stood like that for a while, breathing, watching lights flicker on and off, cars gliding along the streets. From seven floors up, Hollywood looked like a bejeweled toy model town against a painted backdrop. Cities at night are always beautiful, but LA stays purple and pink in the dark, glowing from some untraceable origin. Miniature palm trees were lit with amber from bulbs embedded in the ground. The flat, ordered blocks of the city gave way to skyscrapers downtown and staggered strings of colored lights coming from mansions in the Hollywood Hills. The hills themselves, in silhouette, roundly cradled all the activity. In the cooling air, I felt the presence of the ocean behind us like it was a person, watching. A multiplicity, all somehow functioning as one.

"I'm trying not to be too cynical for this," I said.

"For what?"

I imitated someone's optimistic mother: "See all the beautiful people Tam, you're not alone, everything's going to be fine!"

He laughed and it made me a tiny bit happy. He had little crows' feet forming.

"Don't be too cynical for beauty," he said. "In other parts of the world, people dream of one day seeing LA like this."

I suddenly wanted to prove that I *had* been seeing the beauty, but then I would have had to admit that I was trying to impress him by acting like I hadn't.

"And," he said, "I thought you might find it empowering to be taller than everyone else." I rolled my eyes. "If it's so awful for you here, why not move back to New Jersey? I think about moving home when things get hairy."

I told him there were three kinds of people born in West Courtney. The first were the faceless who stayed there. The second were the slightly more interesting set that went on to New York, Boston, or another East Coast city for a slightly different lifestyle in or after college. My best friend from home, Grant Rose, had considered herself one of these when we were kids. She knew she had the ability to transcend the West Courtney strip-mall culture, but she never had ambitions to do anything important. She'd pop her gum in homeroom and tell the college counselor she was fine with the idea of being someone's secretary. But she was also the only girl I knew who talked about "them" and meant the same baseball-hat and push-up bra gang that I did.

"The third type of people are the real eccentrics, who leave for good, for somewhere exotic," I said. It didn't really matter where they went— Tokyo and LA were about the same psychic distance away: far. For me, Los Angeles had existed in a nostalgic fantasy world, in Raymond Chandler books I bought for fifty cents from the library and burlesque reels I found mislabeled "musicals" in the only independent movie store within twenty miles. Los Angeles stayed abstract, a backdrop for Bettie Page, Lili St. Cyr, Marilyn Monroe, Grace Kelley, and so many others. I was smitten with old pictures of Olvera Street, the El Capitan Theater, the Santa Monica Pier. I wanted to walk down the Boulevard of Stars in T-strap shoes and buttoned gloves.

I told him that when I was younger I would rifle through postcards at antique stores near the shore and buy anything from Southern California. While winters in New Jersey made me feel fat and bored, people all along the West Coast lived lives free of wool and down feathers and I envied their carelessness about weather. I decided in college I was one of the third type of people, who would leave for good, to go somewhere crazy.

Although I thought of it, I didn't mention that as a kid I'd watched mostly black and white movies about Hollywood because they had no colors to deal with, that I especially loved *Sunset Boulevard* because the idea that one could be fabulously selfish and insane, and still have people love you, was deeply appealing to me. I didn't know a good way to explain.

I did say that going back to Jersey was the last thing I could do, because it would mean I'd failed. It would mean I'd failed in exactly the way everyone always expected me to.

"Look out there again," Bow said, nodding toward the city. "You made it."

"It's not what I thought it would be," I said. I felt like a traitor.

"Where's your friend now?" he asked. "Did she get out too?"

"She's still in our hometown," I said, "and she's married, with kids."

"So she's a failure? She's the first type?"

I told him she ended up wanting that life.

He asked if I thought she was happy.

I told him I had no idea, I hadn't spoken to her in a few years. We were quiet for a minute. Then he turned to face me.

"I think you're beautiful."

"Oh please."

"I'm not rushing off to be with Naomi," he said.

I told him he was being very smooth.

He said he wasn't trying to be smooth. And what was the difference between being smooth and telling someone the truth, if either way they heard what they wanted to hear?

I didn't have a comeback for that one.

"Can I kiss you?" he said. He said it from where he stood, without leaning in. He wasn't assuming I would say yes.

"Not yet," I said. "I want you to tell me a story from your life."

"What kind?"

"A juicy one." But now that the kissing was even more likely, adrenaline shot down my legs and through my back.

He turned and faced the street again. "Easy. I used to do way too much coke. I have an ex-girlfriend from that time who still does." He had thought he could help her quit. He hid their relationship for almost year after everyone else thought he'd left her.

The whole time he was talking he stared out at the hills and picked at his thumbnail.

He let her move in when she lost her job.

He sighed and rubbed his face. "I let her hit me when she was angry and high. I thought I was a superman for not getting high with her. I thought I was a saint for helping her out. Then one day I lost it."

"Meaning?"

"I fought back. I broke my hand hitting the wall. I would have hit her face if she hadn't moved fast enough." He kicked her out, after that. He said there was nothing redemptive about ending it, because he never should have been with her in the first place. "That's part of the reason I'm so blunt now," he said. "I'm afraid I'll catch myself in a delusion like that again. It was the only time I've ever been moved to violence, and it felt like I had to purify myself from an evil possession afterward."

"A lot of people feel that way about coke," I said.

"That's the wrong way to think about it," he said. "I don't have prejudice against any drugs. I have suspicion of people who do them without clear intentions for themselves."

"But some drugs are just worse for you than others."

"On an individual level, sure," he said. "Like now I know I shouldn't do coke, unless I want some Herculean task of resisting addiction again. But there's nothing inherently wrong with the *drugs*. It's us doing drugs badly that causes problems. We lie to ourselves about how addicted we are as a culture to things like TV and sugar, and then criminalize drugs that would hurt us far less if they were regulated and people knew enough about them."

It sounded like the argument I'd had many times with conservative parents about sex. I was surprised to find myself in the "wrong" position.

"Don't get stuck thinking like an American on this one," he said.

"Meaning?"

"Our government is so paternalistic on this issue we're all raised to be terrified, and that's how people get stuck without enough information or support. It's ridiculous."

"Hey," I said, pointing down the street at a stretch Hummer limo, "would you ever want to ride in one of those?"

"I think they're ugly, and of course they're gas guzzlers," he said, "but I wouldn't turn down a freebie."

"You came up with a story pretty fast," I said.

"Would you rather I took forever to inventory them all? Or was secretive and had to fight the urge to hide away the bad things?"

I said no, and told him he could kiss me.

"Yesssss," he said, and pumped his fist once. A mockery of machismo, and also, an expression of genuine delight.

He snaked one arm around my waist, put the other on the front of my neck, thumb and middle finger on my collar bones. When he was an inch from my face, I smelled something rich and sweet.

"You smell like honey," I said.

"It's Eidel amber-honey shave cream."

He pulled me into the kiss, his hand between us.

We both took a breath as the warmth of our mouths pushed together. He bit my bottom lip, just slightly. We negotiated our tongues slowly, like feeling for the switch in a dark room. I finally got to bury my fingers in the dark waves at the back of his neck. My body temperature shot up. I hadn't noticed closing my eyes until the kiss ended and I opened them again.

"I like how strong your heart is," he said.

"I like how metaphorical that sounds," I said.

"I just got an idea," he said softly as he moved to tuck a curl behind my ear.

"I'll bet you did," I said.

"You could make some of your rent money by Monday modeling shoes."

EIGHT

ow's great idea, which he explained as we got back into the car, was for me to squeeze my perfect sixes into a few pairs of stripper heels for a catalogue shoot Naomi was doing on Monday. She modeled "specialty" lingerie for a Hollywood Boulevard shop but her feet were too big to do their shoes. Apparently, their foot model was routinely hung over and unreliable, and it was likely I could replace her, if we asked. They paid seven hundred dollars for all rights to the photos from a single shoot.

"The pictures must go on a fetish site," I said.

"So what?" Bow asked. "Your feet are amazing," he said. "Why not share them? Why not make a killing with them?"

"I'm not sure I'm ready to make the leap from voyeur to exhibitionist," I said as we pulled up in front of my building. "But thanks for noticing my fancy tootsies."

"You're a voyeur?"

"Isn't everybody?"

He cocked his head and narrowed his eyes, a little mischief curling the corners of his mouth. "Think about it. Let me know tomorrow," he said. "I'll call Naomi and I'm sure she could work it out." He parked in the driveway, behind my car, and with his hands on the keys, asked if he could walk me up. There appeared an opening for me to cut the night off. Or not. He had those lips. I tried to remember if I had ever slept with someone on a first date. Not unless I counted some guy at a party when I was nineteen. It seemed like an experience I should have, considering my career field. Plus, we might not see each other ever again.

"Sure, why not?" I said. If I was left alone I'd only stay up worrying anyway. Janet wouldn't be home after her stunt this afternoon.

At the top of the stairs, there was something wrong. The porch light was out. The door was unlocked. I stepped one foot in and flipped the lights.

Janet's moving boxes were upended or sideways. Piles of dishes, clothes, and CDs leaned perilously against each other. My clean canvas wall covering peeled down halfway to the floor, and all the furniture had been shoved around randomly. I had to step over a pile of what appeared to be Janet's photo albums and my biology texts from college to get into the room. I'd walked into a crime scene from *Law and Order*. Except there was no one in a trench coat blithely explaining what had happened.

My first instinct, which I suppressed, was to call my mother and cry.

I yelled for Janet. No answer. Gone or dead.

"Don't go in," Bow said, but I did. I walked around and around and couldn't fathom what was going on. The Tasmanian Devil had come through our house. Then I realized there was nothing of any value missing. My laptop was at work. The TV sat on its little cart, maybe there were things missing from the boxes, but it appeared, as I threw open both my and Janet's bedroom doors, that whoever had torn apart our living room had not the time to get to the rest. I found my phone, which I silently vowed never to leave at home again, under a pile of jeans, and called Janet. Straight to voicemail. I hung up.

I had one message, but it was from Todd, so I hung up on that too.

I deflated on the couch. Bow sat next to me and put a hand on my arm.

"You need to call the police," he said.

I whined and flopped over sideways. I covered my face with a pillow and screamed. Where was Janet? Why did she give John a key? I threw the pillow.

"I'm sick of police," I said. "I want Janet to deal with this." But Bow already had his phone out. I walked into the bathroom, sat on the edge of the tub, and breathed through the urge to vomit. When I came out, he was hanging up.

He told me that because we didn't see anyone, the police weren't going to come. I could file a report tonight or tomorrow and they recommended I stay at a hotel until my landlord replaced the locks.

"Great." I couldn't afford a hotel, and the thought of staying in our apartment as it was made me lightheaded. My landlord was not about to change our locks; or, he was, but not until he was rid of us next week, the way things were going. At least I could lock my bedroom door.

"Stay at my place," Bow said, "and then I can bring you back to your car in the morning before I go to work." He could tell I shouldn't drive.

I searched for other possibilities. I should call Todd. "I'll be fine," I said. Todd's house was nearly monochromatic black. I could stay there.

"Come on," Bow said. He noted how late it was. "It's not smart to stay here." He was right. He was also probably still trying to seduce me. I couldn't decide if that was exciting or inconsiderate. I'll turn his lights off right away, I thought, so if his place clashes, it won't matter.

"I need my toothbrush," I said, and went into the bathroom again.

Four years earlier, when I was moving to LA, my mother had secretly baked me a batch of chocolate chip cookies, packed them into a Tupperware, and slipped them into my carry-on. I never sent the Tupperware back, but I didn't want anyone else to use it. I put it in the bathroom where it held all the little hair clips and tampons and other bits that end up under the sink. Reaching into it to grab my travel toothbrush, I decided not to call my mom, and felt better. I was finally old enough to not need my mother, even though I'd thrown a kid-worthy tantrum on the couch a few minutes before. This, I realized, must be why everyone hates their twenties.

On the drive to his house, Bow told a story of a robbery that happened to him when he was six or seven. He and his mother had been walking around the Presidio in San Francisco and came home to find their front window broken and everything but the furniture gone.

"Everything," he said. "They took coats, dishes, some of my toys."

I had a hard time listening, because it had occurred to me that Nathan might have figured out where I lived and come after me.

We drove north on the 101. As Bow was talking, Janet called.

When I asked her if she'd seen our place, she said she was sorry, and she'd clean it up tomorrow.

"You did that? You threw everything around in the living room?"

"John and I had a fight," she said, "and it got pretty bad. We had to get out of there. I'm at his place now." I pressed her for an explanation and she finally told me that John's little brother had been arrested, and John had gone into a rage. "But it's okay now," she said.

I told her I had no idea what that meant.

She asked if I was home.

I told her no, I was staying somewhere else tonight, and when she asked where, I said it was none of her business.

We hung up.

"No need to go to the cops tomorrow," I announced. Bow was pulling into a parking garage. He asked why not, and I told him.

"John is the roommate's boyfriend you hate?" Bow said.

"Yes," I said.

"Doesn't sound good."

"Not at all."

"Do you want to go back home?"

I told him no.

In noir films, when the main characters have a near-death experience, they hold each other like they might never touch another warm body again. After a year of celibacy, the resurfacing of Nathan, a bizarre first date, and a non-break-in, I wanted to get rocked into that same passionate oblivion, tearing clothes off and biting and knocking the furniture over. In an annoying moment of girlish insecurity, I regretted the underwear I had on, and wondered if I would have time to brush my teeth.

Bow lived in one of those Studio City complexes with a landscaped center courtyard that circled a pool. All the front doors and living room windows faced the courtyard, so no matter which floor you lived on you always knew who was swimming, leaving, doing laundry, or coming home with a new girl, because everyone could see into everyone else's front room. It reminded me of the Panopticon, an eighteenth-century model for a perfect prison, where the cells are arranged in a circle and the guard tower is in the center—prisoners can see each other, and the guard can see all of them, but because of the tower's design, the prisoners can't see the guard. Eventually, the model predicts you don't even need a guard in that tower, because once everyone feels that they could be watched at any time, they'll behave as if they are. In a prison, that means prisoners stay docile. In a city, what kind of authority was analogous to the guard? The superego? There was something enticing about how many spaces in LA were designed that way—for optimal viewing of the people inside. Gyms, malls, storefronts at the Grove, all had plenty of windows, and people looked in, while the people inside rarely looked out. There was no way to know if those inside the fishbowl were truly behaving the same way they would if they weren't under glass.

Disappointingly, in Studio City, as opposed to the Panopticon, occupants could close their blinds.

Bow had to push the front door with his shoulder. "Sticky," he said.

His apartment was like a friendly opium den—a maroon and gold tapestry covered the wall behind his couch. He had plants. A heavy wood-bead curtain hung over the entrance to the hallway that led to his bedroom and bathroom. All his furniture was a rich, dark teakwood. The only reminder that we were not in Casablanca was the standard beige carpet. His colors stayed close enough to harmonious for me to be able to function. I complimented his decorating skills and felt relieved.

"I got most of this stuff on trips," he said. "Back when I was studying Southeast Asian religions I went to Thailand, India, and Indonesia on a Watson fellowship."

I asked him if he was trying to impress me, and he said yes.

He bustled around, brought me a glass of water, asked if I wanted a glass of wine or a bowl to smoke, I said yes to both, he rummaged in a hall cupboard for some blankets and pillows, and made a nice nest on the couch. Normally he would put me in his bed, he said, but he'd bought a new one a few weeks ago and only had one set of sheets, which were dirty. It felt wrong not to give me clean ones, plus the couch was really comfortable, he'd slept on it many times. Then he reconsidered, trying to figure out if he pulled the sheets off and then put me in the bed with the blankets—the couch was fine, I said. The blankets smelled like lavender, I didn't mind being on the couch. But I did, if he was going to leave me there alone. He poured us two glasses of something red.

I sat.

He pulled a purple velvet bag from inside a drawer in the coffee table and packed a bowl into a hand-blown pipe. "This is from a Humboldt friend," he said.

"The weed or the pipe?"

"Both. A high-school buddy. Blows glass and grows his own."

"Tell him thank you."

"What a night," he said, and handed me the pipe and a lighter.

I took a hit, passed it back, blew the smoke away from Bow, and confessed that I didn't smoke that often.

"Too bad we're not staying up late to read or talk," he said. "But you'll get some good sleep tonight."

When I got high, I got more paranoid about colors. "Usually I cough like an amateur," I said.

"Amateurs smoke terrible weed. And," he smiled, "they smoke it poorly."

"You're trying to tell me you're not a pothead."

"I'm trying to fend off any judging, period."

We finished the bowl. I watched Bow's hands, sure as a dancer's, as he cleaned and folded the pipe back into its purple pouch.

"You take good care of your things," I said. "Earlier, when you said you wanted to help reinvent America's relationship with its things? I think you could."

He slid off the couch and kneeled on the floor in front of me. He leaned so that his chest rested against my knees. He kissed my cheek, my ear, and the softest place behind my jaw. I slid my arms up around his neck and opened my knees so he'd be closer. He stopped kissing and held me. Our cheeks pressed together. It was the most natural, intimate way to be touched, and I couldn't remember it ever happening before. We stayed in that embrace far longer than I would normally have hugged anyone, and when he started rubbing my back, I wanted his mouth, his lips, his tongue. I wanted him to swallow me whole.

I thought we'd start kicking over the furniture, or at least roughing up the couch-bed, but before it could happen he pulled away and held my face in his hands.

"Do you have sex to escape your life?" he said. I leaned backward, sinking into the couch.

"Sometimes, probably," I said, although I hadn't had the opportunity to use sex as an escape for quite a while. "Don't you?" My thoughts refused to organize.

"No," he said. Just like that. "I think there are right pleasures and wrong pleasures," he said as he sat next to me again. "I'd rather ruin the mood than follow it into something empty. I get very vulnerable, open, during sex, and doing it casually has been terrible for me." He started explaining that at this point in his life sex was very intimate, and I interrupted him again.

"Either you want to or you don't," I said.

Bow sighed. "It's not that simple."

"Like hell it isn't," I said. "I'm the sexpert here."

"I'm surprised you're so offended," he said. "Most people are grateful to know I take it so seriously."

Again, he'd called me a chicken. I pulled my legs up to my chest and held on to my knees. "Most people?"

"I'm going to let you sleep," he said. "If you want to talk about this tomorrow I'd love to." He kissed the side of my head.

I was furious. And curious. And frustrated. I'm being ridiculous, I thought. I should be relieved that he doesn't want to rip a girl's clothes off and do it on the floor on a first date. But what was wrong with me that he didn't want to rip *my* clothes off and do it on the floor on *our* first date? Maybe it was my whining. Maybe he was in love with Naomi. Maybe I'd been too cranky, preoccupied.

I wanted to go home. I tried to imagine Janet and John after the violence in our apartment. She probably ran out of our place after him, trying to calm him down. What did they do then? They weren't going to stop off at Roscoe's Chicken and Waffles for a snack, to chat about the heat wave. He probably drove his truck fast and angry, swerving through that intersection at Gower to get on the freeway, while Janet gripped the handle above her window and kept her mouth shut. She had waited to call me until they got back to his place, and she could sneak into another room, because he'd gotten trashed and passed out. She seemed very far away. I had a pang of worry, imagining how lonely she must have been, and then anger at her stupid, stupid choices. Things are changing, she'd said. The sinking, sickening dread of Nathan crept back in, with the certainty that I'd have to deal with him somehow, "signs" or not. For a second, I imagined him following us here, waiting outside for Bow to leave the room so he could come in and kill me.

The light coming through Bow's miniblinds made orange lines across his wall. I considered going into his room and taking my clothes off, to see what would happen. He would probably stick to his guns.

I kicked my way deep into the blanket nest, turned my face toward the back of the couch where there was less visual information to process, and fell asleep.

NINE

When I woke up at Bow's, I wanted to slip into the crack between the couch cushions and hide. I'd said too much, shown too much. He walked into the kitchen from the shower a few minutes later, shirtless, in the black pants he wore to Bitsy's, and as I watched his body, I tried to remember the last flat male stomach I'd seen outside of the clinic. His sexuality was so effortless, so frank. In daylight his apartment seemed a little shabbier. The glow of candles had hid frayed carpet edges, scuffs on the furniture.

"Morning, sunshine," he said, and asked if I was hungry.

I told him no, even though it was a lie, to shut down his good humor. I stared at the couch's hypnotic pattern of small squares and walked my fingers through them one by one. With the blankets tangled in a big wad near my feet, it was clear I had tossed around all night. I started folding things.

"Don't worry about it," Bow said from the kitchen.

I snuck into the bathroom and glanced at the bottles on the counter—all white labels—he did have an obsession with Eidel. I was a mess: mascara rubbed onto my cheeks, oily nose, frizzy hair. Squatting awkwardly to pee semi-silently against the side of the bowl, I considered locking the bathroom door and not coming out for, say, two or three weeks. He'd probably feed me. Instead I fumbled through an improvised getting-ready routine, using his fancy products.

I would go to the clinic. Saturdays it was quiet, and I could catch up on paperwork. I kept an emergency outfit in the trunk of my car, but Bow was driving me back home anyway, so I might as well go inside my apartment and change.

"Ready?" he said when I came out. I nodded, too embarrassed about getting rejected to try any light conversation.

We made it to the freeway before he started talking.

"I was thinking about you becoming a doctor," he said.

"What about it?"

"I always wonder where that dream comes from. It's one of those basics that's implanted when you're a toddler. No one ever tries to get their kid to grow up and become a graphic artist or a book publisher. People who want to be doctors have to wade through a lot more questions about whether they really want it, or if they've just been told they want it."

"Can't it be both?"

He shrugged. "Sure."

I asked him what he was trying to say.

"I guess I'm asking you a question, which is: How much of the doctor dream is really yours? How much is from other people?"

"You think I haven't thought about that? I just said I think it's both."

He nodded and stopped talking.

The sky was that perfect blue, but the trees seemed fatigued somehow, dry and dusty. When he pulled up to my apartment, after twenty minutes of me staring at both of our reflections in the window, touching my hair, and not making conversation, he brought up shoe modeling again.

"You'll have fun," he said. "You'd make a good chunk of your rent money."

"I don't know," I said.

He asked me to call him today if I changed my mind so Naomi would have time to talk to the store owner.

"Of course," I said. I worked up some nerve and hugged him. "Thanks for the ride."

He laughed. "You don't get it," he said. He slid a hand around the back of my head and kissed me. I let him. Then he pulled away and said, "You're not getting rid of me by having some little life crisis on our first date."

"Slightly threatening," I said.

"I like you. I like the anticipation."

"Are you getting into your Buddhist-waiter mindset?" I was trying too hard to play.

He locked eyes with me. My stomach twisted. He moved a hand up the inside of my thigh and rested it gently, deliberately, on my vagina.

"Now you want me?" I said. "What a mind-fuck."

He pulled away. "Wow."

I got out of the car. He rolled down my window and said he hoped things calmed down for me so we could try again.

I told him I needed to get to work and walked up the stairs to my door, feeling him watch until I got inside. He wouldn't call. Or, he'd want to process everything, and be compelled to call. I certainly wasn't going to reach out to him now.

Nothing would be fixed by escaping into the crazy lives of my patients at the SLLC, but I wanted to anyway. At least when I was solving their problems something was getting done. Janet was still not home. The apartment smelled like dirty clothes. I threw on my most basic work uniform (black pants, gray SLLC T-shirt) and got barely outside my front door.

"Tamina?" my landlord called from the sidewalk.

"Hi, Gary," I said, "I'm late for work." I locked the door behind me, fast.

His face was shadowed by a baseball cap so I couldn't tell if he was feeling friendly. He wore a faded AC/DC T-shirt. He was young, maybe two years older than me, and had inherited the building from parents who died in some kind of accident. He, Janet, and I had all been chummy together, even after our rent checks started coming in late.

"Hey, I've been trying to get a hold of Janet," he said. I suddenly wondered if Janet had slept with him.

"Hasn't everybody!" I said cheerfully, making a beeline for the car.

"We gotta talk," he said, walking behind me.

"We're going to pay," I said, turning to face him.

"I'm sorry, but this just isn't working out." He sounded like he was breaking up with me.

"If I can get a rent check to you on Monday, can we make something happen?" I hated myself, for needing to beg.

"It's been almost three months," he said, and paused. "Look, I've got people interested in the place. They've filled out a credit check already."

I opened my door and started sliding in. "Let's talk Monday, okay? I'll make sure Janet's around." I slammed the door and started the car. His phone went off and he started up the street, left hand gesturing. I had to turn the air conditioner on full blast for a minute before I could touch the steering wheel. While the air changed from furnace strength to tolerable, I worried that something bad happened to Janet after she got off the phone with me last night.

What if she lied about everything being all right to make me feel better, and as soon as she hung up she and John were in another screaming, violent fight? What if she drank herself into a stupor and passed out, and John was too drunk to know how drunk she was, and she choked on her own vomit? It seemed a fitting death for her somehow, since she was always reporting the sordid details of real-life tragedies she saw on the news. I had to stop conjuring horrible images of a mutilated or dead Janet. Money. Money was my problem now. Gary was clearly ready to evict us.

When I got to the SLLC someone had already taken the best parking space, which was usually vacant on Saturdays. Someone who drove a brand-new, powder-blue, BMW convertible. I wasn't sure if I'd intimidated most of the staff out of taking the space, or if I was always in it before them, but either way, parking down the street felt wrong.

Todd was at the desk, which was also strange, but the BMW couldn't be his. Maybe he'd borrowed it from Derek.

"Thank God you made it," he said, half-whispering and shaking his hands at the wrists.

"What are you doing here?"

His eyes darted around. "Linda Green is here," he said, with an intonation that indicated I should have known that already.

My face confirmed his fears.

"I left you a message!" he hissed. "And, you're late. You're never late!"

"Why are you being so flamey?" I asked.

"Shut up! I'm nervous," he said.

Linda was the former porn star who had built the clinic from nothing on her own dime. The education outreach program was her idea, originally. When I was hired at the SLLC, they had a proposal for the goal of the assemblies, but no real curriculum or teachers. I had to get trained through any and every other channel and then build our program from the best pieces of those other curricula. Linda hadn't been personally involved, but she often sent supportive sentiments through Helena. In fact, in four years, I'd never met Linda directly. I'd seen her in passing and had some email and phone contact, but she was very hands off, usually.

When Todd and I had first started dating, one of our regular Friday nights had involved bags of caramel corn and Linda's old pornos. She had big fake tits and a pretty face. Neither of us found her attractive, but she was a legend at the SLLC, since she'd transitioned from sex work to sex education. Only a few did that. And now she was here, watching us.

Which reminded me of Nathan, which reminded me of Juno, and the creepy news that Nathan had been stalking me through the clinic window, and my stomach scooted upward against my ribs. I glanced out at the street, but it seemed normal except for what I understood now was Linda's car.

"Who's she with now?" I said.

"Helena."

"I'm going to get some work done," I said, and walked to the end of the hall.

It was incredibly satisfying to me, when I first landed the job at twenty-two, to have my name engraved on a wood grain plate on an office door that I could close. A few years later, at nearly twenty-six, it reminded me that I was still not in medical school, was not on my way to medical school, and might never see my name on a bigger, fancier door.

My office was about the size of a kiddie pool. When I pushed my chair out from my desk I hit the opposite wall. Decorated with black and white pictures—one of my parents, one of me and Grant Rose at fourteen, one of me and Janet at Disneyland, and then cutouts (some of them photocopied from magazines to take out the colors) of various places in the world I wanted to go (one from each continent except Antarctica) and one old pinup of Bettie Page—it recalled collages titled "All About Me" I'd had to make in middle school. There was also one Polaroid of me and Todd in our SLLC shirts, laughing and doing a double thumbs-up sign.

I only spent about one or two hours in my office on a weekday since I was always in the clinic rooms with patients or at the front desk or out running assemblies and classes. Saturdays I often stayed in there all day, making sure my files were up to date, my emails answered, my appointments for the next week in no conflicts with each other, my messages deleted. I wore too many hats at the clinic, and didn't multitask very well because I was compelled to finish things I started.

That day, I longed for the comfort of paperwork. Everything felt like it was teetering on some kind of edge—I was at the end of living with Janet, maybe the end of my ability to support myself, and the end of my ignoring Nathan Reggman's existence. I tried not to turn my night with Bow into a symbol of the end of my dating career, but it was difficult not to.

I sank into my chair with intentions to fill in boxes, color-code patient files, answer seventy-five emails from high school administrators and parents about our classes, and start crossing things off my list. But as soon as I began, Todd appeared.

"It's our turn," he said. "She wants to see us."

I followed him out to the front desk where a familiar tall, brassy blonde, with a perfectly toned and bronzed body, was leaning against the counter, chatting with Helena. Linda was wearing a black velour track suit with "Juicy" embroidered ostentatiously in pink on the ass and black Puma running shoes with hot pink logos. Helena's white lab coat seemed to blaze in contrast.

"Linda?" said Todd.

She turned toward us and smiled a lovely, glossy smile. She still had enormous fake breasts. She also had a perfect French manicure, very white teeth, and a diamond on her right hand. There was no irony in this embodiment of traditional Los Angeles sex appeal. I remembered a scene in one of her movies where a guy had licked the sweat from her back tattoo and felt myself blushing.

"Are you Tamina?" she asked.

"I am," I said, and held out my hand.

"Linda," she said as she shook. "I'm *so* happy to meet you, thank you *so* much for all of the incredible work you've done."

"I'm going to get back," Helena said. Linda smiled and waved.

I mentioned some charts I needed Helena to review and she nodded as she brushed past us.

I wondered who had told Linda I was doing incredible work. I was Todd's immediate supervisor, although we performed many of the same tasks. My immediate supervisor was technically Helena, the clinic director and an MD/MPH, who spent only a few days a month at the clinic to see her own patients (like Layla) and sign the paperwork our Nurse Practitioner, Robin, had filled out. We had a few interns who worked the front desk and did some filing. It was not a large staff; it was not a large clinic. We outsourced budgeting, billing, and payroll. Todd and I worked the longest hours.

I thanked her, and asked as politely as I could what brought her to the clinic on a Saturday.

She produced an irritating grown-woman giggle. "I'm working on plans to expand some of my businesses in order to better fund this place," she said. "So I thought I'd come take a look around and talk to you guys about what you need. I know that you pretty up for site visits and I wanted to catch you a little by surprise."

"Sneaky," I said.

"Helena wants me to be happy," she said. "But I know that the clinic is struggling with allocating funds and I don't want to be kept in the dark about what's really wrong here."

I wondered exactly what she knew about our day-to-day operations.

"Ask me anything, I'm happy to spill," I said.

"I was hoping you'd be like that," she said, "and I'd like to take you and Todd out to lunch? Chat about how things are going? Can you guys get away?"

The fact that going over Helena's head to talk to the founding director of the clinic could be job suicide didn't bother me much for two reasons. One, Todd would be there, and he was great at politics; two, I had a meeting every month with Helena during which I told her, repeatedly, all of the problems with the clinic. If Helena came back to me angry I could always play innocent.

"Lunch sounds wonderful," I said. I still hadn't eaten.

Todd agreed.

Silver Lake didn't have many air-conditioned places in the clinic's neighborhood. Afraid Linda might melt in the heat, I tried to think of somewhere nice.

"I have to tell you guys," she said as we walked out the door, "what I really, really want right now is Tommy's."

So instead of lounging in a cool restaurant with white cloth napkins on our laps, we piled into Linda's BMW, sped down the street, plopped into hard plastic seats bolted to the table, and slurped on chili burgers while we talked.

Tommy's was red and yellow on the inside, which hurt me. The ultimate symbolic fast-food pair of colors. I couldn't ignore it. Todd was wearing a bright blue shirt that complimented the yellow and waged an all-out war on the red. My eyes moved around the room, searching for things to focus on, and I knew I'd started to seem strange. I gave up and stared at my food.

"Okay, here's the deal," Linda said, licking chili out from under her nail. "Helena is a good friend, but she's embezzling money."

Todd and I both coughed a little. "But we're a nonprofit," he said.

I tried to look up from the table. Looking down seemed guilty. My stomach lurched at the red/yellow wall behind Linda.

I suggested we sit outside. I convinced them it was too loud and I couldn't hear. Todd rolled his eyes when Linda wasn't looking. We wiped off some dusty patio furniture outside the door and I sat facing the street.

"She's not taking a lot," Linda said, "and actually most of it is going to help another project she has been trying to start for ages downtown. So I don't care as much about the money as I care about her lying to me."

I wanted to know what the project was. I couldn't imagine Helena doing anything but starting another clinic. I realized I had no idea where she was from. Maybe she was going into her old neighborhood? We were veering into very dangerous places, if Todd and I wanted to keep our jobs. Linda's involvement in the SLLC was invisible, financial, and we didn't know the extent of her hiring and firing power. Helena, on the other hand, could axe us both.

What concerned Linda was that Helena wasn't putting enough time into running the clinic well. "I'm especially worried about her misrepresenting your needs, areas for growth, you know, the problems."

My phone rang. I apologized, saw it was Janet, and turned the ringer down. Both Linda and Todd took those seconds to check their own phones.

"I don't need you two to worry about the money," Linda said. "That's my job. What I need you to do is tell me, straight up, what the clinic needs."

"More space for file cabinets," Todd said. "I'm stacking files under the front desk and legally, we have to lock them up."

"It would be great if we could have a conference line," I said.

"A new exam table," Todd said.

We looked at each other. "I want the rapid test for HIV," I said.

Linda urged us on.

"We need better equipment for school assemblies and classes," I said. "We could use a projector for PowerPoint."

"And we need more trained staff for assemblies," Todd said, "so Tam and I don't have to do them all."

"Better health coverage," I said. Todd nodded.

"You don't have health insurance?" Linda said, shocked. "You're supposed to!"

"I have it, because I'm full time," I said, "but even the PPO I have is the bare minimum, the coverage is worthless. Todd technically works thirty-six hours," at which Todd snorted, "so he's high and dry." I thought about the pile of medical bills and collection agency letters in my room. Already sweating, trickles making my back itch, I started feeling woozy. I ate a french fry.

"I'll look into that." Linda pulled out a legal pad and started writing things down. "I want you to tell me your fantasy for these assemblies." Todd raised his eyebrows at me. Go ahead, his face said.

So I told her. "We need to always do them in pairs," I said first. I told her we needed better-looking uniforms, girly tees for me, maybe even T-shirts to give away. We needed more giveaways—higher quality condoms, gloves, and dental dams.

"That's only what you need," she said. "Those things sound reasonable. I want to hear your big fantasy, the totally crazy idea for how you'd do an assembly if you could spend as much money as you wanted and didn't have to worry about the politics."

I told her I wanted a sound system, a DJ, and a book we could give away—a funny, well-researched, and well-written one like *The Guide to Getting it On*, except in a condensed, pocket-size edition. We definitely needed a book with pictures and easy, understandable stats. Something the kids might actually read. The handouts we used always ended up covering the floor of the auditorium—it was like someone dropped a roll of penis and vagina wallpaper when we left.

They both laughed. "It's true," Todd said.

I wanted celebrities to come speak for the first five minutes of the assembly; preferably hip-hop artists or actors, people who were not embarrassed talking about sex. I wanted a sign-up table where kids could get on an email list, and every few months we'd send out a brief, well-designed newsletter that reminded them about safe sex practices and kept track of their testing for them. I wanted to make follow-up visits. This meant we needed a better website too, with online appointment requesting.

"And video tutorials," Todd said. "So they can watch a condom demo anytime they want."

I wanted incentives for volunteers, so that some of the high school kids would come sort our mail. We could work out a partnership with the schools that gave the kids course credit, maybe in the sciences, for working for us. If we could get a group of kids who hung out at the SLLC, we might interest some of them in the work we do, and we might build a new kind of educational community for them.

Both sexually active and inactive kids needed to be able to talk about their bodies and decisions with authority and self-respect. It's impossible to tell high schoolers who have already begun to experiment to back off and stay abstinent. It makes you sound like a grandma. But, if they are waiting, they need a community that doesn't degrade that choice. Although we used inclusive language, the gay and lesbian students needed more attention in our assemblies, too. Abstinence-only education was failing everywhere, the data was rushing in to support comprehensive programs like ours, but still, parents and teachers and policymakers acted as if a conversation about sex equaled a permission slip for the country's little babies to start having babies of their own. At least in California there was a bit less conservatism, I said, but certainly there were hotspots of homophobia, and a disturbing percentage—from 40 to 55 percent, depending on the source—of teens still reporting having unprotected sex. We needed tools that could integrate with their toys—current music, technology, language—to reach them.

Linda wrote things down, nodded, made interested faces. Todd offered approval noises. I finally stopped talking for a second. Then I said, "I guess I started preaching a little there."

"It's fabulous!" Linda said. "We are totally on the same wavelength here."

"Why are you asking about all this?" I said.

"Because I have a plan to make a lot of money in the next few years with my production company," she said, "and I really want to expand the clinic's reach so that we have the most in-demand private sex education team in Southern California."

"What about Planned Parenthood?" Todd said.

"What about them?" she said. "They're wonderful, and I'm grateful to them for providing a model. But they aren't underground anymore. They aren't edgy. They're important—they're lobbyists! But they don't have the same kind of appeal for drug users, porn stars, kids in the ghettos, homeless kids. I want the SLLC to be truly available and attractive to everyone."

I looked at Todd's bright blue shirt, tried to lose myself in it, tried to quiet down the nagging feeling that the yellow and red tiles of Tommy's were waiting behind me, stalking, ready to pounce. The whole time I'd been talking I'd forgotten about them.

I told Linda and Todd about a sex education curriculum review I had read recently. The goals always seemed reparative: reduce teen pregnancy, lower risk for STIs. None of the curriculums reviewed had a component that emphasized sexuality as part of your general health or put a positive spin on masturbation or pleasure. Those concepts seemed to be reserved for "experimenting" adults only.

"It's crazy, isn't it?" Linda said. "To act like kids, especially adolescents, shouldn't be interested in pleasure?"

Maybe I was starting to fall quietly in love with her. Even with the heavy eyeliner and bottle-blonde hair. Someone with some power who understood.

She made a joke about the big deduction she'd take for the lunch bill. She said she'd be in touch with us, and we could expect to see more of her as "changes" started happening at the clinic.

We returned to the office, I said goodbye to Linda, who waved me along and told me to keep thinking, Todd ran in to answer the phone, and I sat at my desk to listen to Janet's message. The air conditioning turned my hands clammy. She wanted me to come pick her up, but I couldn't hear from where. I called her.

"Where are you?" she asked. I was instantly annoyed.

"Work," I said, "like every Saturday?"

"Can you come get me?"

When I asked if she was okay, she paused for too long. I had no way of knowing if it indicated her quietly considering the question, getting distracted by something, or attempting to answer without incriminating herself in John's presence.

"Janet?" I said.

She had hung up.

Possible scenarios included everything from Janet being clumsy and stupidly hitting a button on her phone to her getting smashed on the back of the head with a bat and bleeding to death while I sat at my desk. She was probably still at John's, which was somewhere in the hills. I'd never been there. I didn't even know if he lived in the same place he had before. I called her. No answer. I called her again.

"Tam?" she answered, "Can you come get me at the Denny's on Gower? I'm going there right now."

"I'm at work," I said, trying to communicate that I couldn't take an hour off to go pick her up and take her home, especially from a place that was a walkable mile from our apartment.

"That's okay," she said, misunderstanding, "just get there as soon as you can." It sounded like she was talking into a pillow. She hung up again.

I put my head on my desk. On the one hand, when she moved out,

I wouldn't need to deal with this kind of situation again. On the other, where would I live? The apartment felt like one of the few friends in LA I had found on my own. I couldn't invite a new roommate who wanted to throw all of her ugly, clashing tapestries on the walls of my living room, and potheads with tapestries were just the types to respond to an ad for my neighborhood. If only I could get a pothead who didn't need colors to look at. I couldn't afford a new place as close to the SLLC, especially one that required first, last, and a deposit to move in. I could move downtown, but I'd be commuting for over an hour. I could move to the Valley. Every option depressed me. The phone rang again, and I hit the talk button before I noticed it was Bow.

We said hello, him a little too boisterously.

"So have you thought about the shoe thing?" he asked. Pots clanked in the background. He was still at Bitsy's.

"No," I said.

"You mean you haven't thought about it, or you don't want to do it?"

"I mean I haven't thought about it, but I also don't think I want to do it."

"Sure?"

"No."

He paused. He asked if he should call back a little later. I told him that was a good idea. I put my head back on my desk.

In fifth grade my teacher, who had the worst outfits of any woman I had met, visited my mother and father to chat about my sleeping habits. Teal blazer, loud print blouse with orange flowers. When my father said that I slept fine at night, the teacher made him aware that I slept in class nearly every day. It had something to do with the fact that once my eyes were closed no colors could harass me. My parents pressed for answers, I gave them a story about nightmares, and then I took Benadryl every night that year. I got better control over sleeping in school by staring at my desk, or bouncing my eyes around the room, but I still felt the urge to nap when the visual noise of a room hit high intensity. Eventually I started shutting my eyes when anything overwhelming happened.

I was dead asleep when Todd walked in.

"Tam, sweetie," he said quietly into my ear, "today is a bad day for desk napping." He held a thick leather portfolio. "Look at this," he said. It was a projected clinic budget for the next three years, with increases in almost every area, and an especially large one for assemblies. Drawn up before our meeting with Linda.

"Where is this money coming from?" I asked, instead of how he got his hands on the budget.

Todd shrugged. He said he didn't know, and didn't care. "Let's get a digital projector!"

"Is she still here?"

He shook his head. "Had a doctor's appointment." He made a shooting-collagen-into-the-lips gesture. He stepped back and assessed me. "You look beat."

"You don't happen to have like sixteen hundred dollars lying around, do you?" I asked.

"If I did I'd be in Vegas with Derek right now," he said. "You got a gambling problem too?"

"Remember how I told you Janet's moving out?"

"You owe back rent," he said. "Shit."

"Know anyone who needs a room?"

"Who could live with you? Nope," he said. "Sorry, no offense."

"You know, you should date Remy, my other really bitchy gay friend," I said. "Oops, sorry, no offense."

He backed out of my office with his hands in the air.

I tried Janet again. Nothing.

I was running out of time. The three-day eviction notice would arrive this week. Janet wasn't going to pay our landlord a cent.

I called Bow.

"Change your mind?" he said.

"Yes," I said. "Do you want me to call Naomi, or will you?"

He said he would do it. He sounded thrilled.

I asked him why he was so excited.

"You and Naomi in the same room, in sexy clothes, in front of a camera?"

I tried to be charmed.

"Also, I like helping people."

It was probably true.

"Plus, I get more reasons to call you," he said.

I said I couldn't imagine why he'd want to keep calling.

"Let's not sit around being insecure together," he said. "Let's assume the other thinks we're wonderful, until notified otherwise."

I said I would try. He asked if my apartment was okay, and if I'd gotten in touch with Janet. I said I was on my way to find out what was going on.

We said goodbye, and then I left a pile of unfinished, unfiled folders locked in my desk. I took a list of things I was going to do that day, with too many items not crossed off, waved to Todd, got in my car, and drove to the Denny's where Janet said she would be. I tapped on the steering wheel. I couldn't tell if I was feeling jittery because of leaving everything undone at work or worrying about Janet. It all felt the same. Bad.

Denny's was packed with brunchers, the especially lazy ones who stayed in bed until two or three in the afternoon and then rolled over in their sexy undies and decided to get some pancakes. They were young, wearing hats over their matted hair, impeccably rumpled in little jersey dresses, expensively ripped jeans, and studded belts. Many of them kept their sunglasses on, inside. The air conditioning hummed, but it couldn't combat the heavy smell of something deep-frying. Janet sat hunched in a corner table, drinking coffee with both hands like she was cold, which she couldn't have been, watching out the window. She waved enthusiastically when she saw me.

When I got within earshot she started rummaging in her purse. "Let's get out of here," she said, throwing down three dollars. "This place sucks."

She could have walked home from there.

"Now is when you tell me what the hell is going on," I said.

"Nothing's going on," she said.

I drove us home.

"Thanks for the ride," she tossed out as she opened the door. She hopped out.

"Hey," I said, "are you going to be safe here? Doesn't John have a key?"

"What the hell does that mean?" she leaned her head in.

"Didn't he tear our place up last night? You hung up on me today, asked me to come get you at Denny's? These are not normal things, Jan."

"I told you, he was just mad, I'll clean it up."

"I'm worried about you," I said.

"Worry about yourself," she said. "I'm not one of your patients," and she started to shut the door.

"That doesn't mean you don't have problems I can help with!" I yelled after her.

She leaned back in, her face ugly with rage. Her voice came out like nails. "John's mother died. His baby brother's in jail, all the money they were supposed to make this month is getting smoked up by some asshole cop, and he's stressed out, okay? He's trying to help me move so we can live a kind of normal life. I don't need your arrogant, self-important, half-assed therapy speech you learned in a video training at your porn-star clinic."

Surprisingly, she waited a second for me to reply. "Maybe John shouldn't sell weed for a living," I said.

"Fuck you," she said. "You are such a hypocrite."

"What?"

"You pretend you're open-minded, like you give a shit," her voice got hotter, "but you're just a fucking conservative bitch!" She slammed the door. She ran up the stairs.

I sat for a few seconds in the car, my back sticking to the seat, the vents blowing chemical-smelling, dusty air at my face. My neck was rigid.

She'd never been angry with me before—she sometimes pitied me, or was disappointed by me, or thought I was boring. But she never yelled, not like that. I felt like I'd caught a baseball with my chest. Either she'd been dishonest with me for years, and had been harboring resentments silently, or John was terrorizing her. Maybe both. Even worse, she might be right about me.

My phone rang.

"Hi, beautiful," Bow said.

"What's up."

"Naomi says to be at Paradise on Monday at two o'clock, can you do it?"

I had one assembly that would be over by noon. I'd have to leave work early. I glanced at our landlord's window.

I told Bow I could do it. "Do I need to bring anything?" My voice was shaking.

He didn't seem to notice. "No, just make sure your toes are nice and they'll take care of the rest. Don't wear tight sandals or socks or anything that will leave marks on your feet. They'll pay seven hundred. Naomi says she doesn't know how long you'll be there but it will be at least three hours, probably four or five. Okay?"

That was more money than most strippers I knew made on a Friday night.

"Where am I going?"

"Paradise Clothes and Shoes, on Wilcox just off Hollywood. Naomi will be around when you get there."

I thanked him. He asked if it was too soon to make plans to see each other again.

"Try me tomorrow," I said. He seemed cheerful about that. We got off the phone.

The to-do list pulled at me like a magnet. I drove back to the SLLC and spent hours getting everything done in a numbed daze. Janet could have called and apologized whenever she wanted to, but my phone stayed quiet all afternoon.

TEN

I came home at six-thirty to an abandoned natural disaster site in the apartment. Of course Janet went back to John's without cleaning up. I threw on her *Best of Queen* CD and started sorting through the detritus.

Although on the weekends I usually chatted with my mother, I decided against calling her. It would take too much energy to hide how badly everything was going.

I knew my parents were boring people. My father worked for H&R Block and my mother was an administrative assistant at a lawyer's office, but the jobs weren't the problem—plenty of interesting people had to earn money in annoying ways, and even those jobs could have been sources of great conversation. My parents never once acknowledged that their work was tedious, nor did they speak of their work as interesting or important. They didn't demonstrate a grand, romantic love together. They had no strikingly dangerous or even marginally artistic hobbies. At least Grant Rose's mom had done some needlepoint. My parents watched TV, and rarely expressed opinions on it.

When I graduated from Rutgers, my mother sat my college diploma on her kitchen windowsill. No frame, no special box. She displayed it carelessly in a place where it would slowly fade in the sun, as if the ambitions and accomplishments of youth simply didn't matter, in the long run. As a team, my parents were excellent at reminding me of my limitations. The day before I left for LA, they faced me at the kitchen table and offered me a chance to take the easy way out if I was too scared to go.

"If you want a big city, you can go to New York," my mother said, "and then you could still visit."

I assured them I would buy a plane ticket to see them now and then.

"You can work for a doctor anywhere," said my father. "You'll probably end up wasting your time at a plastic surgeon's office."

"Experience with different populations makes me more attractive to med schools," I said.

"You'll stick out like a sore thumb," said my mother, nodding at my black outfit.

"I can handle it."

"What will you do when something bad happens? Who will you call? We don't have any friends out there," my father said.

"Is this really necessary?" I said.

They didn't answer me for a few seconds.

"We worry about our girl," my mom said to her hands. It might have been the most truthful moment she'd ever had with me. I realized later she'd already packed the Tupperware full of cookies in my bag. Sometimes I felt a poignant longing for her, an endearment that broke through my disdain for her pedantic choices.

Of course underneath my defiance, I also feared my parents were right to be concerned. California had become a utopia in my head—diverse, beautiful, tolerant. But what if it wasn't? What if I got there and everyone was as conforming and oppressive as they were in West Courtney? Or, what if I got there and couldn't take care of myself? I'd already begun my habit of over spending.

As I reattached my white wall covering, I saw a new pile of mail under some clothes by the couch. Something in my stomach snapped, my heart raced, and I wanted to go to sleep, throw up, run. Another collections letter. There simply wasn't a way for me to save this apartment, or find a new one, until I had a grip on the level of debt I was actually in. I carried the letter into my bedroom, where the unopened stack of envelopes from the hospital, credit cards, banks, and other collection agencies seemed like a gun pointed at my face. I had been hiding from the stack, and hiding the stack from myself, by shoving it into the corner.

I pulled the whole mess out, sat on my floor, and started sorting. My hands shook and I kept swallowing, but I knew that I'd get through the entire stack that night, because now I had to.

My problem with money was the opposite of my other problems—where

I was fastidious and detail oriented with colors and lists, I was hopelessly reckless and distracted when dealing with money. My bank balance always surprised me. I never understood where my money was going, or how my work hours translated into a paycheck. Once I moved away from home, I never let my father do my taxes because I was too embarrassed about how badly I kept track of my spending. He had file folders dedicated to all his categories of receipts.

Janet's theory was that my lack of awareness with money was a compensatory pathology to balance me out. My theory was that I associated money with lying and death and a selfish part of myself I didn't like.

I'd inherited a chunk of money when my grandpa died, and my parents hadn't told me. I hadn't been too fond of Grandpa since I'd started wearing all black and he'd decided my nickname should be "Dracula." Not "Bride Of Dracula." It had struck me as a double insult. He was a fixture in my childhood. He sat in the same chair, wore the same dark slacks and button-down shirts, and smelled of the same vanilla Dunhill tobacco in every memory. When he died during my sophomore year of college and my cousins, all strangers from South Jersey, seemed to grieve him terribly, I was ashamed. I couldn't conjure up a respectable level of sorrow.

I concentrated on comforting my mother, who never cried where I could see her. Her pain came out as a listless, distracted grumpiness. I missed the last few classes before spring break and stayed home with her while my dad ran all the errands, arranged the memorial, dealt with the relatives. My mother and I spent a stretch of days in the living room, shades pulled against the sun, eating Ritz crackers, not talking about her dead father. My mother's way of grieving was to watch television and criticize the sitcoms.

"This is ridiculous," she said of *Friends*, the hour before the memorial service. "Like those people would really want to spend all day and night together. They're sick of each other, believe me." I listened to her without commenting. She talked about *Friends* all the way to the Methodist church my family had stopped attending in the early 1980s, where my grandpa's memorial service was officiated by a pastor none of us had met before.

My cousins wept, my mother stared at her lap, I tried to remember nice things about Grandpa and could only come up with a card trick he used to do, when I was very little, that involved a story about the Jacks falling in love with the Queen of Hearts. I felt like a cheat, telling the story to a room full of people who were feeling actual pain. That night I called Grant Rose, let her take me out to a bar that didn't check ID, and drank Guinness until I threw up in a bright red bathroom stall. I ended up alone in my childhood bedroom, grateful for the colorless walls, reading my old high school biology textbook. My parents stayed distressingly quiet for my entire visit. I failed to help either of them.

Grandpa left me eight thousand dollars, but my parents kept it secret until I was ready to graduate from Rutgers. In an uncharacteristic fit of disclosure my parents told me he left far less, and in some cases nothing, to the rest of his grandchildren, for which no real explanation ever surfaced.

"He always wanted a doctor in the family," my mother offered, when they finally told me. She was worried that if I got the money halfway through my degree I'd leave Rutgers and move away, but she knew I wouldn't drop out of college with only a few months left. It would offend my need to finish things—the most "normal" of my compulsions, which had grown powerfully as I'd aged. The money impressed me too much to incite any anger at their manipulation, at the time.

I graduated from Rutgers with a biology degree and a philosophy minor, spent half the money on a used Honda Civic in decent condition, and developed a plan to leave the East Coast. I moved back into my room at my parents' for the summer, avoided conversations about medical school, and told them I needed a few months to save a little more. I worked in a bookstore, where I watched classic movies on a tiny TV/VCR in the stockroom, and read mysteries or philosophy while I was supposed to be shelving new books.

I never thought I'd stay too long in California. I truly believed I was on my way to med school in a few years, and that living in LA would be a temporary moment, a postcard, in my life.

At the end of that summer, I should have saved more than six thousand dollars, but I only had three. I'd built a secret Betty Page shrine in my closet that included a pair of five-inch heels I bought at a garage sale and never wore. I could not understand how my little purchases had so depleted my income. The only thing I was aware of wasting money on was food, since I rarely ate at home with my parents. I had enough money to buy gas for the drive west and put down a deposit on an apartment, but that was it.

My parents kept money a secret; my grandpa gave it to me even though I was a bad granddaughter; I spent it irresponsibly. Money made everyone guilty.

Now, I had four credit cards completely maxed out, and one more nearly there. I grew dizzy looking at the bills. So many pedicures. Sometimes I used a credit card instead of a debit at the ATM. I often bought supplies for the clinic and forgot to submit reimbursement forms. The new envelope was from the hospital. A sour mix of shame and anger made my stomach growl.

I went through everything—the medical bills from my hospitalization after the attack, student loans from college—and added it up. Even without the $1,600 that I needed by Thursday to pay one month of our rent, not to mention the back rent we owed, it was going to cost me nearly $4,000 a month simply to maintain my current level of debt. That $4,000 wouldn't even cut into the principal balance on my loans, or the balance on my credit cards. It would pay finance charges, late fees, and interest.

I made $2,300 a month, before taxes.

Maybe Bow had been right—I could always quit everything and go back to New Jersey.

If I did that, I would have to face my parents, and Grant Rose. My parents would be disappointed but unsurprised. It was Grant I dreaded telling my story to. I was the one who'd really gotten out, and she was the one who'd convinced me to do it, before the money, before Rutgers, before I was ready. We were in her car, on our way home from a movie during our senior year of high school when she asked me when I was going to move to California.

"You have to do it," she said. "You'll always wonder what might have happened if you don't." She'd been so powerful then.

I left the pile of bills in my room and cried, on the couch in front of the TV, with a pint of ice cream. The tears came from fear and loneliness, and also from shame, for not having a more interesting method of coping with my problems. If I was a drama queen worth her salt I'd at least find some sleeping pills to take. I had only a sort of bleak self-loathing and self-pity, nothing motivating enough to be that destructive. It occurred to me that people who committed suicide in violent ways were far more self-important than people who trudged through their lives depressed or took too many pills one night. Feeling you didn't deserve a violent end, shouldn't attempt the grandiosity, seemed even more self-deprecating than writing a histrionic letter to posterity and bleeding out in a hotel. There was nothing remotely creative about shoving Janet's Ben and Jerry's into my pouting face while watching how other people worked up all kinds of aberrations on the news. I was truly ashamed of being so boring.

Before I went to bed, I left Janet a note on the front door telling her she'd have to call me to get inside and I flipped the deadbolt. I also set the chain lock for the first time. I locked my bedroom door, too. But I knew I couldn't lock out the future.

ELEVEN

I spent Sunday in a melancholy haze, thinking about what Janet had said, waiting for her to call, cleaning, repacking her boxes, watching TV, and about every two hours, laying in bed. Bow called, but I didn't answer. I occasionally looked out our front window for John's truck, for Nathan, for Gary and his prospective tenants, for some other threat. Normally I would have been out running errands, eating brunch, meeting up with Todd and Derek for drinks, something. Instead I fell flat under the weight of my debt and fear. I went to bed without changing clothes from the night before.

Monday morning I woke up tasting sour fuzz in my teeth. I needed to teach a small assembly at a downtown school. After getting ready without breakfast since the milk was gone, I went to pick up the kit, which I'd left at the SLLC, and ran into three of our regular protestors outside.

The organizer's name was Doris, and she'd made a new sign that read GOD LOVES YOUR CHILD, with hand-drawn pictures of a fetus that had wide-open cartoon eyes. With eyelashes. Usually, we said hello, I reminded her not to harass our patients, she agreed, and then I took my silent rage inside.

"Hey Doris," I said to her, and she nodded back at me. "You know, we don't actually do abortions here." She looked at me blankly. Her hair was sprayed into a stiff wave on either side of her face. "We refer to another clinic that has a surgical wing."

"What?" she said, blinking. Her two friends, with signs that read YOU HAVE OPTIONS and EVERY CHILD WANTS TO LIVE started moving in.

"I'm saying, the volume of babies you'll save, by standing in front of the

SLLC, is small. You want to see a lot of desperate girls getting abortions, why not go to one of the clinics that does them all day long? More souls to save there. We're like a regular doctor's office."

"You teach contraception classes," she said, rallying a bit in the midst of her bafflement.

I laughed a little. "True," I said. "I'm about to teach one right now." I stifled a desire to raise my hand in an absurd high-five.

"I wish I could help soften your heart," she said.

I restrained an impulse to push her. "I wish I could help bring you into this century," I said, disappointed at the lack of zing in my comeback. "Don't you get it that people like you are the *reason* fifteen-year-olds get pregnant? Almost every teenage abortion that isn't a rape case involves some terror of parents, many of whom are religious."

She actually gaped.

"Let me ask you this," I said. "Who do you care about?"

"All God's creatures," she said. "But especially the innocent."

"Fine," I said. "If that's true, then I suggest you figure out a way to take all the money you spend on these Photoshopped atrocities," I smacked her sign, "and put it into education."

"We educate too," she said, and pulled pamphlets from her apron.

"Not on our property," I said, and pointed toward the edge of the sidewalk. She backed up. I fumed in to grab my kit.

Todd, on the phone, nodded and waved, and I left for downtown LA with a box of supplies I hoped would be sufficient.

I led a distracted assembly. It had begun to sink in that later that afternoon I would be allowing someone I didn't know to take pictures of my feet. The auditorium was only one-third full, and someone inside had managed to smoke a cigarette for a few seconds, just long enough to make the air stink. I couldn't keep the students' attention, even with the condom demos. I allowed the bitter realization that they were all just going to keep fucking without them anyway. I ended the assembly early, forgetting to hand out cards until most of them had paraded out with their cell phones flashing, fists balled up in pockets, eyes down or searching for someone—a friend, an enemy, a victim.

I tried to change my mood by listening to ABBA in the car, but it only annoyed me. I decided to get a quick pedicure before the shoot.

At Fancy Nail, Anh pretended to clip excess skin from around my toenails (how could there be any?). I stared at the wall of polish, determined to get a different, new, sexy color. Red? Pink? Suddenly the perfect idea came: A French manicure. Like Linda's.

"Anh," I said. She stopped air-clipping.

"What?"

"I want a French manicure on my toes," I said. I was frantically trying to remember all the toenails I'd seen in the past day to make sure it was still in style.

"Sure, five dollars extra," she said. In adolescent rebellion against the debt, I agreed. She kept my normal skin-tone polish out and picked a bright white off the wall.

It also took an extra fifteen minutes, which she didn't tell me. I endured a special kind of paralyzed panic. Rushing nails ruins them. Bumping them on something before they are dry can spoil the entire investment. So I sat in a vinyl chair with my toes under a UV light and a fan, eyes glued to the clock, immobile, for ten minutes. The ten minutes that were going to make me late. I kept a pair of flip-flops with my emergency outfit in the trunk, which I would wear to Paradise even though they weren't cool.

A new fear: Naomi's people would make me walk in those stripper shoes. Regular heels I could balance in, but six or seven inch platforms? When my drying light went off I ran to the car barefoot. I drove to Paradise in what felt like a six-coffee buzz, trying to take deep breaths. I fed a meter and found the store. I had no idea what to do next.

At first glance, Paradise Clothes and Shoes seemed like a department store. A shoe section, a clothing section, and an accessories section blended together on one huge floor. Instead of twin sets and clunky clogs, all the merchandise was sexy, or intended to be so. I wanted to walk around and check out the theme outfits (nurse, cop, taxi driver), but it was already after two o'clock, so I scanned for Naomi, who was not there, and then went up to the counter and told a thin woman with an enormous pile of braids tied together on top of her head and hoop earrings grazing her shoulders that I was there for a photo shoot? And did she know anything about it?

"They're all in the back," she told me.

"Could you show me?" I said.

"Sorry, are you new?"

I introduced myself.

Her name was Sandra. She slipped out from behind the counter and suddenly towered over me. She could have been a runway model. She was more beautiful than Tyra Banks. I was a sweaty, dorky midget in flip-flops who didn't know where "the back" was.

Sandra walked me through the store and opened a door that was flush with the wall, the kind you push on to release the lock. It was like the secret passageways in *Clue*, one of the movies I'd watched over and over as a kid. The Paradise wall-door opened onto a brightly lit, slightly chaotic storage/office/studio space. Boxes of inventory covered the left and back walls, three desks were buried in papers, and nice Apple flat screens blinked through pictures of various women in bikinis. The studio side was open, spare, with some light rigging and wooden stools.

Sandra waved her hand at the room and said, "We're the largest distributor, we rent to every studio, all the magazines use us."

I had no idea what that meant. "Sounds like a lot to keep track of," I said.

Once upon a time the room had been a warehouse. The owners rented a bigger one downtown and chopped this up into offices and a photo studio. The studio felt more inviting than I expected—concrete floor and spare, white walls, with long rolls of colored paper? Vinyl? I couldn't tell which, piled in the corner.

"This is where you'll be," Sandra said, pointing toward the studio side.

"Where is everyone?"

"They shot accessories this morning, so they might be out getting lunch. You can hang out here."

I sat on a wooden stool and waited for forty-five minutes.

During those minutes, I wondered if Bow had played a vicious trick. I imagined him at Bitsy's, or working on a user manual for a new cell phone, looking up at the clock and laughing, waiting for my desperate phone call.

It didn't seem likely. I defiantly didn't call, anyway.

I wondered where Janet was, and if she'd come home last night, seen my note on the dead-bolted door, and left again. Maybe John had convinced her not to call and apologize for yelling at me. Maybe she really did believe I was that much of an asshole. Maybe I was.

I was still sitting on a stool, ruminating on the to-do list left on my desk, when two sexy young guys, one really large man, and Naomi walked in through another secret door behind me. They came in laughing, carrying bags of equipment, all mercifully wearing black and brown work clothes, except for Naomi, who held a little pink purse that matched her top. Her hair was twisted into about twenty tiny buns all over her head.

"Tam!" she said when she saw me, "you are awesome for being here on time!"

"I thought I was supposed to be here at two," I said, trying not to sound petulant.

"Oh shit," Naomi said as the men all chuckled.

"We went a little late on the last shoot," one of the sexy guys offered. He was black with bleached-out corn rows. "And Slim here," he punched the other cute one, "needed In-N-Out."

"Andy," the other cute one said, holding out his hand. He was thin, freckled, had brown spiked-up hair and enormously long eyelashes. "We should have brought you some food! How rude of us."

"I'm sorry I didn't call," Naomi said. "if I'd known you were going to be so punctual, I would have."

"It's all right," I said. Hearing about In-N-Out burgers reminded me that having no breakfast before the assembly was not my best choice.

The fat man held out a hand, big as my face, and told me his name was Gordy. Short for Gordito, he said.

"You know what it means?" Andy said to me.

"Fat," Gordy said, before I could answer. Suddenly I felt guilty for my appraisal. "It means 'little fatty.' My fuckin' mom called me that."

The one with corn rows told me his name was Russ. I told them they sounded like a comedy troupe.

"We are!" said Russ, and punched Andy in the stomach. "A black, a Mexican, and a towelhead. Now we just need a bar to walk into."

"Fuck you," Andy said to Russ, "We're the fatty, the stud, and the fag."

So Andy was from somewhere in the Middle East, which told me next to nothing. Living in LA taught me I held no authority with which to guess someone's background. I had not yet gotten to the point where I felt "in" enough to make race jokes like these guys were, although I wished I was. It seemed to be some kind of badge of brotherhood, to make racist or xenophobic jokes about your friends. My background was so steeped in silent white guilt that I felt stupid and awkward attempting to make light of racial stereotypes. However, after a few years at the SLLC, I was somehow in the club that could make jokes about sexual orientation.

"Who's the fag?" Russ said.

Andy told him to shut up and started moving camera equipment around. "Who's the fag? Don't listen to him." Like it was obvious.

"I apologize for my colleagues," Gordy said. He ushered Naomi and I to get into wardrobe. "Sweety will be here in a minute to tell us which shoes she wants us to shoot."

Naomi and I walked through the secret passageway. She squeezed my arm and whispered that it was good to see me, and then she moved through the racks, pulling down short hangers with mostly red fabric on them.

"You seem like the retro type," she said.

"Probably," I said, realizing that Naomi was expecting me to wear a bikini, or a short skirt, or some other stripper outfit. I asked just to make sure.

"It doesn't matter much what you wear," she said, "since they're only going to do your feet today, but if they decide they like your look and want to use you for other stuff, it can't hurt, right?"

I suggested an all-black outfit for me.

She said that was fine, and led me over to the monochromatic section of the store. I pushed through the racks. There were at least six different styles of bottoms to cover my small but not-so-toned butt, and as many types of tops. I wanted to close my eyes. Naomi offered to help.

"How about this?" she held up a low-cut leotard, a halter connected to shorts. A 1950s bathing suit for Marlene Dietrich.

In the dressing room I spun around, stared at myself, and decided I'd never been so foxy. I needed more eyeliner, red lipstick, heels, and a tan, but the suit fit me perfectly. It left just enough of my butt showing. I thought about the dancers I'd seen at strip clubs, and how their bikini bottoms were cut like that. The halter made my boobs round. I wanted to stay in that room.

"Lemme see!" Naomi said from the outside.

I cracked the curtain a bit. She wore the same suit, in red. I did immediate, reparative self-talk: you are smaller, and you have a very cute body, and she has a different look. Not a better one, necessarily, but definitely different.

I didn't believe it, but I'd read an article once in the counseling journal we got at the clinic about how effective affirmations could be.

She's a dancer, I continued silently. Obviously she's going to be beautiful without her clothes on.

I opened the curtain.

"Hot!" she yelled.

Sandra glanced over at us and smiled.

Naomi linked arms with me. "Let's wear these, okay?"

"I like it," I said.

"You should, it's perfect on you."

"Not as perfect as it is on you," I said, immediately wanting to smack myself.

"Oh, shut up," she said. She tossed a black silk robe into my hands and then pulled a red one for herself out of her dressing room.

The studio had changed. Russ set up a table with a make-up kit and tied on a black apron. Andy clipped long pieces of light blue fabric to ropes hanging from the ceiling. Gordy plugged in lights. A short Asian woman with tight white pants, a white T-shirt tied in a knot at her waist, and a side ponytail with green streaks in it was rooting through some boxes of shoes.

"Sweety!" Naomi called.

"Hi, hi, hi," Sweety said without looking up.

"Meet your foot model," Naomi said, pulling me over. I held my robe closed and tried to walk lightly.

Sweety turned around, bent to inspect my feet, said they were nice, and then put her hand on my chin and turned my face side to side. "A cutie," she said to Naomi.

A blatant, objectifying appraisal. Normal for models, maybe, but not for me.

"This is Sweety, owner and designer of Sweety Shoes," Naomi said.

"Nice to meet you," I said.

"So polite!" she said. "Like she's not a real model!"

I wondered what Bow had said to get me the job.

Sweety said she liked me, I thanked her, and then she handed me a pair of enormous white strapped-up heels to try on first.

Black and white was not my favorite combination. Zebras, bad 1980s outfits. The shoes had a two-inch, shiny white plastic platform; the heel itself looked seven inches long. Thick white patent leather straps criss-crossed over the foot twice before maybe going around the ankle. I couldn't see how to put them on. I wouldn't know how to walk in them.

"Hot!" Naomi said again, and nudged me to take the shoes. Sweety went back to the boxes. I asked to sit down.

Naomi led me to a couch that was pushed up behind the desks on the other side of the room. "You haven't done this before, right?" she asked.

"Nope." I felt thirteen, trying to appear as if I already knew how to smoke.

"Put your weight on your toes when you walk. The poses will mostly be seated anyway, so no problem!" She cheerfully strapped my feet into the monstrous white heels. My legs were transformed. I was shocked to discover that when I stood up I felt remarkably sturdy. The tricky part was not dragging my toes.

"I'm ready for one of you!" Russ hollered from his make-up station.

Naomi told me to go ahead, since she only needed a touch-up, and wasn't in the shoe shots.

I walked gingerly to Russ and sat in the chair next to his table. It appeared that he'd bought out the MAC makeup store and dumped it into a huge silver trunk with wheels.

"Just the feet?" he said.

"I think so," I said.

He picked up my right and inspected it. He complimented my pedicure, and told me I had perfect bones.

"No one has ever said that to me before," I told him.

"Whoever booked you on this job knew it," he said.

He took the shoes off, and rubbed honey-scented lotion onto my right foot. I exerted serious self-control, trying not to start breathing too heavily. It was so different from having Anh touch my feet—she was skilled but Russ was also so, so attractive. His long, elegant fingers were stronger than they seemed. He wiped the lotion off my nails with a cotton pad. Then, he pulled out a fat make-up brush and a compact of bronzing powder. He gave my right foot a lovely tan and then brought the color up my calf to my knee. He repeated the steps with my left foot and calf. He sprayed them both with a fixative that smelled like Aqua Net and blotted them.

"Wait a minute for this to set," he said. I could have waited hours. He puttered around his make-up, taking caps on and off, dusting the stray eye shadow off containers, fluffing brushes.

"So how long have you been doing this?" I asked.

"Been a stylist six years," he said. "I used to do hair at a place not too far form here."

"My soon-to-be-ex roommate is a stylist at StageRage," I offered, hoping it was a piece of common ground and not some kind of social blunder. I didn't want to bring up any bad blood, if stylists at competing salons had bad blood.

"Fun place," he nodded. He didn't know Janet. He lightly insulted the StageRage manicurists.

I agreed. As we talked about why paraffin was such a scam, I wondered briefly how Janet had gotten to work, or if she'd gone at all.

"Ready for your shoes?" Russ said.

"No," I said, and let him think I was kidding.

"Let's do this!" Gordy yelled from fifteen feet away. Russ told him to hold onto his dick, and then he strapped my shoes for me. That paired with the lotion added up to the most erotic moment I'd ever had with a stranger. The most erotic moment I'd experienced without letting the other person know they were participating. My entire lower body was throbbing and I knew I was blushing. I hoped the modeling part was as easy.

I sat on a box covered in a satin sheet. Gordy took the pictures. He'd hooked his camera to a computer so after a few minutes he imported all the pictures, sorted through them, and knew exactly what he wanted to do next.

"Toes pointed more," he'd say, or, "Try your left toes touching your right ankle."

For an hour, no one looked above my knees. I kept my robe on. Sweety appeared every few minutes with different shoes. Russ would put them on me and brush on a little more bronzer. Gordy would say some directions, and then dozens of photos of my feet appeared on the computer, where Andy would speedily change the light, orientation, and label the good ones. Because the shoes kept changing, my color sensitivity lessened. As each pair came off, I felt less need to fix them.

One pair was exactly like Bettie Page's classic black round-toe fetish heels, with red cherries on the heel. Gordy told me to stand up, and Russ drew a black seam up the back of my calves with eyeliner.

Naomi watched, smiling, from the couch. At first I was terrified of her expert eyes. She had to be judging my every move. But her face was so relaxed, and occasionally she'd say something like, "Yes, girl," or "That's it," so eventually I accepted, was even excited by the idea, that she enjoyed watching. By the seventh pair of shoes, I was doing everything mostly for her. The thrill was completely new.

"Can we get some with Naomi too?" Sweety said.

"Two pairs of shoes?" Gordy asked.

"I want two pairs, with their legs kind of twisting around each other," Sweety said, making a snakelike motion with both hands. My first worry:

white thighs. The bronzer stopped halfway up my legs. Second worry: how to behave with Naomi.

"Awesome!" she chirped from the couch, and tromped over to where I sat. She took off her robe and said to Sweety, "Where do you want me?"

I dropped my robe too, and tensed up immediately. No one in the room appeared to notice that I was now wearing a very small black bathing suit.

Sweety placed us, suggested things, pushed on our knees and hips. Naomi had no problem responding to these proddings, maybe because of being a dancer, maybe because she liked her body being touched. I felt stiff and somewhere in my mind was a voice saying Janet's right, you wanted to have these big crazy adventures, and you're so *bored* by normal heterosexual sex, and now you're getting to publicly rub up against the most beautiful woman, ever, and you can't even enjoy it, because you are, deep down, a prude. Also, I couldn't help thinking about Bow, and how his body had already been every place mine now was.

I wasn't jealous, exactly, of either of them, but of both of them together. I wanted to be that sexy. And I wanted to see them—the way they looked at each other, the way he held her, what her mouth would do.

Sweety finally found a position that she liked. Naomi was half on my lap, our arms around each other, one of her legs pressed between mine. I breathed in her vanilla and tried not to sweat. Gordy shot us. We crowded around a monitor while the photos imported. Naomi's dark skin and black shoes next to my lighter skin and white shoes transcended any matching problem I might have had. The photos were stunning.

Russ started singing "Ebony and Ivory."

Andy sang back-up for a few bars.

Gordy told them both to fuck off, he was going to put that picture on his wall.

"Yes, yes, yes," Sweety said.

Naomi pinched my butt. "We're fantastic," she whispered in my ear. My skin electrified and I wanted her to kiss me, in the soft place under my earlobe. It was disorienting. What was I doing, standing in a Hollywood stripper store back-office studio with people I didn't know, in seven inch heels and a black shorts suit, having fantasies about rolling around in a bubble bath with Naomi?

We all exchanged cards.

"Hey, I know this place," Andy said when he read my card. "I know a girl who does calendars, she comes to the SLLC. She told me about it when I got Hep C."

"Hep C's no joke," I said.

"From a dirty Tijuana tattoo," he said, turning around. "It was a bad fucking deal." He pulled down his shirt collar. The word "Diablo" was written across his neck in old English lettering.

"Man, that's not even right," said Gordy. "It should say 'el,' first. 'El diablo.' You got that shit in TJ?"

"That's what I told you," Andy said, "it was a bad deal, bro."

"But a Mexican dude didn't write 'el'? I don't believe it," said Gordy. "Illiterate motherfucker."

Andy shrugged. "Maybe he thought I'd never know?"

"You want a diablo, check this baby," Russ said, and pulled up his pant leg. Bugs Bunny in a devil suit posed on the back of his calf.

Naomi giggled. "You guys are so stupid," she said.

"Take a picture of that one," Sweety said, pointing at Russ's leg. "I can tell my son if he ever does that," then she made a cutting sound and swiped at her throat.

"You got any?" Gordy said to me.

"Nope," I said.

"Me neither," said Naomi. "Piercings, though, that's different."

Sweety rolled her eyes. "Bull," she said. "All ugly."

"Such a purist," Russ said, shaking his head. He patted Sweety on the shoulder. "You're going to run out of models in this town."

TWELVE

Janet still had not called. Worry began to erode my pride, but Naomi offered an escape, and I took it. She wanted to go to some dive bar off Melrose.

"It's happy hour!" she said. "We worked hard. We deserve it."

I carried seven hundred dollars in cash in my purse and had a plan to model again in two days, in outfits this time, with Naomi, because Gordy thought we worked so well together. Tiny seizures of adrenaline kept shooting up my middle. Anticipation and terror.

Had we worked that hard? Some days at the clinic I worked thirteen or fourteen hours, because of morning assemblies and afternoon appointments. I listened to personal details all day long. I told people test results, and then counseled them when they started to panic, or smiled at them when they sighed with relief. Some nights I came home and couldn't do anything but sit on the couch. Nevertheless, I never felt as naked as I had with Naomi. I was tired.

I followed Naomi to a place with no sign out front on a mostly residential block. She said she knew the bartender, although I didn't see anyone behind the bar when we went in. Dark wood paneled the walls and a few deep, high-back booths across from the bar were covered in black vinyl. The jukebox rattled a bit with "Cherry Pie." Cloudy with the acrid smell of stale beer and bleach, I scooted into the back booth and decided to get trashed. I'd get my car later. If I sank into the corner with my back to the entrance, all I could see was the seat across from me and the door to the bathroom. I was still painfully hungry, so it wouldn't take more than a drink or two to cultivate a nice buzz. When Naomi appeared with our first round, I had devoured a small bowl of pretzels.

She bought two matching apple martinis. I could have sucked them down by the barrel.

"So," she said, suddenly conspiratorial, "how was the date with Bow?"

I couldn't tell if she was asking as my friend or his.

"Odd," I said.

She was amused. "Tell me."

I told her the fun version.

"Did you sleep together?"

"Does it matter?"

"I'm nosey and he'll probably tell me anyway."

"Then no."

"Did he tell you he doesn't like casual sex?"

I answered in the affirmative, afraid she would out Bow as a former sex addict, or worse, as completely disinterested in me.

But she nodded, and said it was par for the course with him. "I'm assuming he told you something about me too," she said. "I want you to know that if you guys are getting together I think it's great."

"He did talk about you," I said, realizing she wasn't asking me to report it.

"You're so cute," she said, and tugged my ear.

"You're a goddess," I said before I could stop myself. She got us another round of drinks. We kept talking about the photo shoot, about her dancing, about my clinic work. We laughed at ourselves, downing fruity martinis in the late afternoon at a black hole of a bar. On the third round, she sat next to me, instead of across, and when the conversation lulled she leaned in, all sweet musk and heat, and kissed me. Her lips were unreal—smooth, strong, enveloping. Everything about her was softer than the men I'd kissed. Her skin was covered in the finest peach fuzz, her scent was light. My muscles tensed up and burned. We caressed each other's faces, necks and shoulders, and giggled with our foreheads together.

"He won't mind," she whispered, when I mentioned I might be breaking some dating decorum rules.

I didn't tell her she was my first girl. I just kept breathing her in.

On the fourth martini, Naomi returned from the bar with her phone propped under her ear.

"She's fabulous, get over here!" she said, set down the drinks, and hung up. "Bow's coming!"

"Oh god," I said.

"And Juno, my bartender friend, says hello. I forgot you must have met him at Wacko the other night?"

"Of course," I said. I leaned out of the booth to look, and he waved. And in that moment, I knew I would throw up.

I ran to the bathroom, shaking, holding my breath, while the back of my throat dilated. I heaved those drinks into the closest toilet, and when I stopped coughing, I sat on the floor and cried. The metal stall was cold against my shoulder. I started rocking back and forth, my head buried between my knees. I couldn't get enough air. I was imploding. When I opened my eyes, the bathroom glared so brightly, so horrifyingly pink, and the walls slowly pushed toward me—I knew they couldn't be, but I was seeing it happen—so I shut my eyes again and tried to count. I got to five before I was having uncontrolled visions of Nathan's face, his arm raised at me, the asphalt, the hospital. I threw up again, remembering the doctor debriefing me about my injuries, saying I'd be fine and at least I wasn't raped. I pulled out a wad of toilet paper and tried to blow my nose. The sticky bitterness coated my throat. I couldn't spit enough of it out. My entire body burned, and hundreds of needles pierced out from under my skin. If I moved out of the stall I would have a heart attack. My heart was working too hard to last. Bodies are so frail. I couldn't believe I relied on a little bag of organs to keep me alive, it seemed so arbitrary that I hadn't died yet, my heart had never beat this hard, there was no way it could keep going. They would find me in the fetal position on the floor of the bathroom, powdered bronzer on my legs, too much cash in my purse. Too young, they would say, shaking their heads. They'd think I'd OD'd. I would become a news story for Janet to see at six o'clock tomorrow, and before she realized it was me on the floor, she'd think, I'd like to tell Tam about this crazy girl who died at a dive bar somewhere off Melrose, and then she'd see that it was me who had died. With my arms around my shins, I kept rocking, whimpering no-no-no-no-no into my knees.

There is always some tiny part of your brain, people say, that knows you'll live through a panic attack, but 99 percent of your body believes you are in immediate risk of death. I'd seen enough clients with anxiety to know what was happening. That was the worst part—understanding, underneath it all, that I was experiencing a slight malfunction, an overload of some brain chemical, and that when it passed everything would be as it was before. No, my body told me, nothing would ever be the same. All I could think about was the incessant, hyperactive thumping in my chest.

Naomi came in the bathroom, knocked on my stall, called me honey, and asked if I was okay. I tried to think of a convincing response. I wanted her to crawl under the door and hold on to me. I wanted her to get the hell out and leave me to my pitiful death.

"I'm fine," I said.

"You don't sound fine," she said.

"I need a minute."

"You're sick?"

You have no idea, I wanted to say.

"I'll be right out," I said.

She left. I felt relieved, then totally betrayed. I'd escaped embarrassment by not asking for her help, but what kind of friend would leave me in the bathroom to die? Oh, that's right, I remembered, she wasn't my friend. I wasn't her problem. I wasn't anyone's problem. I briefly wondered if Bow was already in the bar, telling her what a basket case I'd been on our date. I flushed the toilet twice, for dignity's sake, and wiped the floor with a wad of tissue. I felt a heavy grief about not calling my parents more.

Then Naomi came back. She placed a glass of water and a clean bar towel under the door, without scraping the tile. "Can you tell me what's going on?" she said. "Did you drink too fast?"

If I said yes, I was a loser. If I said no, I had some bigger weakness.

"I don't know," I said, since it didn't matter.

"Do you want an Advil or something?"

I told her no.

She suggested a Xanax. The first ray of light.

"You have Xanax?" I said.

I heard her rummaging in her bag and then the beautiful plastic popping sound of a prescription bottle. She held the tiny pill in her palm under the door. She asked how many milligrams I was used to.

I told her I didn't know.

"Then take this one, and I'll give you some room to breathe, and when you feel like it, come on out and we'll leave the bar, okay?" She sounded so cheerful, in control.

I took the pill. I couldn't bring myself to put the towel on my face, after it had been behind the bar and then on the bathroom floor, but I was endeared to Naomi for producing it. I felt very, very guilty for thinking mean thoughts about her.

Less than five minutes later calmness held me like a winter coat. The part of me that knew I wasn't going to die came into larger, clearer focus. That part suggested that I was having posttraumatic stress symptoms, probably triggered by meeting Juno and having so much adrenaline in my system all day, and I should see a doctor about it.

At the same time, the part of me that had thrown up said fuck that, I'm finding Nathan and kicking the shit out of him. I decided to have this argument with myself later. All parts of the self agreed I had to get out of the Pepto-Bismol-pink bathroom.

I emerged with a rinsed mouth, hands still a bit gritty from the soap-dust that came out of the antique dispenser, face wiped down with wet paper towels, ready to go home. I was now in the middle of what was objectively an embarrassing situation, without having any feelings of embarrassment. My heart was normal, my breathing fine, and it seemed utterly ridiculous that I had feared I might die only minutes earlier.

Bow and Naomi sat together, both wearing serious faces. I expected to become very nervous. I did not. I slid into the booth and went into my purse for some gum.

"Feeling okay?" Naomi said.

"I don't feel anything," I said, "which is way better than what I was feeling before."

"Panic's a bitch," Naomi said. "I get attacks like every week, and I completely freak out. Bow's seen it."

Bow reached out and squeezed my arm. "Hey there," he said. I said hello and tried to smile brightly.

"That's a lot of panic attacks," I said to Naomi.

"My girlfriend likes Klonopin," Naomi said, "but Xanax is like my most favorite drug, ever." She had a girlfriend.

While Naomi and Bow paid our tab and made plans, I thought about how many women I knew through the clinic who had serious anxiety. I wondered if women who got naked in public for a living, and especially women who had sex for money, were more likely to experience clinical anxiety than women who didn't. I suspected so. I also suspected that there was no reliable data on it, except what was in our and other clinics' patient files. The problem was that if I ever found that trend, people would automatically think the anxiety stemmed from the sex work itself—but I knew that it was more complicated. It was the stress of being socially judged, of knowing you couldn't fit anywhere in mainstream national culture, that caused at least part of the anxiety. It was the legacy of Christian morality, so embedded in our culture, that made women unstable. If they felt pushed into the industry, they would suffer for it, of course, because lack of choice causes depression. But if they wanted to do it because they liked it, because they were exhibitionist or experimental, they would also suffer consequences as everyone, even other sex workers, made judgments about them. People like Naomi, who seemed to inhabit both the stress and the joy of being publicly sexual, were heroes.

Maybe my contact with strippers, porn stars, and working girls made me more vulnerable to the same kinds of problems they had. Was there a proximity risk for mental illness? We talked about "burn out" in our medical assistant training, and the importance of having a supportive community to talk to about the difficult issues we would face. Maybe that was the PC way to let us know it was far easier to wash off your patients' fluids than their feelings.

When Naomi and Bow led me out of the bar, I was still inside a nicely padded mental cell, seeing the world through a sense of grand perspective. Naomi hugged me, warm and still sweet-smelling, and handed me a small white packet she'd made out of a napkin.

"Two more, just in case," she said. "Take it easy, and give me a call later?" She kissed my cheek and handed me to Bow.

Bow drove me to my car, which had a parking ticket. Somehow, that was no problem. He suggested leaving his own car, driving me home in mine, and then staying with me for a while.

I noticed, out loud, that that was an intimate thing to do. I said also it was fine with me. How would he get back to his own car? I didn't care.

He asked if I needed to eat.

Yes, I told him, I probably do.

At my apartment, a manila envelope taped to the front door contained our three-day notice. *Sorry*, the handwriting at the bottom said, *Gary.* I wondered if three days included today. Move out Wednesday or Thursday? I'd have to check.

I called Janet from my couch, while Bow made toast. She didn't answer. I left her a message that said something about not being angry with her for yelling at me (I wasn't, I felt light and totally fine) and I hoped we could hang out and talk before we moved all the way out. We might want to talk about the money we owed.

More boxes of our things had been scooted around the apartment. It wasn't an issue; most of my stuff was incidental, unsentimental. She could have it.

Bow made perfect toast, buttered right out to the edges. I ate fast.

"I wish I felt like this all the time," I said.

Bow told me I wouldn't think like that later. "You'd miss feeling passionate, or filled with joy," he said. "Numbness only feels good when you've just felt terrible."

I told him I thought I might feel terrible most of the time, because this numbness was bliss.

"Maybe you should get a scrip of your own," he said.

"Maybe," I said, and we turned on the TV.

Victims of sexual assault often had panic attacks. Being a victim of an assault that wasn't sexual meant I should have suffered less severe emotional consequences. According to my own timetable, I was allowed to be a little squeamish at assemblies for a few weeks, which I had been. I also allowed myself to request not to do them alone, which I'd given up since we just couldn't afford it. I had considered taking self-defense classes, but they were too expensive. The general feeling of unease, vulnerability, and suspicion I carried after the attack would pass eventually. I was functional. Rape victims often weren't. Women who hadn't been raped, but had been sexually assaulted in some other way, often weren't. Battered women who survived, and didn't kill their husbands, had a hard time bouncing back. But women like me, who got the shit kicked out of them one time, because one person was pissed off about something? Where were we in the community of victims? Nowhere. I was part of no club, no codified group of survivors. The LA police did not offer a hotline for me. I was merely the owner of one very fucked-up anecdote.

I hated myself for behaving like a regular victim, for having no control over my body or my brain at the bar. I hated Nathan Reggman for ever giving me victim symptoms. I hated myself for hating myself, because I knew that it wouldn't help me get stronger. I hated needing Xanax or attention to calm down.

My face must have started clouding.

"So how was being an exhibitionist?" Bow asked. On TV, a car chase had started to drag on.

"What did Naomi tell you?"

"That you were really, really good."

"I was a pair of feet."

"And calves," he said, patting me.

"It's not that difficult."

"You'd be surprised how many models show up strung out, or not at all, or talk incessantly, or refuse to wear what they're given."

"The money is so good, why would they do that?"

"Because most fetish models are dancers or actors or escorts too, and they don't need the money."

I didn't want him to think he knew more about the sex industry than me. I needed some area of expertise, especially since I'd bared nearly every unattractive quality I possessed in the few short days I'd known Bow. But I didn't know that much about sex work, really. I'd treated patients, not worked on sets or in clubs.

"Does Naomi work in Vegas?"

"Sometimes. She hates it."

"Why? Lap dances?"

"No, that part's fine, usually. She doesn't like how the women treat each other. She says it's worse than high school."

"Then why do it?"

"She can make a thousand in a night."

"Right." We went quiet.

"Hey," I said, "Do you want to go outside and walk around for a while?"

"Walk?"

"Too rough for you, San Francisco boy?"

He asked if I was okay, turning from the TV to face me.

"I'm fine," I said. "I don't need a life coach." Then I hated him, for making me treat him badly, again. I didn't like being bitchy. I didn't like how he rolled over and took it. "Don't feel like you have to stay here and babysit," I said.

He took my dish into the kitchen. "I'm not babysitting," he said.

I asked him if he wanted a ride back to his car. He came out of the kitchen, drying his hands, and sighed.

"Don't worry about it, I'll call someone," he said, throwing the towel over his shoulder. "It's a good sign that you're all feisty again."

"What's that supposed to mean?"

"You were numb, now you're irritable. I think it's better."

"I don't."

He smiled. "You will, eventually."

"You're arrogant."

He nodded. "Occasionally, yes. I'm not a peacekeeper. Neither are you."

I offered to drive him back to his car again. He tossed the towel onto the kitchen counter and told me to take it easy for a while, he'd be fine. While I scowled, he kissed both my cheeks. He said he'd call me later and shut the door gently behind him.

THIRTEEN

A s I lay on the couch, with the high over and Bow gone, something I was supposed to do that day started nagging. I could tell by the quiet way it pulled me that I hadn't written it down anywhere. I'd taken the afternoon off, but there weren't any appointments on the books. I'd left Janet a friendly message. Maybe I felt strange because of all the cash in my purse.

Then I remembered: a restraining order against Nathan. I ran into Janet's room to turn on her computer.

It was already on. The bunnies-with-guns screen saver vanished, and a recent chat with John sat open on her desktop. Normally, I would not invade her privacy, but these were different circumstances. She might need me.

Hoping a clue to her current location would pop out, so I could justify prying, I read through a few lines of high-school clichés before things got interesting.

JohnBoy76: would of gone crazy w/o u

Janokins: why

JohnBoy76: ur my life.

Janokins: not true, you lie

JohnBoy76: sorry for everything. really you can't understand how i feel i'm so in love w/u it hurts. i want to marry u!

Janokins: you serious?

JohnBoy76: come see

I restrained the impulse to smash the screen with her keyboard. Janet had lied to me. John didn't show up one day, sober, and ask her to get back together. They'd never broken up. She'd hid their relationship. He wanted to marry her?

Why hadn't I figured it out? Janet was terrible at keeping secrets. The day she'd told me he was out of her life we'd been watching AMC and drinking cheap shiraz. I'd done a little congratulatory dance for her. We'd toasted her independence.

She was afraid of my judgment. I had not tried to understand. I wanted to talk to her so badly I called her voicemail again and told her to get back to me right away, not disguising the urgency in my voice.

Hurriedly, I went to the LAPD website and looked up information on restraining orders. The more I read, the clearer the picture became: This was not the answer to my problem. Papers had to be served to the offender directly, and you had to know a good deal of their personal information. Maybe it was the answer to Janet's problem. I left the website up and wandered back into the living room.

Flipping through channels got me nowhere—no old movies.

I still wanted to go for a walk. My body couldn't stay still. Jittery and so, so hungry, I picked up my bag and got one step outside before I saw Bow, sitting on the curb, leaning back on his hands. He turned as I came down the steps.

"No ride yet?" I asked.

He shrugged. "Traffic."

"Call it off," I said. "Stay with me."

He squinted at me for a few seconds, looked at his watch, then pulled out his phone and sent a text message. I didn't ask to whom.

We started out toward Sunset. "Maybe I'll score some free boxes at a restaurant," I said. "I'm moving out."

"To where?"

I shrugged.

Even in neighborhoods like Hollywood and Silver Lake, where the stores were small and stacked together like dominoes, people didn't stroll. No street felt like a real boulevard. LA city planners had to build places specifically for walking in, like the Grove or the Santa Monica Pier, because once you stood alone at a streetlight waiting for your turn, you realized everything in the city was too large, fast, and heavy to contend with unless your body was encased in metal like everyone else's.

The sidewalk changed color and texture about halfway through every block. I wondered if there had been accidents, broken pipes underground, a shortage of cement. I noticed all the faces. I tried to fit the people into old movies. They were the extras filling the late-night diners, the couples in the park, the families falling over each other at store windows. I couldn't make it work—the real faces were too filled with stories. Movie extras were blank—responding only to what happened in front of them. These faces knew things. Bow stayed quiet, and I didn't look at him.

I smelled trash, in the way that you can truly smell the rotted remains of someone's life when it's hot out. Black cords from neon signs snaked across windows, white bubbles of caulking stuck to the frames of repainted doors. Colored stucco stopped right before the crumbling, dirty edges where buildings met the ground. The sun sat low in the sky and streaked the world with deep orange light.

We walked into Thai Town.

"I'm starving," I said.

"I could eat," he said.

We walked into the first restaurant we saw, and sat in a booth next to a window full of dusty satin flowers. The sun had finally disappeared behind the city, but the place wasn't air conditioned and the vinyl felt slightly melted. I ordered peanut noodles and studied the walls. A perfect collage of greens, yellows, reds—everything gilded with gold paint. The whole room was garish, greasy, and somehow still pleasing.

I wondered if my time in California was coming to a shuddering end. I imagined the flight back to Newark. The bleakness of New Jersey turned my stomach. Not again. I breathed through it.

A pile of pink noodles, steaming, sweet, and dusted with peanuts, arrived in two minutes. I slurped with a fork instead of the chopsticks I'd finally learned to use. Bow picked at some pineapple rice.

"Do you feel like we've known each other longer than a few days?" he said.

My phone rang. A Los Angeles number I didn't recognize. I answered.

"Tam?" It was Janet.

"Where are you?" I said, trying not to sound as worried as I was. Bow speared a piece of pineapple. Where was her cell phone? Instinctively, I looked out the window. Only twilight and cement.

"Can you come pick me up?" her voice shook. She was crying.

"Where? Are you okay?"

"I'm in the ER."

"Jesus! What happened?"

"I'm at Sunset Urgent Care, can you come?"

"Are you okay?" I asked again.

"Yeah, just please get here."

She hung up. I shoveled three oversize bites. "I gotta go," I said.

"Should I come with you?" His mouth full.

"I don't know."

He swallowed. "I'll come then," he said. "I don't have to be anywhere until later tonight."

"You want to drive?"

He nodded, and paid, over my conflicted protest. I didn't feel I deserved the kindness. While we half-jogged the blocks to my car, I tried to call the number back, getting the Sunset Urgent Care switchboard, and filled Bow in on as much detail as I could remember.

If Janet was hurt, I had to take some of the blame. We weren't far, but every creeping car ahead of us seemed menacing, an obstacle, and I imagined us driving up and over them. Bow swung the car around in front of the ER and I hopped out, flew from the lot to the waiting room, and scanned for Janet.

She looked horrible. Strung out from crying, if nothing else. As I sat next to her, she told me John was inside, getting stitches. The story came out in jumbled run-on sentences that I had to keep interrupting to understand. A fluorescent bulb on the ceiling behind her was sputtering, like in any scene in any scary movie where something terrible is happening.

They had been arguing at John's place. John put his fist into the wall. When Janet tried to calm him down, he raised a hand to hit her, but he didn't get the chance, because she pulled a bookend out from a box nearby and clocked him above the eye with it. She'd cut him pretty badly, driven him to the hospital in his truck, the whole time listening to him scream about how he was going to call the cops and tell them she'd attacked him. She sobbed, hyperventilated, curled over herself like her appendix had burst.

I gave her one of the Xanax in my purse.

Over her protests I pulled her outside. "I'm so glad you're not hurt," I said. But as my adrenaline pumped, I secretly feared she might be worse off than if he had actually hit her. Then, at least, she'd be able to walk away clean. Traumatized, of course, but with a clear enemy to blame, a framework for understanding what had happened, support groups to go to, the whole therapeutic community trained to deal with her. Now what would she do? If he convinced a cop she'd attacked him, she was screwed. If he didn't, which was much more likely, she would feel guilty for the rest of her life. If she didn't get out of the relationship now, this would only bind her to him more tightly.

Bow had been circling, and he pulled up to the curb seconds after we walked out.

Janet froze.

"This is Bow," I said, as he got out.

"From Bitsy's?" Janet said.

"Nice to meet you," he said, walking around to offer her his hand.

Janet looked at me in utter disbelief. Then back at him. "Hi?" she said, as if it was a question.

And I couldn't explain to her why I'd brought him with me.

"Let's go," I said.

"I'm not leaving John here," Janet said and started inching toward the hospital.

"He's got his truck," I said. "You two need a break."

I plopped into the driver's seat, adjusted everything so I could see, and after a few seconds, Janet got in the car, slammed the door, and slumped against the passenger window. Bow watched her from the backseat.

"How much of your stuff made it over to John's place?" I asked, nearly backing into someone's already-dented BMW.

"A couple boxes," she said. "Not a lot."

I asked if she had the key, and she did. I told her to give me directions.

We drove into the hills of Los Feliz. My first question was how the hell could John afford a place in that neighborhood.

Janet sighed and rubbed her face. "He inherited it."

"Like Gary," I said. She nodded.

I did not mention that we had now officially been evicted. I did not mention my inappropriate thoughts about John and Gary's parents dying together in the same plane crash or hotel fire. I wondered what Bow was thinking.

John's house had a 1970s polished-rock driveway and expensive colored-glass windows. The inside smelled like thirty years of weed smoke. I imagined if I licked the walls I'd get stoned. The colors were too loud:

avocado and mustard wallpaper, bright orange and brown patterned floor. I couldn't stay inside.

"Assembly line," I announced, and stationed myself in between the car and the house. They followed me.

"Thanks," Janet said stiffly to Bow, as he wrestled for some space in the trunk. "You didn't have to do this."

He smiled at her, and told her it was no problem.

She avoided my eyes and went back into the house.

We got as many of Janet's boxes as we could fit in my car, stuffed them in as fast as we could, and took off.

John still had a key to our apartment, so I told Janet I wasn't taking her home. I asked her where she wanted to go.

"Call Remy," she said, and closed her eyes. I felt a twinge of pride that she'd come to me for help before dialing through her friends from work.

Remy was home, watching James Bond movies all night.

"Can I bring Janet over for a while?" I asked him.

"Is she troubled?"

I said yes, she was. I looked in the rearview to merge onto the freeway, and saw Bow's profile—consternation, or concern, lining his face.

Remy refused to fix any fashion emergencies. I told him okay.

Janet's eyes fluttered open and she turned to stare out the window. I darted in and out of traffic, bile hovering in the back of my throat. I tried to ask a few questions, but Janet shook her head and closed her eyes again.

Remy lived in West Hollywood, in a gorgeous apartment north of Santa Monica Boulevard. He liked to talk about how WeHo was the oldest gay neighborhood in the country. Established even before the Castro in San Francisco. WeHo men carried Chihuahuas in sweaters when Castro boys were still learning how to match their belts to their shoes, he said. I was gambling that Janet had never taken John there. Remy's huge, perfectly landscaped building had been painted fashionable neutral tones: sage, umber, ivory.

Janet navigated the paisley-carpeted hallways of the enormous condo-plex. The redesign must not have been finished—the inside hallways sported distinctly early-80s modernist wall sconces and primary-color-block carpet. Remy answered the door in silk pajama pants. His pompadour was slightly less exaggerated than my memory.

True to stereotype, he had a fluffy white dog, smoked, and made constant sex jokes. But he was an East Coast transplant, like me, and small scars peppered his arms from knife fights he got into as a kid in Brooklyn. Remy seemed like a peacock, but I knew that he'd break anyone who threatened his friends.

"Drinks?" was the first thing out of his mouth. Then, to Janet, "Honey, you look terrible." He poked my shoulder. "What have you done to this girl?" And seeing Bow, "I'm terribly sorry, but you can't see me in my pajamas."

"Not now," I said, and nudged Janet inside. The wide-neck shirt she wore had slipped off her shoulder. She didn't appear to have noticed. I turned and motioned Bow to follow.

Bow and Remy shook hands.

Remy and I deposited Janet on the couch, in front of *Octopussy*. She hadn't said a word for almost a half-hour.

"I'll stay in here," Bow said, "if you two want to talk?"

Remy thanked him, walked me into the kitchen, and leaned on his polished granite counter.

He asked if I was going to tell him anything.

"I don't know much," I said. I told him as much as I knew.

"She's like that after only one Xanax?" he said.

"What do you mean?"

"She's a zombie."

"Isn't that kind of what it's supposed to do?" I said. Then, "Is that the most important issue here?" The kitchen was entirely stainless steel, and I felt like I'd walked into the control room of a spaceship.

"Did you ask her if she was already on anything?" Remy said.

"That would have been smart," I said.

"Don't you work for a doctor?"

"What am I supposed to do about John?"

"Why do you need to do anything? He's her problem."

"Whenever I think that way she ends up in more trouble."

"So what?"

"She sent him to the emergency room!" I yelled. Then, getting back in control, "You don't think that's kind of a reason for us to intervene?"

"What is it you think you're going to be able to do?" Remy said.

I didn't know. Still, I told him, it felt wrong to do nothing. I moved my feet symmetrically inside two kitchen tiles.

"It's none of your business," he said.

I said of course it was.

"Who are you to tell her what's a big deal and what's not? Who are you to say what she should do?"

"I'm trying to watch out for her," I said.

"You'd never let anyone treat you like this," he said, rolling his eyes. Dismissive, contemptuous.

"Like a friend?" I said.

"Like a child."

I put my face right next to his. "Then whose problem is she?"

"Back off," Remy said.

"You have no idea what I've been through today," I said, starting for the kitchen door.

"Leave her here," he said. "Go home and calm down. John's not going to do anything."

"Fine."

I went through the living room, past catatonic Janet, hollered at Bow that we were leaving, zigzagged back and forth through the hallways until I finally found an exit, and then had to go back around the block to find the car. Bow trotted a few steps behind me. Had I been treating Janet like a child? Was that why I wasn't more angry with her? I couldn't tell if Remy and I were disagreeing about whether Janet needed help, or whether the kind of help I'd offered was wrong. He was helping her too, by letting her stay over.

"Are you okay?" Bow asked, as I gunned through a red light.

"I want friends who will *tell* me when I'm doing something stupid," I said, "not just leave me to rot in my own bad choices."

Maybe I shouldn't have made her get her stuff out of John's. My backseat was crammed with it, and pulling out onto the street I tried to think of somewhere to go that wasn't home or the SLLC.

"I need a vacation," I said.

Bow checked his phone.

"Remember Franco, Betty Page, from the show?" he said.

Of course I did.

"We could go to his party tonight," he said. "That would get you out of the house." When I didn't respond, he added, "Or you could always come hang at my place."

I said going to a party now was absurd.

"I was thinking 'vacation,'" he said.

Then I remembered Juno saying he'd be at Franco's to bartend. Instead of fear, nausea, or a desperate need to sleep, I suddenly felt tingly, kinetic, enraged. I could ask big brother about Nathan coming to my work. I'd get the story Nathan had cooked up for his family, and then show Juno a scar up on my hairline from when I fell. I wanted some answers, and I could get them. If not from Janet, then from him. I had run out of reasons not to try.

"I think you're right," I said. "Let's go to the party."

"Really?"

"Yes."

"There's just one problem here," he said. "Do you have any white clothes in your car?"

I asked why.

"It's a white party," he said.

"For real?" I thought that was an old rave-scene fad that was over.

"Franco's for real. Everything's going to be white."

I suddenly yearned to see it. My instincts said I'd feel an almost supernatural force of calm. "You won't want to do coke there?"

"I will want to, but I won't do it."

"Good man."

FOURTEEN

On our way to my place, Bow and I drove past Todd's favorite sushi bar. I peered in the windows like a stalker, but didn't see him or Derek, only bamboo wallpaper and bright aluminum counters. Outside, the streetlights were on. One amber, two blue-white. I judged the person in charge of ordering replacement bulbs harshly.

"Can I say something about Janet?" Bow asked.

I told him to go ahead.

"She's gone," he said. "At least for now. You know that, right?"

"I don't think she is," I said. "She called me tonight, didn't she?"

"She didn't call you to help her get out of that relationship," he said.

"She doesn't want to live like that," I said.

Bow nodded. "I hope you're right," he said. He didn't believe it.

I changed the subject. The only all-white party outfit I had was an old Halloween costume—the famous Marilyn Monroe dress. My other white outfits were for sleeping in.

We made an elaborate transportation maneuver. We unloaded Janet's boxes into my apartment, I changed into the dress, we drove my car to Bow's, I locked mine up in his parking space, he ran up to change, and he drove us to Franco's, talking excitedly about the city adventure we were having together after I rebuffed his invitation to keep discussing what had just happened with Janet.

"I need some time to think about it," I had said.

"Fair enough," he had said. Then, after a few minutes of mumbled talk radio piping through his speakers, he pronounced, "You might like to know that Franco's a monochromatist."

148

I said I'd never heard of that.

"He prefers things to be all one color. You'll see. Each room in his house is completely monochromatic. The only time he'll wear two or more colors is when he's in drag."

Was he like me, but even worse? I couldn't believe I'd never heard of this. He must have made up the word. "Does he have OCD?"

"Probably. What I do know is that the house is uncanny, and therefore worth seeing."

"Lucky he can afford it," I said, looking at the mansions we were passing.

"The more money you have, the whiter you can make your world," Bow said, craning his neck to make a left. "That was a double entendre about both the party and our racist culture," he added.

"I got it," I said.

It was nearly eleven when we arrived. The block was packed with cars, so we drove around the tangled streets of the Hollywood hills looking for a space. The houses all had such personalities—some hiding away behind protective shrubs, some perched high upon double-car garages, and a few flat-roofed and unpretentious, reminding everyone that once, in the not-too-distant past, LA had been a place for normal people to live.

Bow wore a tight white T-shirt and cotton pants. I was too consumed by adrenaline to fully enjoy it, although I kept wondering when he had time to go to the gym. He found a spot. I got out, slammed the door, and smoothed my dress. I wore silver heels, high ones. Nothing like the shoes I'd worn for the catalog, though I had to do that special feminine prance to walk in them.

"This is nuts," I said, looking down at myself. Ten upside-down smiles beamed at me from my French-manicured toes. My hemline fell below the knee, so my bronzed calves were separated enough from my white everything else, I hoped.

"You look fantastic," Bow said. "I want to put you on a windy subway grate and take pictures."

"I've had enough pictures for the day," I said. "But thanks."

Bow held out his arm. I wanted to find Juno and get some answers. I tried to picture Nathan's face, to see the brotherly similarity, to feel some kind of compassion for either of them. Instead I felt cramped up inside my ribs. I wondered if Juno had any idea that Nathan had kicked me after I hit the ground.

Franco's front walkway was landscaped with pink—pink flowers, pink stone. Even in the dark, I could see the outside paint matched. The door was open.

The inside of the house looked like it had been erased—white coverlets, white drapes, nothing on the walls but white hangings on white paint. White carpet spread from the front door to glass sliders leading onto the back deck. White brocade upholstery buttoned onto every piece of furniture. All the people were dressed in white, with an occasional metallic accent here and there, like my silver shoes, another woman's gold. Their skin tones made up the color palette of the whole tableau. Strings of white lights hung from the ceiling, casting a romantic glow over everything. Speakers hidden somewhere pushed a slow, funky beat into the air. It was just loud enough that people had to stand very close to hear each other. The air smelled clean.

It was the first time I'd been in a room with no colors to deal with. Nothing to actively ignore. No uncomfortable feelings about matching problems to function in spite of. Someone had turned down the visual noise. I felt like my head had been removed from a vise.

"This is unbelievable," I said in real awe, "it's actually all the same shade."

"I have no idea where he gets the money to do this kind of stuff," Bow said.

I wanted to sit down and never leave. Then Franco shattered my peace.

"Bow, honey!" he squealed, in the same voice he'd used at Wacko. A rail-thin, pubescent-looking man in white pants, shirtless and barefoot.

"Hi, sweet thing," Bow said, and they performed air kisses.

"It's your little doll!" Franco said, opening his arms. "I remember you! Nice dress!"

I thanked him for inviting me. He motioned for me to say it right into his ear. He smelled like lavender. "Thanks for having me!"

"Oh! Nonsense!" he clapped his hands. "Darlings, welcome to my home." He waved his hands around. "Bar is outside, et cetera." He saw someone else to greet, patted my cheek, and moved on. Bow raised his eyebrows.

"It's okay to pat your face?" he said.

I shrugged. If Franco set up the bar outside, then that was where Juno had to be. I couldn't go directly for him; it would be too obvious.

I noticed at least three mirror-top side tables supporting stunning piles of cocaine. We started toward the sliding glass, but stopped at a white table covered with white food. A three-layer cake, fluffy powdered-sugar cookies, and yogurt-dipped pretzels in an enormous white bowl reminded me of a table in a fairy tale. White cheese nestled in a bed of white crackers. A platter spilled over with what appeared to be hand-made marshmallows, coconut clusters, and white chocolate truffles. I breathed in the sweetness.

A woman with platinum hair, cut short and spiky, picked up a toothpick and speared a marshmallow off the pile.

"This is the absolute best idea," she said, swaying her hips to the beat.

I agreed, not caring if she meant the party theme or the food. She ate the marshmallow like she was giving head. Another woman, in a white sequined bikini top, reached out with her thumb and wiped some sugar off Platinum's face.

"What do you do?" Platinum's girlfriend leaned in and said to me, licking her thumb.

"She raises hell," Bow said.

"Are you an activist?" she said. Not a trace of humor in her voice. I wondered if working in a clinic qualified.

"Sometimes," I said. I asked them what they did by pointing and making a questioning face. I kept searching through the glass for Juno, but I couldn't see him. I felt less and less brave.

"Excuse me," I said, while Platinum started describing her dog grooming business to Bow, and I headed back the way we came in. Bow extricated himself and followed.

"What's up?" he asked.

"Need to pee," I said.

Bow led me to a hallway, told me he'd stay in the living room, and I moved down door by door. The curiosity won. Behind three closed doors completely perfect rooms offered me new delight. Franco liked lighter colors, for the most part—seafoam green, periwinkle, similar in tone to the pink of the entrance. I marveled at the precision. He must have found an expert painter, fabric dyer, upholsterer.

Then I found the bathroom. Franco had decorated the whole room in royal purple. If Prince had built a house in honor of his own caricature, this would have been his master bath. Thick purple towels hung on purple rods affixed to glossy purple walls, fluffy purple bath mats lay on purple tile. All exactly the same deep shade.

Janet would have laughed so hard. She would have told Franco he was my dream date.

I imagined her curled up on Remy's couch, watching Bond movies, glassy-eyed and quiet. Remy would make jokes, and martinis, and she would be able to sleep. She could deal with John another day. A dull grief settled in to my gut; suspicion that John would reappear, apologetic and even more powerful. That Bow was right.

I needed to start packing for the move. Maybe I'd leave everything for Janet or the police to take away.

Franco's purple hand soap smelled like him. I scrunched my curls with some water. My face looked too worried. I tried to relax my forehead. I rubbed my temples and took three deep breaths. I would say hello to Juno, then tell him I needed to talk to him when he could get a break. Then I'd ask him what Nathan had told him. Then what? What was I going to do with whatever bullshit story Nathan had given his family?

I had one more Xanax in the car, if it came to that. Shit, my car was at Bow's.

Someone knocked.

"Hang on!" I called, assuming it was Bow.

But when I opened the door, instead of Bow's stubbly, beautiful face, a young blond guy stared at me. It took us less than a second to recognize each other.

I grew four inches, lunged forward, and slammed him against the wall of the hallway. The thud from the back of his head hitting a picture frame dimly registered. He was just a squirming shape in white dress pants and a sleeveless tank, making unhappy grunting noises as my forearm pressed into the base of his throat. He pulled at my arm with both hands.

"If you ever come near me again, you little prick," I whispered, "I swear to God I will fucking kill you." I stared at his blue, watering eyes, and I simultaneously felt a grand triumph and a sickening momentum, the sense of things being very, very wrong and careening toward much worse.

I let him go. "What the fuck is wrong with you?" he said as he bent over to cough, gasp, and rub his throat. "What are you doing here?"

I tried to keep my voice down, though the party was loud enough to drown us out even if we'd been screaming. "I was invited," I said, aware that if he lunged for me I'd fall into the bathroom. I'd be a casualty of the purple tub. "What are you doing here?"

"Bar-backing for my brother."

"Are you stalking me at work?"

"You call killing babies work?"

"I do not kill babies," I said through my teeth.

"What do you call it then?" he started yelling. "Fucking Janine would never have done it if it wasn't for you! How can you live with yourself?" He got out a few more lines, at increasing volume. I closed my eyes for a second and did not back up. As he yelled, he started crying. Soon, he couldn't breathe hard enough. Sobbing, with snot oozing down his lip, arms wrapped around his stomach, he slid down the wall. "She left me," he said between ragged breaths, "because of you! I wanted to marry her!" He slammed his head backward into the wall and a horrifying noise, somewhere between a scream and a wail, erupted from the back of his throat.

He was seventeen, and wanted to be a father. The most important thing in the world had been taken from him.

He coughed so hard he gagged.

For an instant, I thought about his girlfriend, Janine. She was one of the braver cases, I had thought at the time. She wanted to go to college, she said. She wasn't ready to be a mother. She hadn't shown any signs of being in an abusive relationship, any more than most high school girls, anyway. We had a long talk about birth control. It was my job to educate. To coach her into making responsible, safe decisions. To give her the referral that would change her life. And Nathan's.

I stared at Nathan, who was furiously wiping his eyes and nose, trying to catch his breath. It was no one's job to counsel him. Because so many teenage fathers abandoned their pregnant girlfriends, we had no safety net to catch the boys who stuck around. I envisioned them like pinpoints on a map: young men all over the country wrestling their own grief and rage without any help. Suddenly I was certain he'd never talked to anyone about what happened.

"Nathan," I said in my counselor voice. When he turned his face up to me, he was completely broken. "I'm sorry this hurts so much," I knelt down to face him. "This has been an incredible loss for you."

"Fuck you," he said. "You do it every day."

I told him we didn't need to make peace between us, but that he should know he'd put me in the hospital for a few days. "You might have killed me,"

I said, "and you've got to deal with that rage or you might make an even bigger mistake in the future." I told him to picket with the pro-lifers if he wanted to, or study law and fight for father's rights, "but don't be violent. Just don't. You'll end up in prison."

He didn't look me in the eye. He sniffled and hiccupped. "What about you?" he said. "You just jumped me."

"Stay away from me," I said. I told him if he showed up at the SLLC I would call the police.

No answer. I nudged him with my foot. He grabbed my ankle. "Don't touch me, bitch!" His fingers like a bear trap.

"Stay away from me," I said again, this time a little louder. "Don't come to my work. Do you understand?" He threw my foot forward. I stumbled, steadied myself against the wall. He wiped his face with the bottom of his shirt.

"Yeah, I get it," he said.

I turned and started to walk toward the party, to get Bow, and to get out. I felt shakey and feverish.

"You should watch your back," Nathan said.

"Get some help," I said, without turning around.

I made it to the doorway that led into the living room. Bow stood two feet away, talking to someone I didn't have time to notice before Nathan hurled himself at me from behind and caught me in a choke hold. My neck snapped back and we struggled. I jabbed with my elbow as hard as I could and tried to worm downward, away from him. We crashed into the wall and stumbled to the floor. I landed hard on my knees. I punched back with my elbow again, felt Nathan loosen, and scrabbled away from him, coughing. Then Bow was in between us, and an enormous red stain splashed the carpet, where he'd dropped his wine, and the happy noise of the party turned into a strange, hushed questioning. I couldn't get my footing, so stayed down, stunned. A thumping beat still breezed through while voices from beyond Bow rose in concerned cadences:

"What's going on?"

"Is everything okay?"

It only took a second before they sensed that the worst of it was over. People who couldn't see us started milling out to the pool. Bow held Nathan around the chest with both arms, like a lifeguard, although Nathan seemed to have exhausted himself, and slumped against Bow, deflated, eyes to the ground, one arm folded over the place where I had elbowed him.

Bow asked if I was alright. I had no voice. I had no words. I couldn't feel my body enough to know if I was hurt. I patted around for my dress, to cover my thighs. What a ridiculous instinct, I thought.

Bow asked Nathan what the fuck he was thinking as he shoved him hard against the wall and held him there. Nathan's face shined with sweat and tears and snot.

"Fuck off," Nathan said, but didn't fight back.

Juno and Franco appeared from outside. Above me a new rush of activity and raised voices swirled. My neck hurt. I stared at the wine stain. The whole scene had taken place without any blood or snot or sweat staining any of the perfect white clothes, perfect white walls, and the only proof that anything bad had happened was the wine on the carpet. Bow's glass lay on its side, a trail of wine leading to its lip, like the cover of an old murder mystery.

The feeling was of being way too stoned. I worked hard to identify the voices.

"What the fuck's going on?" *Juno.*

"Your brother's out of control." *Bow.*

"Fuck you, asshole." *Nathan.*

I stood up and bent my knees to check for wobbliness.

I interrupted everyone to ask Bow if we could go. Nathan was now slouching behind Juno, and the space between Bow and Juno had closed, while they argued, and Franco made attempts to divert their attention. I knew it wasn't over, but I couldn't stay there.

"Please," I said to Bow, "let's just go."

"What the fuck did you do?" Juno said to Nathan, and Nathan stared at the ground, mute. He looked like a ten-year-old waiting for his punishment.

Franco's voice was the clearest then. "This was all very entertaining, my darlings, but in very poor taste. Juno, get back to the bar. Nathan, you will not leave his side. Bow, my dear, please take your little gladiator home."

"You're serious?" Bow said.

Franco didn't answer.

"Your little party is more important than this?" The few anonymous faces in the room seemed demonic to me then.

"Just go," Franco said.

"Fuck you, Franco," Bow said. "You're a piece of shit."

Bow held his hand to me. He was breathing hard through his nose—

maybe because he was biting his tongue. I wove my way to him and we got outside.

Once he'd established that I was physically unhurt, he vented some rage about Franco, offered me apologies, and asked again if I was okay.

I told him I felt terrible.

Bow drove me to his house. That's where my car was, and LA people need to end up wherever they've left their car.

He asked me to come inside, and I did. He put in a homemade CD, skipped a few tracks, and turned it down low, while I folded into the couch. Leonard Cohen's hypnotic voice smoothed the air. After two glasses of water, and a few minutes of not talking, Bow finally broke into my fog by sitting next to me and taking one of my hands.

"Can you tell me what happened?"

I told him he saw most of it.

He had forgotten Juno was bartending, hadn't even been in the backyard before I came out of the bathroom, and said he felt like an idiot for inviting me.

"This is when I can't justify being a pacifist," he said. "I should have punched that fucking kid in the face."

"I knew Juno would be there," I said. I confessed that I'd wanted to confront him with questions about Nathan. But Nathan's appearance had caught me by surprise.

"Nate doesn't usually come with him," he said. "Still, why would you do that?"

"It was a bad idea," I said.

"Obviously. I asked you why you once thought it might be a good one."

"I don't know," I said. "I was desperate for information." Then I asked how well Bow knew Juno, and how well he knew Nathan.

Juno was an acquaintance of a few years, he said, although more a friend of Naomi's, but he'd only met Nate once or twice, when his parents kicked him out and he stayed at Juno's until they calmed down.

"You acted like you knew him better than that," I said.

Bow said that's how this group of friends all were. Affectionate. "Nate seemed like a regular high-school prick," he said. "Juno's the black sheep of that family. God, what a mess." He went quiet for a few seconds. I tried to envision another way it could have gone, a way that ended with agreements and understandings.

I ran my hands over my neck, started poking the old places where I'd been hurt, then found the new.

"Do you need ice?" Bow asked. He started to get up.

I shook my head. "Can't deal with ice on my neck."

Then Bow said, for future reference, that he'd like to be notified when he was being used.

"What?"

"You didn't trust me enough to tell me you had an agenda."

I stared at him, amazed. He met my gaze.

"You think I'm being harsh," he said.

"I don't like being told what to do."

"All I'm asking is that as long as you're dealing with me, you're telling me the truth." He put his glass on the table. "This whole thing could have been avoided if you told me what you were doing. I'm happy to offer you the same respect."

"It wasn't your business," I said.

He said that was unfair. "I didn't get to choose whether to be involved."

That was true. "Okay," I said, wrenching my pride. Then I had to tell him, "I pushed Nathan in the hallway. I started it. I mean, this time."

"You did?"

I nodded my head and started crying, quietly and slowly, at first. But the more I thought about that day, that evening, how furious I was that my chance at some answers had been ruined, how terrifyingly immediate my own response had been, the harder it came. Bow pulled me into his lap. He kept a hand in my hair and said gently, "Get it out. This is good."

I saw Nathan's face twisted with grief, and myself, knotted on the floor of a dive bar bathroom, afraid. I saw another me, curled up on the ground next to my car at Greenvale, breathing tightened by a broken rib. I saw Janet, asking Remy to drive her back to see John, and I saw John, letting her into his house, his face dark with anger. My mother and father sitting in front of the TV, not talking, not looking at each other, not caring about anything, not changing. I saw all the patients at the clinic, all their scared, twitching hands, their bravado, their blood oozing into test tubes and their prayers to whatever God they'd grown up with, please, please don't let it be bad. The high school kids, holding on with all their might to some scrap of loving attention, the girls getting pregnant, the guys hoping no one ever saw their softness. I saw their slouching shoulders, heard their guarded voices. I saw Todd at home with Derek, asking for more, knowing the answer would come silently, in days of being ignored. I cried for every memory of any pain, mine and everyone else's, and I screamed, and sobbed, and yelled it into Bow's shirt, my face straining against the force of it all, my body buckled as if my stomach had been torn away.

After a few eternal minutes, when my breathing started evening out, my cries turned to strained little whimpers. I felt limp. I'd made two large, dark spots on Bow's chest. I wiped my face with my hands and took a few shuddering breaths.

"God," I said, my nose stuffed and my throat sore. I tried to chuckle; I still sounded like I was crying. I slid off Bow's lap and leaned back on the couch, his arm still under my back.

"How do you feel?" he said.

"Exhausted," I said.

He smoothed some hair from my sweaty face, and said he was getting me some water. I didn't want him to let go of me, and said so.

"I won't," he said. "Not really." When he walked into the kitchen my body ached. Raw, exposed, I wanted him to crush me, cover me.

"Here," he said, handing me a glass. I drank half in one breath.

My head was full of the way he smelled, his wine breath, his almond warmth. I sank my face into his neck. My chest felt like it had cracked open and spilled. I wanted to tuck myself into the crook of his arm, hibernate under his weight, but I couldn't stop sniffling.

"I'm getting snot all over you," I said.

"Salt water and dirt," he said, rubbing my back now, "I'm not afraid of it."

I said I really needed to blow my nose. He kept one arm around me, reached to the other end of the couch, and produced a box of tissue.

There were boxes hidden all over, he said, because he got bad allergies in the spring.

I said that was one of the few ways we got to notice the seasons change in LA. I blew, and wadded the tissue in my hand.

"Do you miss having seasons?" he asked.

I told him I went to New Jersey in the winter every year to visit my parents and got reminded that it wasn't so awesome to be cold. He wiped under one of my eyes with his thumb.

"You use waterproof makeup?" he asked.

I told him yes, I did. When he asked why, I said I didn't know why; it was what my mother had always used.

"What if I kissed you," he said, "right now?" Would it be too much? Was it too predictable if I was a woman who had just cried, and we kissed? He was kidding, and also, not.

No, I said. I mean yes. It's okay to kiss me, please.

He kissed my eyes. Then he kissed my mouth.

My body ignited immediately.

He took the tissue out of my hand and tossed it toward the kitchen. He pulled the halter of the Marilyn dress over my head, pushed the dress down to my waist, and ran his fingers lightly over my neck before kissing me there. He kissed each inch from my ear to my shoulder, breathing in as he touched me and out as he pulled away, slow breaths, two fingertips tracing along with his mouth.

"Oh shit," I said. "Are you rescuing me?"

"No," he said.

His tongue flicked behind my ear. Then he pulled back. "If I'd been a real rescuer, I would have pounded Nathan into the floor. All I did was drive you back to my place."

"That's good," I said, "because I don't want to play that game." I could feel the heat evaporating, and didn't know how to sink back in.

He sighed and said that was all wrong. "Role-playing is fine," he said. "It's all fine. It's about *you* doing what *you* want. You play a femme most of the time anyway. When you don't want to, you don't have to. Will. Choice. Consciousness."

I would have been indignant, but his frankness was too much of a relief. I realized I was ashamed that I'd wanted him to physically protect me.

His hands left warm prints on either side of my neck. He nudged me back onto the couch and kissed his way to my breasts. One hand over my heart, one tracing light, slow lines around my face. I kept my eyes closed, felt them burn from the crying, felt my skin burn from the promise in Bow's touch. He pressed tongue to nipple to teeth and I sucked in some air.

"Wait, wait," I said, and scooted up and away. "I have to tell you something."

He raised his eyebrows.

"I kissed Naomi," I said, "at the bar today, before you got there."

"Really." He turned away a bit and sighed through a chuckle.

I tried to come up with a reason for not mentioning it earlier, but couldn't.

"Anything else?" he said. "Any husband or girlfriend I should know about? Are you on parole?"

"No," I said. I had almost gotten sexually involved with him without having The Conversation. I said that regardless of what we got into tonight, I'd like to check in about our sexual health. I told him I got tested every six months for everything, because of work, because I needed to know when new types of tests came out, because I was curious.

"Everything?" he said.

I nodded. "It's not bad," I said, "I just have a blood draw. Regular Pap smears. I'm on the pill. I use condoms, always. What about you?"

He said he was surprised I hadn't asked sooner. "Haven't been tested for HIV for a few years. Haven't been screwing a lot though." Then he shook his head. "I didn't always use condoms. Got chlamydia once, got it treated. I'm lucky I don't have anything more serious."

I asked him if he'd ever had an antibody test for genital herpes and he said no. I asked him if he'd been swabbed in the last year, for gonorrhea and chlamydia, and he said no, but he hadn't been with anyone new since the last time he'd been tested.

"I always tell people they need to get comfortable talking about these things," I said, "but I've never actually tried to have sex directly afterward. I think I'm kind of a fraud." The tears started rising again. I reached for Bow's hand. He intertwined our fingers.

"I'm not uncomfortable," he said, and smiled at me. "I'm not even turned off."

"The Naomi thing doesn't bother you?"

"Only that you waited to tell me, because it seemed like it was a weight on you. She kisses people the way most of us hug or shake hands. It's her way of getting to know someone. It's a good sign, actually."

He nestled in closer.

"I'd never kissed a girl," I said.

"Let's go to bed," he said. He stood, and pulled me with him. "My condoms are less than three months old," he said as he steered me around the corner into his room, "just in case you were about to ask."

A part of me worried that in the morning he'd tell me what a mistake it all was, that he'd done it for the wrong reasons, and that it could never happen again. The rest of me was on fire.

I loved watching violent love scenes in movies like *The Postman Always Rings Twice*, when Jack Nicholson and Jessica Lange stage a car accident to kill her husband. They are about to cry to the police, but first they have to show that they got hurt so no one suspects them. Lange breaks a bottle on Nicholson's head, he hits her square in the face, and then he rips off her panties and they fuck in the mud next to the busted car and her husband's corpse. That scene horrified me and turned me on.

In reality, what I wanted in bed was a quieting of all the voices that told me I was too short, or too crazy, or not sexy enough, or missing some essential piece of understanding that governed normal people's feelings. I had no memories of being able to fully concentrate on enjoying being naked with a man without constant evaluation of my performance, his performance, our achieving either his or my orgasm, the colors in the room, the consequences of what we were doing, the methods, be they conventional or more experimental, by which we were doing it, and whether the scene of us together was a bad copy of something I'd seen in a movie. I wanted passion, but somehow I always ended up in a negotiation of identities.

His bedroom smelled like incense. He announced that he was lighting candles, and then flicked a lighter at a few votives on a dark wood nightstand. The bed was unreasonably pliant, almost squishy, and he had beige jersey sheets, the softest I'd ever felt. I slipped off my dress and crawled in. Just a few days ago I'd been sitting at Bitsy's wanting to touch Bow's body.

He pulled off his shirt.

"Pants, too," I said. He complied. Dark hairs grew thicker on his legs than I'd imagined. A thin silver chain I hadn't noticed before glimmered from his chest. He jumped, arms out, and crashed onto the bed right next to me.

Then we were kissing hard, rolling over each other, struggling to pull the blankets from between us, our breath pushing through our noses, in between our tongues. He tangled a hand in my hair, looped an arm under my leg, bent me and squeezed me and buried his face in my chest, in my stomach. He pulled me to the edge of the bed, knelt on the floor, and just as I became aware of the fact that it had been hours—many stressful, sweaty hours—since I'd showered, he was pushing my legs over his shoulders and inhaling, his nose against my crotch, one thin layer of cotton between us. He breathed me in, rubbed my legs, my ass, my stomach, pressed on the outside of my thighs as if to say, *do it*, and so I squeezed his head just slightly, and he moaned into me, the buzz traveling from my clit to the back of my own throat. He pulled the thong off, caught my eyes, and his warm mouth opened onto my vagina. When my back arched against him, straining, he cupped my ass and held me up. I grasped for the bed, yanked on the sheets, every circle of his tongue pushing me up higher, and then he slid his fingers inside and moved in rhythm with my hips. He brought me to the panting, clenching edge of an orgasm, then slowed down, pulled away, and reached into his nightstand drawer for a condom, a bottle of lube, and a foil-wrapped Cadbury Egg.

"What are you doing?"

He bit off half the egg and held the other half to my mouth. He grinned.

I took it, running my tongue on the ends of his fingers, a little shocked by the sweetness. I rolled the chocolate shell in my mouth and let my tongue dig out the cream the way I used to as a kid. Bow crawled on the bed and I pushed him onto his back, watched him chew and suck and swallow tiny sips of sugary syrup. I chewed the chocolate shell slowly, feeling my mouth water.

He tugged on my hips. "Get up here," he said, and I knelt over his face. This time he moved his mouth agonizingly slowly, and I could feel the egg rub against my skin as he let it dissolve, inside me, against me, under his tongue. While I finished my half, almost overwhelmed by the sugar, he nibbled, explored, a languid cat enjoying a delicacy. I stayed put, breathing slow and deep, until I could feel the texture on his tongue change—he'd finished the egg. He rolled me over, then bolted out of the bed and reappeared in seconds with a warm washcloth. He cleaned me with total attention, then threw the washcloth over his shoulder to make me giggle.

I pulled him down, pushed him onto his back, and knelt over his hard-on. He wiped his mouth and hummed, almost a tune. I rolled the condom on and smoothed extra lube from the tip down.

"Glycerin free," Bow said, his breathing ragged, "and organic."

"Eidel?" I asked, and he spanked me.

I poised over him. I guided his penis in an inch, just enough for us both to ache, and then I held him steady with my legs while I slid down slow, bending to kiss him. In the slippery heat of our mouths, I tasted myself and the candy together, sweet-savory, a fullness and extra sensation, totally brand new. The feel of him, the heat, everything buzzed and crackled in me. We savored it for a few gorgeous seconds, eyes open together, before speeding up.

I watched him bite his lips. His eyes rolled back. He scrunched his nose and let out his breath. I rocked faster and faster to see it, to feel him get there. But again, he slowed us down, and rolled us over, and then, he pushed a pillow under my ass to lift my hips. On his knees, he reached for my feet and held them to his chest. He pushed into me at a steady beat, kissed my toes, and going just a bit faster, took my big toe all the way in his mouth, which was too much for me, and I came, my body contracting with and around him, the relief of it shooting through every joint, every vein.

I was miles away from the party, from Nathan, from Janet, from everything, and the images that fluttered through me were all warmth and wet and sweetness.

He went slow and gentle until I'd landed, then asked, "Okay if I take a turn?"

I said yes, please, and with five or six hard thrusts he came, and collapsed on me, and let out a few loud, groaning sighs.

"I liked that," he said into the bed.

"Me too," I said.

"Explain yourself," I said, as he reached in between my legs, pulled out, and started tying the condom off.

"The egg?"

I nodded.

"When I meet someone I'm attracted to, I think about what they might taste like. It's like a game, to see if I can pick a candy that will taste like them?"

I laughed. "How do you know if you've won the game?"

"You liked it, right?"

I said I did.

"Then I won," he said. "I don't usually involve the other person, but," he flopped down next to me, "you're up for new experiences."

"You have a list of women and the candy you think they taste like?"

"And men," he said.

"Written down somewhere?"

"No."

"Hilarious."

"Not gross?"

"No. Fattening, maybe."

"Like I said, I don't get to test my accuracy too often."

Leonard Cohen was still singing in the living room.

Bow asked if it was too much.

I told him that as far as I could tell there was no Too Much category in his worldview. I was beginning to understand it.

"That's why I love this city," he said.

I snuggled in. "Makes sense."

"I'm taking you to see the dolphins in Malibu," he said.

"So I'll believe you're not a lunatic?"

"So you can be overwhelmed by the beauty."

We were quiet for a few moments, tracing light circles on each other.

"Every heart to love will come," Bow sang in a flat tenor as he pulled on my curls, "but like a refugee." He tapped my head. "I love that line."

"I can't even say the word 'love' without feeling self-conscious," I said. "It sounds like a silly thing people say in bad romantic comedies."

"That's one of the perks of not being a cynic," Bow said. "I get to love everyone and everything. Even myself."

"There is a crack in everything," I sang along. "That's how the light gets in." Bow kissed my hair. I asked if I could tell him something strange. He said of course.

"I have this problem with colors," I said, barely above a whisper.

"Meaning?"

I explained it, as best I could. Describing my sense of relief at Franco's house seemed to help him understand. I told him most people didn't know.

"You certainly are multifaceted," he said. Then he thanked me for telling, and the absolute anticlimax of the conversation struck me as very, very funny. My laughter sounded a little maniacal, but he kept his arms around me and chuckled along, and then exhaustion descended, like a heavy velvet curtain.

Bow warned me that he snored, and gave me permission to roll him over if it kept me awake. He said sleeping next to someone was the most vulnerable thing you could do. "People fart," he said. "They grind their teeth, they drool. I used to never fall asleep first, I was so afraid that I'd be too disgusting."

"Please," I said. "I'm a medical assistant?" I ran my hand over his stomach and smelled our sex, mingling with latex and sugar, as he pulled the sheets up over us.

It wasn't until we were still, and Bow's breathing had become deep and steady, that the cramping, nauseous dread of Nathan, of Janet, of the future, took over my body. I lay awake then, wishing Bow would wake up and keep talking, so I could pretend for a few minutes longer that the next day was not ever going to come.

FIFTEEN

Collese in New Brunswick, New Jersey was only somewhat different from high school in West Courtney. I even resented the place names, the way they echoed some other, more important Old Brunswick or Old Jersey. I knew Jersey wasn't all bad—at least New Brunswick had better restaurants than the chains my parents supported. There were a few more interesting characters, too. In my freshman dorm, I met three art students who were into making heavy, wiggly Jell-O sculptures and then taking photos of themselves, naked except for aprons, holding the molds out on cafeteria trays. They recruited me to assist in the mold-making because I inadvertently criticized their colors.

"Did you do that on purpose?" I asked innocently, pointing at a shiny green mound that had a distinctly blue ring around the edge. They hadn't, and hadn't noticed.

"We need that eye," one of them said, then told me her name was Sunny. We spent three weeks trying to set various molds in our dorm kitchenette—and eventually abandoned the project because anything that actually held its shape looked like psychedelic breasts, which made for one or two great pictures but not many more, and anything that lost its shape was the scat of some rainbow-dwelling Sasquatch, which couldn't be construed as social commentary on America of the 1950s, according to Sunny. I thought the project was a springboard to friendship, but Sunny didn't stop by my room after her art class ended that semester.

I found a coffee shop to study in that was painted a color of blue I could ignore. I decided to pursue biology on my way to medicine.

Most of the kids I'd known in West Courtney were headed to blue-collar jobs at eighteen. Grant Rose went to community college, took one class a quarter, and waited tables at a nostalgic diner that served malt frosties in soda-fountain glasses. I came home from Rutgers the summer after my freshman year, nine months before my grandfather died, with my colors obsession in full flower and an A+ in Dissection. I wore all black and constantly wanted to talk about what I was doing in school. It felt wrong to drink Coors Light with the same old kids at their same old houses and rehash the plots of the same old TV shows. Grant Rose tried to listen to my stories about my classes, my roommate who got pregnant and dropped out—but our lives had diverged irreversibly, for the first time, and our conversations stalled.

Grant and I spent my last summer night before sophomore year sitting on her back porch. We were smoking a tiny joint, not really getting high, sucking in air and trying not to burn our fingers. She'd picked me up after her dinner shift and forgotten to take her little green apron off. She pulled absently on the strings and squinted into the late-summer dark.

"So, you're happy at Rutgers," she said. A statement, not a question.

"I guess," I said. I loved the work, but spent nearly every day alone. I didn't know how to talk about that.

"I thought you might get sick of it and try to get into UCLA," she said.

"What gave you that idea?"

She shrugged, puffed on the joint, relit it, and passed it over, holding her wisp of smoke in until the moment when she might have responded to my question had passed. Slowly, like a fog dissolving, I understood the depth of her fantasies about California. She'd made imaginary plans, and aspired to a different life there, but she'd done it for *me*, not for herself. She never thought she'd leave West Courtney, and had spent her dreams on me. I felt I'd been handed a great responsibility.

Grant Rose stretched out, ran her fingers through her hair and made a ponytail, twisted it around, then let go. Her face was smooth and her lips shone with a drug store miracle gloss. The sticky strands at the base of her neck were the only sign she'd spent the day rushing from table to kitchen to table.

I couldn't tell her how difficult it had been for me to adjust to the new environment at Rutgers—how many dorm rooms I wouldn't enter, how often I had to avert my eyes now from the sloppy, clashing outfits of the students around me. I'd dropped a class after one painful meeting in a room with dark green walls, loud drapes, and wrong salmon-and-grey flecked carpet. I hadn't been able to concentrate, I couldn't listen, I could barely breathe. I left the class halfway through and sat in a bathroom stall. That one was a required writing class. I had to keep my eye on the course offerings, hoping I could take it again, gambling on a new classroom. It, whatever was wrong with me, was getting worse.

"I've been going out with Bill Cransing," Grant said, holding her hand out for the last quarter-inch of the joint I'd been holding. He was a local boy. Nice enough, I remembered. Not particularly attractive. Not particularly anything.

"How's that going?" I asked, feeling a twinge of something sour in my gut.

"Fine," she said. "He's a nice kid."

They dated on and off for the next three years. When I came home to visit, Bill's presence became a ubiquitous, unspoken assumption. He didn't talk much, and would always graciously offer me the front seat when they came to pick me up at my parents' house. He would slide in behind Grant and stare out the window placidly while she and I tried to catch each other up on the mundane details—my grades, her customers, how our parents were doing, what movies we'd seen.

When I returned home for the summer after graduating, finally committed to moving to LA, Grant Rose, who was two months pregnant and twenty-two, married Bill. My last big task before I could concentrate on leaving was being her maid of honor.

She said she was getting married because she was in love, and although I couldn't argue with her when she smiled and calmly announced that it was all happening and she wanted me to participate, I secretly grieved the death of what might have been her life. I also grieved, without consciousness, the end of our real friendship.

Grant and Bill's wedding was traditional, slightly ostentatious, and held in a church. I wore a lavender dress and stared at the amazing maroon of the carpet, overcome with how blood-like it was. I tried to dissociate when they started saying their vows. I shifted around in my platform shoes—as an experiment I had chosen matching my height to the bridesmaid next to me over color consistency (the shoes I had sent in for dying had come back three shades too dark, anyway). I was regretting the shoes. I felt horrible for hating Grant's marriage when she seemed so blissful, but I was already thinking of her in the past tense. I knew she was settling in to become a housewife and I was too angry with her to accept it, be kind, stay close. Her choice to stay in New Jersey only fortified my decision to leave.

At the reception, Grant swirled over to me in her white chiffon gown, blazingly beautiful.

"Thank you for everything," she said.

"It's no problem," I told her. "I'll expect you to make a few phone calls and buy me some bobby pins when it's my turn to strap on the ball and chain."

"Yes!" she sighed, and took both of my hands. "Someone is going to be very lucky to have you someday." The way she said it, heavy with implication, made my head spin with questions. Then she leaned in, and as I breathed her champagne and hairspray fumes, she asked, "Is the dress okay? I'm so pissed that they fucked up all the shoes. You can change now that the ceremony's over, if you want."

"I'm fine," I told her. "I'm lucky weddings have such simple color schemes." I tried to laugh good-naturedly, but felt somehow betrayed that we were discussing colors in public. I searched for some scrap of conversation that would be appropriate. "I hope you and Bill are very happy."

She hugged me. "Send me your new address as soon as you get to LA. Promise."

"I promise," I said.

Then she told me she was proud of me and floated on to have confessions of love and loyalty with someone else.

Bill wanted her to do whatever she wanted with her life, which on the surface of things seemed like a loving, sweet way to treat her. The problem was that after high school, when she was no longer responsible for my well-being or social status, when she found she could make a living using a minimum of charm and keep a husband without making any sacrifices, Grant needed a fire under her ass to do anything at all. Bill's devotion manifested as a nice little house for Grant to sit in. She quit working at the restaurant, had her baby, collected potted plants, and reread the romances we'd shoplifted as kids. She spent time with her mother, cooked with her mother, became her mother.

We talked often during my first year in LA, and she would send me photos of her and Bill and baby Paul. She scribbled notes on the backs of the photos as if she were the baby—*Can't wait to see you, auntie Tammy*—and then her second pregnancy had some complications, and I started spending more time with Janet, and finally, our old intimacy truly faded into awkwardness.

We met for coffee in her bright kitchen after nearly a year of silence, when I was home for Christmas, and I held little Jenny for a few minutes, and fed Paul small piles of Cheerios, and tried to make my life sound glamorous, since it was clear I'd become a character in a story to Grant, as much as she had become that to me. Afterward, neither of us tried to call.

I memorialized her, in a way, by putting a picture of the two of us in my office at the SLLC, taken when we were fourteen and jubilantly brandishing water balloons. I missed the mischievous, curious girls we had been together. Seeing her grow up and choose the life we'd scorned as kids made me feel alone, rootless, and secretly superior.

I woke up before Bow. The sun, viciously bright behind Bow's vertical blinds, told me I was already late to work. That the world was still twirling around its axis, that I had no place to live, that my neck was sore from Nathan's choke hold, and that I'd made love to the Bitsy's waiter were pieces of information trying to connect, trying to make sense, but they failed. I could stay in this bed. No one could find me. I'd let the whole thing, meaning my life, just blow over. Then Bow rolled toward me, breathing deep as he climbed into waking, and the possibility vanished.

His opened his eyes and smiled at me. "You're here," he said.

"It's true."

"What time is it?"

"Late. Probably nine. I have to get to work. Right now my buddy Todd is totally freaking out."

"Your neck," he said and reached for me. I thought he might poke the tender spot, but he pulled me closer to kiss both collar bones. "God, what a bastard." He sighed and met my eyes. "What are you going to do?"

"I don't know," I said. "Go to work, I guess."

"What are you going to do about Nate?"

I thought I'd answered him. "I don't know," I said again. But it wasn't good enough. "I guess I'll go back to the cops?" He made a skeptical face. Faith in the LAPD was deep naiveté. "He's so young," I said, "and if you'd seen him crying, it's like he's this baby flailing around because he can't figure out how to make himself feel better."

"Sounds like most people I know."

"On the other hand," I said, rubbing my neck, "he's dangerous."

Bow nodded. "That's the salient bit." I asked him if he had any ideas, and he said he'd be willing to call Juno. "You could give Juno the whole story," Bow said, "and then let the family deal with him. They'd be tough, I guarantee you that."

I told him I'd think about it. I looked at the light outside. "I have to go," I said.

My phone was dead. I hadn't paid the bill for two months and ignored the messages threatening to end my service. I called Todd from Bow's cell. I sat in the living room, wrapped in my Marilyn dress, and said I was on my way.

Once he believed that I wasn't bleeding in a ditch on the side of the road, Todd told me I was the Worst Employee of the Week. "I need you to hurry," he said.

I asked him what for.

"Your girlfriend is here," he said.

I thought of Naomi, but Todd wouldn't know her. Janet?

"Linda," he said, sounding irritated, "and I've been chatting her up, telling her you were out buying assembly supplies or something."

The time had come to use my Emergency Outfit. My trunk stayed fully stocked with jumper cables, a flashlight, a Mylar blanket, and a few plastic bags filled with survival kit items like a change of clothes, soap, a toothbrush and toothpaste, condoms, and clothes. The outfit included an old pair of low-waist, boot-cut jeans (they still fit, but they were a color I didn't wear that much anymore) and a black shirt. The shirt was tight, slightly shiny. It could be dressed up or down. There was a clean pair of underwear in there too. If I ever got stuck too far from home I wouldn't have to borrow clothes or shop—activities which took me hours. I could say, "I've got a few things in the car," and presto! I was dressed in a perfectly acceptable LA uniform for work or play.

Bow emerged from the bedroom, naked, and walked into the kitchen.

"Hungry?" he said, opening the fridge. He shivered dramatically in the cool air. "I've got granola. Go ahead, make fun of me."

I declined and shut the bathroom door behind me. I checked myself in the mirror. Smudged mascara made dark circles under my red, puffy eyes. A bruise had started to darken two inches of my neck. My hair had formed three nasty dreadlocks in the back.

I washed my face with Bow's Eidel Forest Dew Foaming Cleanser, ran my fingers around my curls, rooted in the rest of the products for some kind of hair gel, found some that smelled like tea, used a little, and tried to put it back facing exactly the same way. He knocked. My heart jumped. He didn't try to open the door.

"Your soap's under the sink," he said.

"What?"

"Your Eidel? You left it in the car the other night. It's under the sink. You should take it."

"Thanks," I said, and found it in a square basket that held his manicure set.

I came out of the bathroom and Bow pulled me into a squeeze. His skin was warm. I spanked him, lightly. "I really have to go."

"Don't play the who-calls-first game with me," he said, holding my hand as I moved to the front door.

"I won't," I said. "I know it's a dumb game."

"Good luck today," he said. "With everything. Stay calm."

I opened the door, and for a few seconds, anyone in Bow's apartment complex might have seen him nude, leaning against his couch, arms crossed. He didn't seem to think about it, seemed to feel as comfortable naked in the late-morning light as he would have in a pair of pants. It wasn't exhibitionist. It was just a total lack of concern. I was struck by the enormity of his accomplishment in overcoming the habits of modesty, and felt something close to pain, like someone had just massaged a muscle I never used. Next time, I thought, I'll stay naked too.

I changed into the Emergency Outfit in my backseat and screamed down the road to work, still wearing my absurd silver heels. I'd missed the morning rush and spent only fifteen minutes on the freeway instead of forty-five. The cars seemed to sparkle and dance around me, like I was cutting through water. The sky was utterly clear, and the bright green hills of the Cahuenga Pass rolled along—colors perfectly complementary, shapes sensuous and round, excellent variation between soft green and hard rock. All the neon signs that blazed garishly at night were now innocuous, quaint, like toys someone forgot to put batteries in.

When I arrived at the SLLC, Linda had taken my parking place again. I swallowed half of the last Xanax before leaving the car. Stay calm.

I walked unsteadily into the office. I wondered if Remy or Janet was leaving voicemails on my dead phone. I tried to predict what Janet might be doing—packing the rest of her stuff at our place? The dread settled below my stomach, as I imagined that Remy had let her go patch things up with John. I supposed he couldn't stop her.

Linda stood behind the front desk with Todd, laughing, holding an enormous Coffee Bean cup in one perfectly manicured hand. A bright green dress wrapped tightly around her breasts and flowed around her legs.

"Tamina!" she said, in a voice that reminded me of summer camp.

"Hi, Linda," I said, perky as possible.

She apologized for dropping in again, and then told me we needed to have a meeting. Like, soon. "I was hoping for now-ish," she said.

I excused myself to check my appointment calendar. I had people scheduled at two, two-thirty, and four. A pile of paperwork to deal with, an old to-do list, and a nervous curiosity about Janet giving way to rising anger.

"I could meet now-ish," I said, leaning out of my doorway.

"It's too freaking hot," Linda said, looking out our front window. "Let's go somewhere beautiful."

We said goodbye to Todd, who gave me a you-are-going-to-come-back-here-and-explain-yourself face, and Linda drove us to Cha-Cha-Cha, a Caribbean restaurant hovering on the fringe of downtown, just south of Silver Lake. The outside could have appeared in a budget travel guide to the third-world exotic, with painted plywood and strings of Christmas lights. The inside exploded with color, too much, too many, bright potted palms and shiny, gaudy oilcloth tabletops in tangerine orange, cherry red, candy grape, printed with cartoon produce and checkers. On another day, I couldn't have stayed inside. On Xanax, I felt no overwhelm. My body throbbed with remembered pleasure for a second, as I flashed back unexpectedly to the way Bow's hands had pulled on my hips.

Linda ordered us a half-pitcher of sangria. I casually checked my watch. It was eleven-thirty.

"Don't worry, I'll drink most of it," she said.

I knew no protocol for this interaction. While drinking sangria with my job's major funding source, on an impromptu lunch meeting with a mysterious agenda, was I expected to come up with an opening topic of conversation?

"So, how are you?" Linda asked.

I told her I was doing fine. She said I seemed tired. I admitted I'd had a late night. She sipped some water.

"Partying?" she asked.

"Well, I went to a party," I said. Our tablecloth clashed terribly with the one next to us. I noticed, but cared very little.

"I hope it was a friend that did that to your neck," she said, and I reflexively covered the bruise. I should have at least put some make-up on it.

"Hey," she said, "I'm kidding. It's none of my business. If choking's your thing," and she shrugged, accepting.

A small rise of nausea constricted my throat. I swallowed. "It wasn't a friend," I said. "A boy named Nathan Reggman attacked me because of the clinic."

Linda raised her perfect eyebrows.

Maybe it was the dread of my financial stupidity forcing me to leave Los Angeles, or the desire to destroy the stereotypes I'd pinned to Linda, or some tiny, almost imperceptible shift in her facial muscles that opened the door for more disclosure. Maybe I did know that Janet was gone. Maybe I was finally tired of all the secrets, or maybe it was the drug. I asked if Linda wanted the story, and she said yes.

I started with Janine coming into the clinic to talk about getting an abortion. I told Linda everything: the attack in Greenvale's parking lot, the days in the hospital, the worthless police interview, going back to work, the desperate search for Nathan's name, the months of ignoring my own stress symptoms, meeting Bow, running into Juno at Wacko. I told her about Nathan and Juno "dropping by" the clinic, and how I'd never seen them. I described the panic attack in the dive bar bathroom, and then my decision to go to Franco's party to find Juno. I even told the truth about Bow, and as I talked, I shredded a napkin in my lap.

After offering validating amounts of outrage and sympathy, Linda sat back and shook her head. "I'm so sorry," she said.

The waiter scooted up to us, taking advantage of the lull, and we ordered—I hadn't read the menu but I couldn't eat anything anyway. I asked for plain rice and plantains. My tongue scraped the roof of my mouth.

"So what are you going to do?" Linda asked.

I told her I was thinking I'd go back to the police. I sipped some water.

Sure, she said, but it was likely nothing would come of that. "He's young," she said. "You work in a clinic that caters to sex workers and delinquent kids. The prejudice in the system is not on your side."

I knew it. I sucked an ice cube from my glass and chewed.

"Let me ask you this," she said, "and I know you can't know for sure, but do you really believe he's going to come after you again?"

I tried to convince myself I didn't. "I don't know," I said.

She nodded thoughtfully and spooned some ice out of her glass, into mine.

"I wonder if the SLLC is liable for worker's comp," Linda said. "Or maybe the school has some liability?"

"Neither," I said. "I checked right after it happened."

"So when are you going to leave?"

I asked what she meant.

"Aren't you quitting?"

"No," I said. "Not unless I have to run home to Jersey because I can't pay my bills."

"Ah."

"I love the job," I said. "No. That's not true. I love the clinic. I love what we're trying to do."

"Well, that's it then," she said. "I want to talk more about this kid sometime, but I need to change the subject, if you're ready."

I nodded.

"It's clear you've got the balls to come along on this plan I've got, the one I told you about at Tommy's? I want to run a few things by you."

She leaned over the table, which squished her balloon-breasts together. Her face was bright and excited and she started detailing an incredibly smart-sounding, well-designed business plan that explained the budget breakdown Todd and I had seen the other day.

"This isn't for public consumption, okay?" she said, dipping her chin.

"No problem," I assured her.

She'd invested money in a production company, an all-female porn studio, and she'd made a killing. She'd gotten a friend with an MBA and an NP in private practice to sit down and help her make a plan to pour the money into the SLLC. It was time for her to delegate.

"I think you're bright enough, you're clearly brave enough, and you've been through so much with the kids you know how important this is."

I thanked her.

"I want you to be clinic director."

I couldn't have anticipated that, not even if I'd been forced to guess the wildest request Linda might make of me. I might have predicted she wanted to cast me in a film before putting me in charge of the clinic. "Helena is leaving?" I asked.

"She will be, yes," Linda sounded certain.

"But, I don't even have a master's," I said. She was talking about my taking on a job that was performed by a person who had been working in the field at least seven years, already had an advanced degree, and usually had some clinic experience as a practitioner. I'd worked in the clinic for four years, with a B.S. in biology, and learned all my patient skills on the job or in Continuing Education training sessions. She could hire a nurse off of Craigslist who would be more qualified.

"I know you don't have your master's *yet*," she said. She looked almost prankish. Her plan was to find a new doctor, maybe a post-doc fellow at UCLA, to team up with our Nurse Practitioner for all the diagnosing and prescribing. What she wanted me to do was get a master's degree in public health and be the administrative director of the whole thing. The clinic would pay for me to go to school. She offered to increase my salary right away, and then again when I finished my degree.

"That's a huge commitment," I said. "For me, but also for the SLLC."

She smiled and half-shrugged. "What other kind of commitment is worth making?"

Our waiter dropped by, poured a half-inch of water in each of our glasses, and retreated.

"I want you to start at about sixty thousand," Linda said, "and then go up to seventy-five when you've got your MPH. If you want to do a different degree, let me know."

Tripling my income. Crazed visions of paying off the credit cards, snipping them with rhinestone scissors, and getting my toes painted bright sparkling purple swirled inside me. But I didn't have a place to live after the next few days. I tried to imagine applying to MPH programs from the public library, sleeping under my desk or on Todd's couch, and I felt a curtain descend on the fantasy.

"I'm flattered," I said, "but I'm just not qualified."

"Bullshit." Linda unfolded her napkin, laid it in her lap, and then leaned on both elbows. "One thing Helena does tell me is how capable you are. You practically run the clinic already. As long as I have a good medical team backing you up, you can do this. Your evals from schools are always outstanding, and we have a great return rate with clinic patients. The kids love you."

Our food arrived. I took a few bites of rice and drank water. My mouth went from dry to sticky. Linda happily sawed away at her mango chicken.

"Not all the kids love me," I said, gently probing my neck.

Linda put down her silverware and reached over the table. She gripped both my shoulders and stared at me. "Now it's my turn to tell you a story," she said. She sat back and crossed her arms. "I'm from Yakima, Washington. Do you know where that is? Of course you don't. Small town. I was molested when I was nine by an older kid who was friends with my brother.

"By the time I graduated from high school, which I almost didn't even do, I was having sex with anyone who would hang out with me." She sighed and asked me if it sounded like a familiar story.

It did.

"When I was eighteen," she continued, "I went to Oregon State. I was raped by a professor who was on faculty for just that one year, at a party he never should have been at. I took his ass to court. You must have some idea how hard that is. I had to drop out of school. The school wanted to settle, but I wanted him locked up.

"My family didn't support me. My mom told me I was a slut. I started stripping to make enough money to take care of it all. I'd been smart enough to go directly to my health center after the rape, and there was another girl at the party who saw a lot of what had happened, but the trial took forever. I was still poor when it was over, and I had no friends."

I told her I was impressed—most girls barely got any treatment, let alone put themselves through the burden of a trial. Even then, many of them quit the process before they could go for a conviction. I asked if she'd seen the process all the way through criminal court.

She nodded. "I couldn't let him go," she said.

"Wow," I said. "And?"

"I won."

"That's incredible!"

She nodded. "Sadly, it is." She told me that after it was over she moved to LA, started stripping at the Body Shop, doing photo shoots, and shooting porn. She stayed drunk or high most of the time for five years, but even then she knew better than to waste her money like the other girls—what they spent on Coach bags she put in the bank.

"I read books on set," she said. "Anything I could find. Business textbooks, medical books, trying to find a field I could go into after I stopped doing movies. I studied the directors, producers. I sat in the editing room for hours, watching them work."

She made thousands a month doing appearances, posing for calendars, and she rode the wave.

"But I knew I wanted to do something bigger. Better. I came up with the idea for the clinic after I had to go to the ER with some nasty burns from an accident on set. Everyone there treated me like shit. I'd come in to the hospital in a silk robe with these fluffy slippers on, and I was nude under the robe. I had this telltale hairdo and skanky make-up. The minute all those doctors' and nurses' eyes were on me, I could tell what they were thinking. *Whore.* I had burns all over my arms, and they thought I deserved it."

She stopped to drink some sangria. I peeked at her forearms.

"I had reconstructive surgery," she said, and turned one of her wrists over. "This is the only one you can really see." A pink scar, too wide to be from a blade and too irregular to be a scrape, made a vague S-shape from the base of her palm around to her wrist bone.

"Did I quit?" she said. "Did I move back to Yakima? No. I opened my goddamn clinic, where anyone can come in and get the attention they need, and not be judged, and kids can get real answers to their questions, and no one looks down on anyone like those people did to me. I started a production company that would make hot movies that didn't degrade women. I still catch shit from the other studios." They were a boys' club, she told me. Other porn producers hated her, parents hated her, even people she used to do movies with hated her, because she did something so different with her life afterward.

She poked at her food. Then she met my eyes. "I can't force you to take this job," she said. "I can't convince you that you deserve it. I don't know that much about you outside of your work. But you remind me of myself, a few years back."

My face burned. I stared past her at a rainbow-light parrot sign flashing from the ceiling beam.

"You basically know what you want to do," she said. "I mean, in the world. You know yourself well enough to know what you're good at, and what you're not. But you haven't decided where to land."

I blinked through some sudden, embarrassing tears, and caught them with the back of my hand.

"That's just what I see," she said. "Stop me if I'm projecting a bunch of bullshit here."

"You're not," I said, sounding more certain than I'd intended. I told her I had always thought of my work at the clinic as a temporary stopover between college and the bigger plan to be a doctor. "Now I'm more invested in the education piece," I said. "We're doing both preventive and reparative work, and I don't know many people who can say that about their job." I told her that I felt productive at the clinic, doing the daily tasks of preventing a few more people from contracting or spreading STIs. Clinic work was ticking things off a list. I did drug counseling, advised on smaller issues, like flus and colds and healthy vaginal discharge. Every patient I saw was another small task accomplished. It was the place where I felt the intersection of the complex real world and my own dreams of some kind of accomplishment actually occurring.

"Yes!" Linda said. "And also, you *should* be thinking about bigger things—more education programs, our web presence, all kinds of stuff. You've got the imagination for it."

I remembered Bow, asking me if being a doctor was really my own dream, or the dream I'd been taught to want. As a clinic director, I'd be accepting a more political path. No one outside my field would automatically respect me. It was that easy, finally, to decide.

"You win," I said, and Linda's eyes ignited. "I'm grateful for the chance."

She clapped and bounced a bit in her chair. "Really? Oh my God! This is so exciting! It's going to be great. I'm so happy!" She started chatting about all the miracles we would work together to save more and more of LA's uninformed and insecure youth.

"I have this idea for a new kind of peer-counseling group," I said near the end of lunch, as Linda finished the sangria. "I want to start a program for teenage boys who have fathered a pregnancy that's being terminated or adopted. Even if there are only two guys willing to come, seems like it's something we should offer."

"That's what I'm talking about," Linda said. She pointed at me, looked around, then nodded and smiled at an invisible audience, as if they'd been there all along.

SIXTEEN

I was dazed and queasy in the car after lunch, while Linda talked about the porn industry of the last five years. I asked her to drop me off at the strip mall near the SLLC, so I could get my phone turned on again.

I put a wad of my shoe-modeling cash on the counter at the cell phone store and told a young guy with a stringy ponytail that I needed service, now.

"Not a problem," he said, and took my phone into some secret back room. A few minutes later he emerged, and told me the phone should work in four hours.

I walked in the heat, phone in hand, imagining the messages. Maybe Janet had a revelation, borrowed some money from her parents, and paid our rent. Maybe Nathan got arrested and was going to court-mandated anger management courses. I couldn't hang on to those hopeful futures, and kept worrying that there were ever more tragedies just beyond my small circle. Everyone I passed on the street, and every face in every car, seemed poised on the edge of grief or panic. Any one of us could be next on the news. I tried to remember that Xanax doesn't last forever, that I'd just taken an incredible step forward into some bright new future, but I felt like I'd shown up at the prom in a pair of greasy Dungarees. There was some fundamental way in which I, just by being myself, didn't match my occasion.

The blast of air-conditioning inside the SLLC gave me goosebumps. There were a few people in the waiting room, all of them young and slightly kinetic—bouncing legs, twirling hair—and Todd looked tense. I leaned in through the reception window and told him I just needed a minute in my office. He nodded.

A few minutes later, he appeared in my doorway. "Room one is all set," he said. He reached to me, and lightly rubbed my back. "Did you have a good time with Linda?"

I sat up. "I had a really good time." I had a pang of missing him, even though he was standing in front of me. I wanted him to know everything, but there were patients waiting. "I've got some stories for you," I said, and he nodded.

"Me too," he said.

I asked if he was alright, and he said no, he and Derek had broken up, again. He looked like he might cry. "This is it," he said. "I can't do it anymore."

"Shit," I said, and hugged him. "We'll talk in a bit, okay?"

I walked past him toward the exam room.

Taking a few deep breaths to calm my stomach, which was doing some kind of acidic tango, I pulled the chart out of the bin on the exam room door. The kid's name was Brian. Nineteen. Wanted to get an HIV test. I held my hand out to check for shaking. Not bad enough to make me screw up a blood draw. I knocked on the door and opened it.

Brian was thin. He seemed very small, sitting on the exam table looking at his knees. He had a trendy haircut, almost a mowhawk. He wore an orange T-shirt with "Fly a Kite" handwritten across the front, cargo pants, and sneakers. He reminded me so much of the crowd I saw every weekend at Bitsy's that I wondered if I might have eaten at the table next to him.

"Hi, Brian," I said. "I'm Tamina. I'll be administering your test today." I looked over his interview notes. Bless Todd for that perfect handwriting. "Is there anything you'd like to ask me before the test?"

He swallowed. "I guess, uh, how long do I need to wait?"

"You'll get your results in one or two weeks," I said.

"No, uh," he looked back at his knees, "I mean how long after I have sex with somebody do I need to wait to get tested."

I had a scripted answer. "If your partner tells you that they are HIV positive or you think they are at risk because of other behaviors, like IV drug use or having anonymous sex with multiple partners, you should get tested about three months after you were exposed. Are you aware that you were exposed?"

"Not exactly," he said.

We still used the EIA test at our clinic—which meant I'd need to take a vial of blood. "It's not the newest or fanciest test," I said, "but it's reliable." I put on a pair of gloves. I told him I was working on getting rapid tests in to the clinic, oral swabs that give results in twenty minutes, but even for those a person had to wait three months after infection for the antibodies to start showing up.

"Let's do this," he said, and held out his arm. I wanted to apologize for chatting, but knew better.

"Hang on a second," I said, and looked at his interview again. "You've never been tested for HIV before, right? Do you want to talk about why you decided to?"

He said that he had recently gotten sober. He was in a band, and had sex with a lot of people. Unprotected. He was always drunk or high.

"Can you tell me which drugs you were doing?" I asked, careful to stay in the past tense with him.

"The regular ones," he said.

"Alcohol, marijuana?"

He nodded.

"Anything else?"

"Sometimes," he said. Then he cleared his throat. "I did some heroin," he said, looking at me briefly. "We'd always get new needles," he said, and cleared his throat again, "at the exchange." I was glad to hear he was using with responsible people.

"And when was the last time you used any drugs intravenously?"

"Almost four months ago."

He said that when he got a wart on his testicle he came to the clinic. "I don't think it was you I saw then," he said. "It was some lady doctor. She was black. That doesn't matter, I mean, I'm just remembering her. She was good. I got tested for other stuff. I had another infection, too." I wondered how often Helena had to deal with people being surprised that she was a doctor.

"Did you get treatment?" I flipped through his chart. Chlamydia. Of course.

He said yes. "It freaked me out," he said. "Got me thinking. I got sober. I stopped fucking around. Excuse me. So it's been a few months since then."

"It's great that you are taking such good care of yourself now," I said. I wiped down his forearm with alcohol. It was smooth, perfectly healthy, a great vein pulsing almost imperceptibly in the inner crook of his elbow. I decided not to tie him off, in part to spare him the sensory memory. He was one of the curious, who wanted to watch it happen. Most people looked away when the needle came out. I asked if he was in a drug treatment program right now, or if he wanted a list of NA meetings in the area, while I slid the needle under his skin.

"I go to meetings," he said. "I've been doing okay." We both watched as his blood pushed its way through a few inches of tubing into the vial.

Patients might be uncomfortable telling medical personnel about their sex lives, but most would end up talking. Usually they would exaggerate or get defensive or provide all kinds of rationale for what they had done. Sometimes I felt like they'd confused me with a priest—and a clean bill of health was divine forgiveness.

I pulled the needle out, covered the spot with gauze, told him to hold some pressure on the vein while I snatched a Band-Aid, and fixed him up.

"Might bruise a little," I said, and he nodded.

I labeled his sample, told him I would be right back, and carried the tube into the office where we packaged labs to send off. I went back into his exam room.

"You are all set," I said. "You'll get a phone call in a week or so, okay?"

He was moving his arm in a circle. "Right on," he said.

"We have some good literature here," I said, pointing to a rack of pamphlets hanging on the back of the door. "You might want to take a look at 'What an HIV test means' or 'Communicating with your Partner about HPV.' Those can be really helpful."

"Thanks." He looked up at me, and one half of his mouth smiled politely. "Take it easy," he said, and slid off the exam table. I told him he should come back in another three months, even if he got a negative result, just to be sure. "And there's a bowl of free condoms on the front desk," I said.

"Free is good," he said, and walked out with his hands in his pockets.

I dropped his file with Todd at the front desk a few minutes later, tried to sound normal as I said hello to Helena, felt certain she could see my twinge of guilt about Linda's plan for me to take her job, and then saw Layla in the waiting room.

She stood up, grinning. Her hair was pulled back into a strategically messy ponytail.

"I called, but I didn't want to leave a message here with, like, personal info in it," she said.

I looked to Todd, who glanced meaningfully at the appointment book—I was running late. "This will just take a minute," I said to him.

I brought Layla into my office instead of an exam room and asked her what was going on.

"I think you should start an advice column," she said. "Martin and I are awesome. You helped me so much."

I thanked her for stopping by.

"No problem. I'm trying out the New Way."

"The what?"

"It's like a new method of relating to people, kind of like karma, but it's all about gratitude. I have to thank people for what they do for me. It's supposed to make me humble." She pulled a dog tag from under her shirt, which had "NW" etched on one side in loopy cursive.

I would not have been able to discuss the New Way without my cynicism leaking. I made a noise of affirmation, said it was good to see her, then told her I needed to see a patient.

"That's cool," she said. "Hey, can I take that *People* with me? Did you hear about that guy who got killed in a bathtub the other day?"

She stood and started twisting her hair. I told her I didn't think I had.

"He was screwing some lady, and her husband found them together. The husband locked the guy in the bathroom and starved him for weeks, then he just went in there and killed him and left him in the tub."

My stomach turned. Layla had reminded me of how badly I needed to talk to Janet.

I told Layla to take the magazine and said goodbye.

I dragged myself through the afternoon. Occasional pangs of excitement when I thought of Bow rippled through me incongruously with occasional pangs of terror when I thought about Nathan. By the time we closed the office, after Helena left, Todd and I both were moving like our shoes were full of sand.

He asked what happened to my neck as he locked the front door.

"I'll tell you everything," I said, "but I need you to do me a favor."

"The robot asks for help?"

"Please."

He chucked my chin and said, "Doll, I'd do anything for you."

Todd followed me back to my apartment and came inside with me to check for John and Janet. They weren't there. My phone was back on. I stifled disappointment that Bow hadn't called. I left Janet yet another message.

"Smells like garlic in the garbage disposal," Todd said, wrinkling his face as we went inside.

"Very specific," I said.

He shrugged. "The nose knows."

I opened all the windows, turned on the fans, and we lay on the couch, our heads at either end, knees bent and feet together. I told him everything I could think of.

He congratulated me about Bow and the promotion. "You can stay with me until you get a place," he said. "I'll need the company." I asked him what he thought I should do about Janet.

"Cut and run."

"I hate that."

"Be a friend."

"I don't know what that means here."

"Cut and run."

"Okay, shut up."

"You asked."

"I'm sorry about Derek," I said.

"Yeah," he sighed. "Don't let me get back with him. He's not in love with me. Unless that changes, this is best, no matter what else I say."

"You got it." Then I asked what he thought I should do about Nathan.

He shook his head. "I wish I knew this Bow guy. I don't like how connected he is to the kid."

"It's a coincidence," I said.

"It's creepy."

"That's not helping."

"I want to meet him."

"Nathan?" I said.

"Bow."

"Come on."

"I'm serious," Todd said. "You've been acting crazy for days. I thought maybe it was because we went back to Greenvale, but this is too much."

I had a flash of Remy's face when he told me I was treating Janet like a child. Maybe I had been acting crazy.

"Fine," I said, and I called Bow, but he didn't answer. I left a message asking what he was up to that night.

He didn't call back. Todd and I spent the night packing my stuff, talking about work, cleaning out the kitchen, and in the end, watching *Cold Case Files* until we fell asleep on the couch. It was just like when we were dating, without the sex.

SEVENTEEN

I woke up just after the sun came up, thinking about Nathan, and decided I needed to try going back to the police. I didn't trust the LAPD any more than Bow or Linda, but abusive men were the one type of person they didn't arrest often enough. The compassion I'd felt for Nathan at the party seemed misplaced. I needed to help boys before they got to the point he was at, if I wanted to help them at all. Deep down, I knew I'd failed somehow, but at the moment that was less important than showing myself, and everyone else, that I was no longer paralyzed by indecision. I wanted to drive out to the Valley to see if I could talk to the same officer who had dealt with me after the attack.

I pulled a blanket from my bedroom and covered Todd, feeling an overwhelming affection for him. I left him a note and set the alarm on his phone so he wouldn't be late to work.

When we were dating, we had developed a morning routine. I always got up first, and Todd would join me in the shower. I never knew when exactly he was coming, so I always had a few minutes of anticipation, during which I pretended to be soaping and shampooing normally. As soon as I heard the door clicking open, I'd duck my hair under the water so that he got a glimpse of me naked, eyes closed, before I acknowledged he was there. It was part performance and part insecurity—I didn't want him to know how eager I was for him to look at me, kiss me, say good morning to me, before the rest of his day took him.

It was early enough that traffic was light, and the heat hadn't quite settled in. I still had the cop's card from the hospital, and had no problem finding the station since it was on one of the disturbingly large streets that fed the highway. Still, it was like the first day at a new school—I couldn't seem to get my clothes to hang right, I was sweating, and the woman I parked next to looked at me too long. At the same time, a deep calm ran underneath my nervousness. I was finally Dealing With Nathan. My plan was to give the cops his identity, and indicate that he'd aggressed a second time. When they asked me what I wanted to happen, I'd tell them I wanted him arrested.

The inside of the station was surprisingly modern. A reception desk swooped in a large semicircle around the front room, and many people, most in plain clothes, bustled in and out of two doors behind it. The Berber carpet had flecks of turquoise and magenta. Three magenta vinyl chairs sat in a line by the window. Industrial décor was so reassuring.

"Help you?" a man in khakis, in his thirties, with a thick moustache, said from behind the desk. He stood, maybe to show me the badge attached to his belt.

I said I'd like to speak with Officer Ramirez, please, and showed the battered card, as if to verify my request.

"Reporting a crime?" he said.

"I guess so," I said. "It's in connection with a report from a few months ago?" Suddenly I had no idea how to explain what I was doing there.

"Theft?"

"Assault."

An older Hispanic woman and a young boy in starchy Dickies came through the front door.

"Help," she said.

"Emergency?" said the reception officer.

"Help."

"Please take a seat, ma'am."

The reception officer disappeared behind door number two, I assumed in order to check for Ramirez.

The woman blew a strand of hair out of her face as she rocked from foot to foot. She looked at me. "My son," she said, and pointed out the door. I looked, reflexively, but the parking lot was nearly empty.

I held my hands open. "Where's your son?"

"My son!"

"Dónde está?" I said.

Then she launched into faster, more terrified Spanish than I'd ever heard. I tried to interject my non-understanding, while the small boy crawled progressively farther and farther under her skirt.

Cop In Khakis reappeared alone, and told me Ramirez was out. He took my name and told me someone would be with me momentarily. I stayed put. The old woman did too, and we shifted our weight, looked out the window, and sighed.

"Necesitas ayuda?" he asked her. She started telling her story to him in Spanish, maybe a bit slower this time, and he clearly understood, or at least made a nice show of saying "sí" every few words, so I clasped my hands and sat. The small boy walked very close to my knees and stared for a second before scampering back to his grandmother.

Door number one opened, and an overweight officer in uniform called for me. His face was a hard pink, like a New Englander after one very intense day on a boat in Florida. I followed him through the door. Behind me, the old lady said "Help," again.

We entered a large office space with no cubicle walls or partitions between desks. The noise of thirty police officers talking on the phone, talking to each other, talking to tired-looking citizens sitting on folding chairs rose with a wave of heat.

"I'm Jorgenson," my officer said, and indicated that I sit across from him. "Our air's out. Sorry for the inconvenience." He plopped behind his desk and asked me what kind of crime I needed to report. He fanned himself with paperwork. I wanted to hydrate him.

The instant I indicated that I'd already filed a police report six months ago, he held up his hand and asked me to wait. He got up, walked into another person's desk area (who pointedly ignored him), and then returned with the largest black binder I'd ever seen. He flipped through it, looking, I guessed, for my name. All the police reports were filled out in various squiggles of shaky blue ballpoint, and had been shoved into plastic sheet protectors.

"You don't keep your records online?" I asked, truly surprised.

He shrugged. "Some," he said. "Not dead ends."

He found mine, looked it over, and refused to let me read it.

"So you have more information?" he said.

I told him I'd encountered my attacker again, learned his name, and wanted to press charges.

Jorgenson smiled blandly. "You don't press charges," he said. "The DA does that, if the DA's office decides there's a good chance they'll win a case. You said he told you his name?"

"No, I found out through some friends of his."

"You're certain it's the same person?"

"Yes."

"And he hit you? Did he use any kind of weapon? Did he steal anything from you?"

"He just hit me. There were a number of witnesses this time."

"New hospital records?"

"No."

"You said he's a minor?"

"Yes."

Jorgenson kept making notes on my old police report, until he had to turn it sideways and write in the margins. After a few more minutes of inane questions, I asked what was going to happen next.

"Honestly?"

"Of course," I said.

"I'm not sure."

I didn't understand. I wanted to slam my fists on the desk and demand justice like a victim on TV.

"These kinds of things don't usually go all the way to trial," he said. "They don't usually go much further than the police report. He sounds like some punk trying to get a rise out of you. We could do a restraining order if you really feel threatened."

Explaining the difference between "getting a rise out of me" and putting me in the hospital was futile—the cop had seen so much worse. I wondered if it would have been different with Ramirez, or if this was some kind of standardized conversation.

"You're really not going to do anything?" I said.

"Lady, there's nothing I *can* do."

I got up to leave.

"Don't hesitate to call if he surfaces," Jorgenson said. He was friendly. He sounded satisfied by the job he'd done.

"Right," I said. "I thought that's what I was doing."

He nodded, as if to say, yes, people often make that type of mistake here.

I got in my car, tears stinging. After all that. The ineffectiveness made me want to rip my hair out. I screamed and pounded the dashboard. Leaning against the steering wheel, I felt the old dread, the fear that Nathan might come find me, start gripping my chest. I was angry with Linda and Bow for being right about what would happen if I went to the police.

I was angry with Bow, because he still hadn't called me back. I was angry with Janet. I was angry with myself.

I drove south on the 101, past Hollywood, Silver Lake, and Echo Park. I drove into downtown. I took an exit I'd never heard of and followed the flow of one-way streets. When I had to pee, I snuck into the bathroom at a gas station, then drove more. I cried. I turned the radio up loud, and waited for a song on a pop station to describe how I felt. None of them did. I turned it off. I drove past blocks of deco-style buildings that had started browning and crumbling, that had bars on the windows, that had mysterious storefronts or no signs at all. No one was walking on the streets.

Close to the garment district, I wedged my car into a metered space. For an hour, I walked aimlessly among the chaos. Every cheap shirt reminded me of Janet. I stared at the "Latin-style" mannequins, with small busts and larger-than-the-average-white-girl butts. I forced myself to look at unmatched outfits. In one crowded clothing stall, getting bumped and jostled by busy women—Hispanic, Asian, black, all trolling carts stuffed with plastic bags—I stayed fixed on a mustard-colored top slapped on a red skirt for so long that I had an afterimage when I blinked. My heart was racing. I wanted to throw up. The air slunk around me, heavy with the smell of sausages and piss. My shoes were sticking to the sidewalk.

I also felt a kind of wild exhilaration, like I'd leaped off a cliff and was about to hit the water.

Middle-class people moved to cities like Los Angeles with fantasies. Even those who could rationally acknowledge the odds against them held secretly excessive dreams. They moved wanting beauty; wanting white linen, fresh fruit, the tinkling laughter of a starlet in their ear. If they were like me, they wanted mist under the streetlights, cool trench coats and fast-talking friends. And sometimes, when the sun went down over the water in Santa Monica and the Ferris wheel rolled along in place, shining on the pier, or the white cross on the hill at Highland Avenue lit up just as I was glancing at it, or the graffiti on the overpass told me to "GET FREE," the city seemed like a fluid, benevolent miracle-worker—a sprawling genie offering up shiny treasures, expecting nothing but my awed gratitude in return. There could be a sense of spiritual fulfillment in LA's effortless aesthetics.

But there was also a more nuanced joy in abiding the city's famed obstacles, and that joy can't be shared by tourists. Those who function through the infinite, miniature horrors of urban life possess an inexplicable power. It isn't born of virtuous patience, or even bitter resignation, it is another thing altogether, a mix of participation and acceptance that simultaneously implicates and vindicates all residents. Every traffic jam is both our fault and our personal inconvenience. Every long line, every fake conversation, every velvet-roped, hierarchical evening is something we both create and endure. We choose the problems of Los Angeles over the problems of other cities, and then we get to complain all we want, like husbands to a particularly beautiful but capricious wife.

I felt a startling pride when my parents asked if I was bothered by LA traffic on one of my early visits home. I waved a hand and called it "normal for me now," not quite knowing how to describe to them the way traffic, and being ceaselessly, comfortably bothered by it, had become woven into the fabric of my days. Los Angelenos rarely talked about traffic except to announce that they'd be arriving before or after it.

I wanted to be a woman who could navigate the neighborhoods, who discovered hidden gems behind ugly hand-painted restaurant storefronts, who suffered the indignity of not being able to find parking on my own block. I wanted all those things to become the unnoticed background noise to my life, because if my background noise was the noise of Los Angeles, then I could count myself among the energetic, capable, independent, savvy, cosmopolitan few who could handle almost anything.

Everyone has to bear the burden of some personal trauma—moments of terror that color their ability to live happily—but it wasn't the act of surviving trauma that indicated true resilience, at least to me. It was the act of surviving, every day, many thin layers of difficulty, and eventually, believing them normal. I'd been doing it silently, for years, with my colors, toes, lists. In LA, everyone was doing it together. I'd lived in a state of overwhelm or numbness, depending on whether I was losing or winning the fight on any particular day. There had to be another way to do it.

I tried to meditatively acknowledge that the colors of the mustard and red outfit bothered me, as I stood still. I fought the impulse to run or double over or shut my eyes. I ignored the stringy-haired sales girl who circled me two, three, four times. Digging my nails into my palms, breathing slowly, I remembered how bad it had been in college and decided this was it, it had to be getting better. If it wasn't, I'd get my own Xanax. I no longer wanted my personality to be defined by all my quiet suffering. There were too many important things to do.

When I got home, Todd was gone, the TV was on, and Janet was slumped on the couch, staring into the space a foot from the screen.

"Hey, there," I said awkwardly.

"I talked to Gary," she said. My stomach twisted. I became suddenly aware of my toenails being too long. Unimportant, I told myself.

"What's happening?" I said.

"He's not going to sue us if we're out by tomorrow night."

That seemed utterly impossible and I told her so. I wondered aloud if John had threatened him.

"Fuck you, and no, actually, Gary fucked up," she said. "Our old rental agreement has some obsolete clause about termination or notices or something that he forgot to change when the laws changed last year, and it would be a huge hassle for everyone if he really evicted us. He'd rather not have to take us to court, even though we'd lose, if he did. We just have to get out now."

Relief stayed in the distance. I couldn't arrive at it, hard as I was trying.

"So, you're going to John's."

"Yeah."

"You really think that's a good idea."

"I'm not talking about him with you anymore."

I sat next to her. "Jan," I said, the emotion welling in my throat, "I can't support this."

She shook her head, didn't meet my eyes, and started picking at her fingernails. "I'm not asking you to support it."

"I mean I can't be close to you as long as you're with him."

"We've already had this conversation," she said. Then, as if it was only now occurring to her, "And we haven't been close for months."

"You're my best friend!" I snapped. I heard the fifteen-year-old in my voice. She met my eyes. The only feeling I could discern in her was exhaustion. Not grief, not love, not hurt, not even regret. Just a pure weariness, settled deep into the muscles of her face. "We haven't been close because of him," I said.

"We haven't been close because of *you*," she said. She accused me of being different since the attack. More anxious, preoccupied. "You were always a kook," she said. "Now you're impossible to talk to."

"You're kidding me," I said. "I can't believe you'd even pretend that I'm more fucked up than John."

She shook her head. "It's not a competition."

"If you stay with him," I said, drawing my back straight, "I won't be around."

"You can't ask me to choose between you," she said. "That's manipulation."

I told her that wasn't what I was doing, although we both knew it was. I framed it as a choice between a life with John, which was unhealthy, and a life without, which was better.

"I can't do that," she said.

"You won't do it."

"I can't!" She got up, and wandered into the kitchen.

I asked her if she'd married him. I looked around at our apartment, at the stacks of books and clothes and things we never thought about—ironing board, footstool, roll of sticky drawer liner. Moving required ten thousand tiny decisions. Strange that we had such trouble making bigger ones, with all that practice.

She opened the cupboard, pulled out a glass, and filled it with tap water. "His anger is getting better. I'm not leaving him now." Her face was tight with resolve.

Too classic, too familiar. "Can you hear yourself? Come on, Janet." I scrambled to figure out a time when they might have snuck off to Vegas. "You can't even tell me the truth?"

"We haven't gotten married yet," she said.

"That's good."

"Fuck you."

"Get out before it gets even harder."

"Leave it alone, Tam!" she put the glass down too hard and I winced. "I don't want to talk to you about this ever again!"

"Fine!" my voice strained. "I give up!"

"Good! You don't know a goddamn thing about us!" She closed her eyes, and again I saw how tired, how unbelievably tired she was. And I knew she was right: I didn't know a goddamn thing about them. I didn't know a goddamn thing about Janet. And she didn't know a goddamn thing about me. The easy, domestic interactions of daily life had been enough for us. "I'll have all my stuff out by early tomorrow," she said. "Whatever you don't want, you can leave on the curb. John's got some friends who are going to pick it up."

Was I supposed to thank her? I said nothing. She left the glass on the counter, grabbed her purse from the couch, and said she'd see me later.

I looked up at her, my heart breaking. "I don't think so, Jan."

Then she left.

Maybe she'd change her mind in another month, or a year, or ten. Maybe not. Years of wasted time, so much of it my fault.

I left Todd a voicemail about the police station, and told him I wasn't coming in. I left Helena and Linda voicemails indicating that something had come up and I needed to take a few days off. Of course, something had been up for a long time. Since before Nathan, before I moved to LA, even.

I went into Janet's room, where the computer was the only functioning surface in a sea of clothes and other chaos, with the intention of sending emails to Todd and Helena about the appointment book and files. I was startled by an email in my Inbox from Grant Rose, with attachments.

She'd included me on a huge distribution list of family and friends, and sent along vacation pictures from Walt Disney World. The kids seemed appropriately ecstatic, greasy with sunscreen. Of course they were shockingly big. Jenny had a toddler belly. Grant's face was radiant, and she looked like a mother. Her note was short and generic. I wrote back: *Nice to hear from you. Family looks wonderful. Let's visit the next time I'm in Jersey. I'd like to start over and get to know each other again, for real.*

Then I dragged my body across the hall and curled into my bed.

I woke up hours later to the phone.

"I thought we weren't playing the wait-to-call game," I said, ready for Bow's story to annoy me.

"I'm sorry, Tam, I had to come up to San Francisco."

"What?"

"My mom's in the hospital."

"Oh no," I said.

A car accident—her spine broken in two places. There was no one else to help, and he was suddenly immersed in the responsibility of making decisions about her care. He apologized for burdening me.

"If you need help," I said, "I could come up there. I know my way around medical people." Was it too soon to offer something like that?

"No, no," he said. "You've got so much going on there. And this really sucks," he sighed. "I'm no fun right now. You'd have a terrible time." But I could hear him struggle with the idea.

"Okay, Mr. Honesty," I said.

"You'd actually drive up here?"

I felt a lightness surge through me. I could do it. I could just leave.

"I want to," I said. "I've never been to San Francisco." Then I realized he may have already called Naomi to come and I braced myself.

His voice was small, the softest I'd heard it. "I would love that."

"I'll leave early tomorrow," I said, and got off the phone before he could get polite and decline again.

I called Naomi to cancel out of modeling the next day. She asked if I didn't want to do it, and I said I'd love to but something came up.

"You okay?" she said. "You want to meet for a drink or coffee or something?"

"Thanks, I'm fine," I said, touched. "I'm going up to San Francisco for a few days."

"Oh! Thank God!" She already knew why I was going. "He's a fucking mess. You're so sweet!"

I thanked her again, and felt guilty for not telling her right away that I was going to see Bow.

"I'm so glad for you guys," she said. "Give him a kiss for me. One of you call and let me know how Cindy's doing?"

"No problem," I said. Uncomfortably, I wished he'd called me first.

Todd came over and we loaded two suitcases, a few boxes, and a laundry basket filled with sundry irreplaceable items into our cars. I left Janet a note reminding her of what furniture was mine, asking her to please take it to John's, promising that I'd come get it soon. We unloaded my stuff into Todd's living room. I'd packed a bag for San Francisco but felt like something was missing.

"Phone? Wallet? Sexy underwear?" Todd suggested. "I'm making gin and tonics."

"Thanks. I've got those things. Well, sort of. I need some new sexy underwear."

"You can ask your fetish model girlfriend to help you there," he said, pulling glasses down from a rack above his stove.

"I've got a jacket, sunglasses, insoles," I poked through my bag. "What am I forgetting?"

"Probably nothing," he said. He plopped ice in, and poured. "But you wouldn't be you if you didn't worry about it."

"Yes, I would," I said. Defensive.

"Oh, honey," he smiled. "I didn't mean anything."

"People change," I said.

"Of course they do."

I left for San Francisco just as the sun came up. I called Bow, expecting his voicemail. He answered in a state of insomniac concern.

"Don't get lost," he said.

"Check."

"I mean it. Cell phone service is crappy for a lot of that drive. Stop and get a map if you didn't print one."

"I'll be fine."

There was a pause, during which Janet came careening back into my mind. There was nothing to do for her anymore but answer if she called.

"I don't want to get off the phone," Bow said, amused.

"That's adorable."

"Shut up."

"I'm going to go," I said. "I'll see you in a few hours."

"Thanks," he said. "I know this is weird."

"I might have seen weirder things."

"Weirder than me?"

"Don't be insecure."

"See you soon." I heard him smiling.

I decided to drive the coast before turning inland to catch the freeway. The sun was hovering a few inches above the hills. I pulled the car to the side of the road just north of Santa Monica, where the rows of houses along Pacific Coast Highway gave way to Malibu's pseudo-ruggedness. I parked in the lot of an expensive waterfront bar, and walked to the edge of a short cliff.

The sound of the waves was hypnotically familiar. To the left, the city lights sparkled right up to the ocean. On the right, the road that would take me north curved around a deep blue hill. A disturbance in the water caught my eye—a black shape appearing and disappearing in the shimmering light. I reflexively searched for a seagull. But instead of finding darting wings ascending the air, I saw more and more sharp black shapes breaking the surface, moving down the coast in an effortless rhythm of rising and falling.

Almost alien, they cut half-circles through the water with singular forward purpose, their hooked fins pointing back toward where they'd been.

A pod of dolphins. Real dolphins, living just outside the city. I laughed out loud. I hadn't believed Bow's story about them, not really. I stood there at the western edge of the continent, breathing the heavy coolness of the Pacific air, watching the dolphins swim along, and for a brief, profound moment, I was freed of the delusion that I knew anything much about what was possible, or what would be.

Vanessa Carlisle is a writer, editor, blogger, artist, and educator. Her fiction and nonfiction writing has appeared in both literary and trade magazines including *NinthLetter*, *Boink Magazine*, *The Catalyst*, *Juked*, *Glossolalia*, *WordRiot* and others. She is the co-author--with her sister Erica--of *I Was My Mother's Bridesmaid: Young Adults Talk About Thriving in a Blended Family* (Wildcat Canyon Press). Vanessa has taught literature and creative writing at several colleges and does editorial consulting on manuscripts for private clients. She holds a sexuality educator's certification from Planned Parenthood and has taught Sex Ed to a few hundred teenagers. Vanessa holds a BA in Psychology from Reed College and an MFA in Creative Writing from Emerson College. She is currently a PhD candidate at UC Riverside in the Comparative Literature program and is the recipient of a Chancellor's Distinguished Fellowship. For many years, she has subsidized her writing and academic work by dancing with live bands and in clubs. Follow her arts and culture blog at gorgeouscuriosity.com, or connect with her at vanessacarlisle.com. Vanessa lives in southern California and writes many of her pages at Stir Crazy coffee shop on Melrose.